THE WORLD'S SHATTERED SHELL

LAURENCE RAPHAEL BROTHERS

Published by Water Dragon Publishing
waterdragonpublishing.com

ISBN 978-1-957146-74-4 (Trade Paperback)

10 9 8 7 6 5 4 3 2 1

FIRST EDITION

For my mother,
my first reader and constant encouragement,
and for my father,
who instilled a love of books and writing,
with all love.

ACKNOWLEDGEMENTS

I am deeply grateful to my friends and colleagues in Seventh Prime, Codex, and the Elementals writing group for their support and criticism over the years. Without these overlapping communities, I might never have published anything at all.

BOOK ONE

THE EGGSHELL WORLD

1

O N THE FIRST DAY OF THE EMERGENCY, I woke a little before noon. I didn't realize it till I made it out of the bathroom, dragging a comb through wet hair, but something had changed. There was something different in the air today. Wasn't sure what, though, and didn't much care. Picked up my phone, checked my non-existent messages. No signal, out of service. Just as well.

I walked down the three flights of stairs and opened the front door of the dismal black-and-white-tiled lobby of my apartment building to stand there blinking in the bright sunlight. Something was different for sure.

My neighbor — I thought he was a neighbor — pulled up to the fire-hydrant in front of the building in an old silver Honda, got out and popped the trunk. He had eighteen gallons of water there in plastic jugs and a few shopping bags full of groceries. He looked up at the fourth-floor windows and then looked back at the jugs.

"Give you a hand?" I don't know why I offered. Usually, I wouldn't even have noticed him or that he might need help.

He looked at me suspiciously, hesitated a moment. I thought his name might be Michel. Swarthy guy, wiry and short. Late twenties, maybe. No idea what he did for a living, no more than I knew anything about any of my other neighbors.

"Eh, sure," he said, as if he were giving me something by allowing me to help. Then, he paused. "Thanks," he forced out. French accent, or that's what I thought it was, anyway.

I picked up four of the jugs, two in each hand, the little plastic handles tugging at my fingers and thumbs. He hefted two jugs along with a shopping bag and slammed the trunk, looking both ways as if someone might be waiting to steal his precious trove. I managed to get a finger around the front door handle and levered the door open with a foot. I glanced at the mailbox labels as I went through the lobby. 4C: Delacroix, M. Down the hall from me. Must be him.

The elevator had been broken for a year now, so I went back to the stairwell. Michel followed behind. The dimly lit concrete steps smelled strongly of mildew and faintly of piss.

I put down the four jugs at his door, figuring he wouldn't want to let me into his flat. He paused for a moment, probably wondering whether the jugs would be safe outside his door for the minute or two he'd have to leave them unattended. But if he opened the door, he'd probably have to invite me in. So we trudged downstairs and out the door, and I waited there by the curb for him to unlock his trunk again.

"Hey Michel," I said, taking a chance. He didn't correct me, which made me feel good about remembering his name. "Why all the water? Stocking up? Iced tea addiction? Tropical fish? What?"

I picked up another four jugs.

He glared at me, suspicious again. "For the emergency," he said. "What do you think?"

"Emergency?"

"Surely you know?"

"I know nothing," I said. "Just woke up fifteen minutes ago. Did something happen?"

"But of course," he said. "It's all in the news. Where do you think everyone is?"

Since he mentioned it, there wasn't much traffic around, hardly anyone out on the street. Wouldn't have noticed if he hadn't said anything, though.

I shook my head. "I don't know."

"They're all on the highways heading out of town. Or else they're queued at the supermarket, buying water and bread."

"Is something wrong with the tap water?" I wondered if that shower I had just taken was a good idea. Not to mention the water I'd drunk out of the faucet.

He shrugged. "It's what you do," he said. "Just in case, you know?"

I didn't answer. We walked up the stairs again, dumped another load of water jugs at his door and went back down. He said nothing, and I had nothing more to say myself. One more load and we were done.

"Thanks," he said again when we returned to his front door. He was out of breath and looked uncomfortable. "You really didn't know?"

"No, really, I didn't. What's the emergency, anyway?"

"I — well, you should probably hear it for yourself. Turn on the news. I have to go inside. Sorry." He said all that in little discrete utterances that could have come out of a machine. He obviously didn't want to talk to me, so I let him go. He waited until I got to my own door before inserting his key in the lock. Just in case.

When I got inside, I powered up my elderly desktop computer. I used it mainly for Solitaire, Minesweeper, and web surfing. Five minutes later, it told me my Internet connection was down. Great. Not that I wanted to waste an hour on the phone with the company, but I couldn't if my phone was down too. So I sighed and walked over to my little television, a flat screen perched on the counter dividing my kitchen from my all-in-one everything room. I hesitated. I hated watching it. Turned it on anyway.

The first channel that came up looked weird. A warping and shearing effect distorted the image and turned it into an abstract smear. Every two seconds, the picture jerked and lost sync, falling apart into a cascade of blocky pixels to reform a moment later, just as distorted as before. The audio was equally messed up, so I couldn't hear what was going on either. I changed channels and saw the same thing a few times — the underlying distorted image looked the same — and then, finally, I got to a channel that was clear, more or less, though every second the picture still gave a weird twitch. The audio worked too.

"... for the duration of the emergency." A well-dressed woman at a news desk was speaking, a video image behind her showing a stopped line of cars on the highway. Many of the drivers had emerged from their cars and were standing on the side of the road.

Next, they cut away from the newsroom to a reporter interviewing a store manager at a supermarket. Lines of shoppers with piled-high carts could be seen, and while most of the aisles were still full of products, there was no water left at all. Michel must have been the early bird.

"Most of my clerks didn't come in this morning," said the assistant manager, a short heavy-set woman with ginger hair. "I might not be able to open tomorrow."

But why wouldn't they come in, I wondered. What was keeping them away?

Then, over to a situation room where the deputy mayor alternately appealed for calm and threatened the use of deadly force against looters. Apparently, the mayor himself along with the police commissioner were safe in a secure, undisclosed location. Sounded like a pretty serious emergency to me. Next up, said a voiceover, was a list of school closings.

It seemed our leaders had decamped. But now I began to wonder. With no immediate danger, was this report even true?

More human-interest reporting from the news, and I couldn't take any more. I shut off the TV, still clueless after half an hour about what had actually happened.

I sat on the unmade bed for a few minutes, trying to motivate myself to do something. There were lots of things I could do, some I should, but that was the way it was every day. Eventually, the combination of boredom and hunger got me off the bed. Yeah, nothing much in the refrigerator. I decided to go to the store to see if it had any food left to buy.

I had to walk past three blocks worth of tenement apartment buildings to get to the closest strip mall. The side street was almost deserted, strange even for a weekday afternoon. No kids around at all. I crossed paths with an old lady wheeling a shopping cart full of brown paper bags. She wore black wraparound shades and a leopard-print pantsuit that might have been in style forty years ago and, for all I knew, they had just come back around again.

"You're too late," she said cheerfully.

"What? Sorry." I hadn't expected her to address me.

"The grocery is closed. I was one of the last people they let inside."

"Oh, well. Maybe I'll find somewhere else."

"Good luck!" She seemed to mean it.

I gave her a little wave, and she returned it. She was the first happy person I'd met in a long time, it felt like. I was about to keep on walking when something occurred to me.

"Excuse me," I said.

"Yes, dear?" She turned around to face me again.

"I'm ashamed to say that I got up late today."

She smiled, making me feel good about the admission.

"I understand there's some sort of emergency, but do you, ah, happen to know what sort?"

"Pardon me, dear?"

"I mean, do you know what happened today? Something bad, I guess?"

"Why, why —" She was perplexed, unable to answer. I felt bad for flummoxing her like that.

"Never mind," I said, and she smiled again, relieved. "I'm sure it's nothing important. I hope you have a good rest of your day."

"And I hope you find someplace that's open, young man," she said, and we parted ways.

I walked the block and a half to the intersection where my street crossed the avenue. The traffic lights blinked red both ways instead of following the usual red-yellow-green sequence, and there was almost no traffic, but apart from that everything looked normal. The strip mall was right there, so I walked into the parking lot. It wasn't much, just a supermarket, liquor store, dry cleaners, pizzeria, a couple of cheap boutiques, and a McDonalds off by itself in an island in the middle of the lot.

There was a cluster of perhaps twenty people standing around the supermarket doors, the remnants of a larger group now dispersing back down the street in both directions. Like me they must have been latecomers to the store. The lights were off behind the plate glass. All the other shops in the row were closed, security grills rolled down and steel shutters locked in place.

As I walked up to the doors, I heard grumbling from the latecomers who hadn't made it into the store in time, but really, these people seemed more apathetic than angry. None of them seemed to know what to do next, and it made me feel unhappy to be among them, because I didn't know what to do next, either.

I briefly considered walking down the avenue to look for another supermarket but decided against it. I still had food at home — just nothing very appetizing. Then, I saw someone walking away from the McDonald's with a paper bag in his hands. Sure enough, the lights were on inside. I tried the front door and found it locked, but from that vantage point, I saw half a dozen people queued up on foot at the drive-through window around the side. I hadn't noticed it until now, but a police car with its blue lights flashing was parked on the far side of the fast-food restaurant. The car had a monitoring-the-situation feel to it. No one would be looting the supermarket, not right now anyway. I didn't usually eat McDonald's food, but I could afford it and I thought it would be better than the can of chili and box of stale crackers I had waiting for me at home. So I got in line.

The last person in line was a white, middle-aged balding man with a walrus moustache who looked like he should have been at work bossing a construction crew somewhere. He darted a wary glance at me as I approached, not quite daring to look at me directly. I must have looked harmless enough out of the corner of his eye, so he turned back to his place.

The line slowly moved forward — more slowly than usual for a McDonald's, I thought — but, even so, no one got behind me in line till I got to the window. I gave the guy in front of me plenty of space, so I didn't hear what he ordered, but he left carrying a pretty big sack of food.

"Welcome to McDonald's! How can I help you?"

The clerk was a young black woman. She was tall and slim with tight corn-row hair.

"Uh, sorry," I said, "I wasn't thinking about my order. Do you have, umm, a chicken sandwich?"

"I'm afraid we're out of everything except hamburgers," she said, "but they're free today."

"What?"

"Oh yes," she said. "We're giving away burgers. For the emergency."

"Oh."

I thought about asking her what the emergency was but changed my mind at the last moment. Maybe she wasn't the best person to ask, anyway.

"Well," I said, "two hamburgers, I guess."

"Just two?" She smiled. "We have plenty. And there's not much to a hamburger."

"All right. Three. No, wait." I had a thought. "Make it six please, in two bags if you don't mind."

"Not at all. It'll just be a minute."

It took longer than that, and she was just standing there with no other customers to deal with, so to make conversation I asked, "Why is only the drive-through open?"

"Oh," she said, "we don't have enough staff to man the registers in front. The management thought it would be better this way."

"I see."

"Oh, your food is ready."

She ducked away from the window and came back with two white paper bags.

"There you go, sir. Have a good day." Strange, but I thought she meant it.

I took the two bags and headed over to the cop car. Made sure I passed in front so he could see me coming and walked up to the driver-side window. Wouldn't want to freak him out. I stopped a yard from the car, gave a little wave. He rolled down his window.

"Yes?" His tone was annoyed, stressed out. The police officer was young, tanned, with thin lips, wearing mirror shades.

"I was just wondering if you wanted any hamburgers," I said. "I got some extra."

He seemed taken aback.

"Oh, yeah," he said after a pause, "that would be great."

I handed the bag through the window.

"Listen," I said, "I don't mean to trouble you, officer, but can I ask you a question?"

I could see him tensing up, like I was going to hit him or something.

"Yeah? What is it?"

"Well, I got up late today," I said. "I don't have a job right now. It was only maybe half an hour ago I heard about this emergency, but I still don't know what it is. Can you tell me what's going on?"

His face froze into a mask for a second, and then he shook his head.

"What the fuck," he said. "Why not? We're not supposed to say anything, but the orders make no sense to me. No one told me anything official either."

He hesitated, then shook his head.

"People have been going missing," he said. "That's what I hear, anyway. All this —" he gestured at the mostly empty streets, "all this isn't just people trying to get out of town or holed up in their houses. My partner didn't show up to work today. A lot of the people who should be around are just gone, is what I think."

"Wow. It's just here in town? Or outside? The rest of the country?"

"I don't know," said the cop. "I'd expect all kinds of outside attention — staties, the feds, all the news people in the world. But I haven't heard anything all day from outside town. Internet and phones are fucked, and the only radio and TV is local. Right now, I just want to finish my shift, if you know what I mean."

"That doesn't sound good," I said. "But if no one knows what's going on, at least that explains why no one's saying anything. Thanks for that, anyway."

"Yeah," he said. "Thanks for the food."

I left him, went back to my flat and had lunch. It wasn't bad. I thought about Michel and his plastic jugs as I washed down the burgers with tap water. Then I boiled some water on the stove, let it cool a little, poured it into a pitcher with some tea bags and let it sit to steep on a sunny windowsill. After lunch, I sat around for a while, wondering again if there was something I should be doing. Couldn't think of anything. Every once in a while, a siren wailed in the distance, but there was no sign of anything horrible happening anywhere I could see.

Usually, I'd spend the afternoon walking around town, but I didn't want to today. It was too strange out. I didn't like the lack of people, the way everything seemed to be closed.

I walked aimlessly around my flat for a while, played some solitaire, and eventually I pulled out a book and started reading it. Swann's Way. Got it on recommendation. I'd tried to read the book a few times before but usually got bogged down on the first page. Today I was making progress. Slow and steady — very slow, in fact — but moving forward.

When I looked up, four hours had passed along with fifty pages, and it was late afternoon.

All in all, it was about as productive and useful a day as ever. I was tired of reading now, so it was just a dull three-hour wait until eight. Couldn't take doing nothing anymore, so I turned on the TV again. The one working station was doing human interest stories now and in no case did the reporters or interviewees talk about what was going on. Orders, or an aversion to facing the facts? Strange, either way.

Time passed with painful slowness. At last, it was eight. I let myself out of my flat and went downstairs without seeing anyone at all. Summertime dark, still some glow in the sky. It was half a mile to Caernarfon. I was almost there, walking the familiar path, when it occurred to me the place might be closed. Caernarfon was a brick-walled corner pub in the middle of a residential section. Being dimly lit inside at the best of times with no plate glass facade and no neon, there was no way for me to tell for sure until I got right to the front door. Open, thank God.

The pub wasn't much, a tiny little place wedged into the corner of an anonymous apartment building, but it was where I spent most of my nights. A minute at home doing nothing was painful. Here it was relaxing ... comfortable, even. Maybe too comfortable, which was why I only came here at night. I had the idea that if I hung out here during the day, I'd vegetate completely.

Rhys was there as usual behind the bar, big bushy red-brown beard and all. He was my closest friend, I guess, in the whole world, even if I wasn't his. I don't know why I looked up to him, really. Looked at logically, he was just the owner of the one place I spent time at. He'd never asked me for a favor, not even once, but if he ever did, I knew I'd do it for him, whatever it was.

Only a few regulars were present and no one I didn't know.

At one of the high, round tables in the middle of the room, Nora was perched, as usual pecking away at her laptop. Slight and energetic, pale skinned, with straight brown hair. Quick to take offense, and a biting wit to her too, but I liked her anyway.

At the bar, Quaid, a big heavy-set black guy with a blocky jowled face, was nursing a beer trying to ignore Steiner, who was talking at him, if not to him. Another silent type, like me. I imagined he concealed some deep sadness, something I'd never dared to ask him about, something he never gave any sign of, but I thought it was there anyway. And I liked him for the strength he showed in bearing up under the burden.

The Professor sat in the corner, a shot-glass at her elbow, playing her endless chess games with herself. Rightfully speaking, I didn't even know her a little bit, as she spoke even less frequently than Quaid and almost never mixed with anyone. Even so, I trusted her and respected her. No good reason, I just did. She'd been the one who recommended Proust to me.

They were all friends, that's how I thought of them anyway, even if they weren't the kind you'd go bowling with, invite for a dinner party, or even ask out on a date. Not that I ever did any of those things anyway.

So Caernarfon felt like home. Rhys nodded to me, drew a pint of pilsner and pushed it to me across the bar. Whenever he had nothing better to do, he stood there in front of a faded old wooden sign on the wall. The thing was grey with age, and you could just make out a red snaky dragon, the paint mostly gone, only a scattering of scarlet flecks remaining to outline the form. I asked for some nachos to go with the beer and, while he was microwaving the sauce, I took out my wallet to pay.

Rhys held up his hand, shook his head and said, "No charge today."

For the emergency. Right.

Steiner turned to talk to me. He had a lined face, not old though, with a permanent five o'clock shadow, black stubbly crewcut, a diamond stud in the rim of his left ear, and steel-rimmed glasses. Always talking, I think to cover up his anxiety. He told me once he was phobic, but what it was he was afraid of kept changing. He never knew what it was going to be. Traffic this week, spiders the next, sharp objects for a month after that. He'd got the stud in his ear to fight his way through that one. The way he put it, the old fears never quite went away, but there was always a new one to worry about. For him, the worst time was in-between, when the old fear was fading and the new one hadn't yet formed. Whatever it was this week, he was here tonight, just like me. I liked him for making the effort, for overcoming his fear every night, for fighting through his troubles.

"You think George will show up tonight?" asked Steiner. "With Patrick? Or Jane and Allen?"

I didn't see what he was getting at. Both couples were occasional patrons at the bar, but not here just now.

"How should I know?"

"Yeah," he said, "it's just they have families, don't they?"

"I guess so. What does that matter?"

Steiner nodded. "I don't think we do, do we? I mean, those of us here now."

"Hey," said Rhys, rumbling through his beard, "I have a family."

"I mean, married-with-kids family," said Steiner.

"Oh."

"George and Patrick don't have kids," said Quaid.

"Yeah, but they do have rings, anyway."

Steiner turned and called out. "Hey, Nora, you're still single, right?"

"So?" She answered without turning her head.

"Just seems like a pattern, is all. Trying to figure things out."

"What," she said scornfully, looking at Steiner now, "you think this is a singles-only catastrophe? Give me a break."

Steiner laughed and tapped his chest to signify she'd scored a hit. After a pause, he turned back to Rhys.

"How long can you keep this place open? I mean, if the emergency continues."

We all looked at the bartender. Nora stopped typing. The Professor even looked up from her game.

"I've got plenty of beer and spirits," said Rhys. "If it's just you five, could last for months. The bar food will run out in a week or two if I can't buy more, but hell, it's not like there's a wall around the city, is there? I don't think we're cut off. It's just the network's down. Power and water are fine."

"For now, anyway."

"Well, if we lose power, you'll have to drink in the daytime," said Rhys. "And if we lose water, well, there's always beer."

Time passed. I ate my nachos and drank my beer, fell into a sort of reverie, not thinking about anything in particular. Steiner spent most of his time talking to Rhys. I overheard him saying his fear this week was drowning, so he made sure to take a bath every day.

"Stubborn bastard," said Rhys, and patted Steiner on the shoulder. Steiner smiled, blushed a little. It didn't take much to make him happy.

About mid-way through the evening, we were interrupted by a stranger's entrance. Nothing much to remark on an ordinary night but tonight we all paid attention. He was in his late 60s or early 70s, with black hair, bags under his eyes, deep jowls, and a big nose.

He stopped at the entrance, looked around for a minute, then walked up to the bar.

"Yes, sir?" asked Rhys.

"I, uh, I want to buy a bottle of whiskey," said the man.

"This is a pub," said Rhys, "not a liquor store. I can serve you a drink if you like."

"The liquor stores are all closed," said the man.

Rhys shrugged. "If you like, but I'll have to charge you like you'd ordered twenty shots. That's how many are in a bottle. It will be damn expensive compared to a liquor store."

The man hesitated, then nodded.

"What do you want? Will J&B do?"

"That'll be fine," said the man. He reached into his jacket, fumbled out his wallet.

Rhys turned to the rack on the wall behind him, found a fresh bottle of J&B.

He turned to the man. "Here," he said. "If you really want it, fifty bucks. I'd rather serve you at the bar, though. Free drinks tonight."

"Free?" the man said, "Really? But, uh, no, I just need the bottle."

He paid for the bottle, turned and left.

"That was weird," said Steiner.

"Not so much," said Rhys. "The guy's a maintenance drunk. I recognize the type. Probably, he's okay most of the day, but he drinks himself to sleep every night. I bet he drinks at least a half bottle, maybe the whole thing. You saw that big red nose, the pores and everything? If he was a regular binge-drinker or a real no-hoper, he'd be happy to drink for free. But he's got his self-respect, you see. Doesn't like getting drunk in public. Hence the bottle. We'd never see him in here except, like he said, the stores are all closed."

"Huh," said Steiner. "I didn't see any of that until you said it, but you're right. And I get the picture too. The poor old guy is going home now. Lives alone, I guess. Maybe he's going to be drinking while watching late-night TV, or maybe he's figured out how it works after all those years and he's drinking in bed so at least he can fall asleep there. Poor bastard."

And that was it for a while.

The others weren't talking much tonight, so I was pretty much left alone. Apart from Steiner's nervous chatter, there was the comfortable silence of people who don't need to talk to each other all the time. I spent my time relaxing in silence, nursing a beer, occasionally ordering a refill, occasionally chatting with Steiner and Rhys. When I looked up again, it was after midnight. Tonight everyone seemed a little hesitant to leave. At last, Nora closed her laptop and put it in her carry-bag.

"Hey, Nora," said Quaid, turning away from the bar. "You want a walk home? I mean, you know, just because of the, ah, situation outside."

"No!" Nora's response was automatic. "I'll be fine." Then she paused, hesitated. "Wait. I'm sorry. Yeah, I think I would like that. If you don't mind."

They left together. I watched them go. Steiner followed my gaze as the door closed behind them.

"Wish you'd made the offer?" Steiner was often obtuse, but other times he could be annoyingly perceptive.

"No. Well, maybe. I don't know. It was the right thing to do, anyway, for one of us."

"Yeah."

Steiner said goodnight then, and the Professor started putting her pieces away. I was about to head out myself, but the Professor surprised me by speaking up. In the last year, we'd exchanged maybe a dozen words total — when she spoke at all, it was usually to Rhys about liquor or sometimes to Nora about poetry — but I never felt like she was cutting me out, just that we didn't need to spend our time chatting.

"A moment of your time, if you will."

I think she was around 60 or so, but at that age it's hard to tell. She had a narrow face, with long grey hair tied back behind her head, and she wore rectangular rimless spectacles. Tweedy jacket with elbow patches worn over a blouse. With her clothes and formal diction, the nickname was inevitable. I guess she liked being called that because she never asked anyone to use her real name, and if I'd ever known what it was, I'd forgotten it now.

"Sure, Professor," I said. "How's the emergency treating you?"

"Well enough," she said, "and thank you for asking. But really I'm more interested in how it's treating you."

"Huh? I'm fine. Why do you ask?"

"Hm." She looked me over carefully. I wondered what she was looking for in my face. "To be honest," she said, "I don't think I can explain myself yet. Intuition, if you will. Please take care, though."

What the hell? But she seemed sincere.

"Well, thanks," I said. "Have a good night yourself."

She nodded, folded her chess set under her arm, and headed out the door.

I went back to the bar. And then I thought, *Why didn't I offer to escort her, like Quaid did for Nora? Maybe because she seemed so self-assured? And why wouldn't I need an escort for that matter? Anyway, it was too late, now.*

"Guess I'll be heading home, too," I said. "Hey Rhys, I appreciate you keeping the place open. Not sure what I'd do if you weren't there."

"S'nothing. Have a good one. See you tomorrow."

The walk home was uneventful. I didn't see a soul the whole way. At one point I could have sworn I heard a horse neighing in the distance, but I looked around and there was nothing. I went to bed a little early and slept through the night with no dreams at all that I could remember.

2

I WOKE UP ON THE EARLY SIDE, for me anyway: around 10 a.m. The feeling of strangeness from the previous day was gone, or else I'd gotten used to it, not sure which. Phone and Internet were both still down, and I didn't even bother with the TV. Despite that, I was expecting to see the whole city back to normal when I went downstairs, but no. There was hardly anyone on the street and the few people I did see were furtive and didn't cross my path.

Down to the strip mall again. The walk was unpleasant today. The neighborhood looked even more down at the heels than usual, and I felt like I was a walking target, all by myself on the street. The supermarket hadn't reopened, but the McDonalds was still working. No cop car today. I hoped nothing had happened to the officer. The girl from yesterday was at the drive-through window again.

"Hi there," I said. "Still open, I see."

"Yes, sir. Can I take your order? Hamburgers are still free."

I asked for two hamburgers. Three had been a bit much the day before.

She placed the order on her machine, stood there smiling at me. There was something different about her today. I wasn't certain what it was at first, then I realized it: one of her eyes was blue. Surely, both had been brown the day before? I couldn't say for sure. I didn't know what teenage girls were into these days. Maybe coloured contact lenses were a thing? But somehow, I didn't think so.

She ducked away, came back with the sack.

"Thanks for choosing McDonald's," she said.

I laughed. "Like there's another choice. Everything else is closed."

"Well," she said, "thanks anyway."

I went back home, feeling happier just for talking to her. Who cared what color her eyes were, after all.

On the way back, I ran into Michel, returning after parking his car. He seemed different today, not so aggressive. Chastened almost. I wondered where he'd been.

"Hey," he said, almost tentatively, "what's that you're carrying?"

"McDonalds. Place right down the street is still open. They're serving hamburgers for free."

"What the hell! I better get down there. Thanks, man."

"No problem," I said, smiling. The wariness he'd shown the day before was gone. Yesterday, I thought he'd begrudged thanking me for helping him with the water but today he seemed more honestly friendly. It was something, anyway. I was going to ask him where he'd been driving, but he was already gone. I shrugged, went on inside. When I got up to my floor, I knocked on all the doors. There were seven of them including Michel's and no one answered at all. Not surprising on an ordinary weekday, but today … well, maybe they'd all fled the city.

Another hamburger lunch, this time with iced tea. Tasty. I turned on the TV afterwards, just for the hell of it, but it was showing old sitcom reruns, and I couldn't take more than five minutes of laugh tracks before shutting the damn thing off.

I went back to reading Proust. Another afternoon of unexpected progress. From chapter to chapter, the thread of the story was a little murky for me because I kept getting distracted by the individual words. Each sentence was a work of art. It was like getting too close to a pointillist painting only to find out that each dot of paint was an exquisite miniature of its own. Something to do with Marcel, and Swann, and some women. I decided I liked it anyway, even if I wasn't exactly reading with comprehension. I wished I had the Internet back, as I wanted to find out more about Proust. I knew that Swann's

Way was the first book in his larger work, but I didn't know how many other volumes there were, and now I was worried about finishing the book and having nothing left to read. I wondered where the nearest library was and if it was open. I pictured myself breaking in just to borrow a book and almost laughed out loud.

There was a knock on the front door, and I nearly fell out of my chair. I'd never had a visitor before that I could remember, not even a salesperson. I got up, opened the door, and there was Michel, holding a bottle. "Hey, man," he said, "I just wanted to thank you for telling me about the McDonalds."

He looked ragged and run down, like the neighborhood I'd walked through earlier.

"No problem," I said.

"Here." He handed me the bottle. Pastis, French liqueur.

"Thanks." I put the bottle on the kitchen counter, which I could reach from the front door. He looked at me a little hesitantly. I wondered what was going through his head. He looked like he wanted to say something, but couldn't.

"Are you doing all right?" I asked, feeling awkward. "I mean, you know, the emergency and all."

Michel's face contorted, and he took a step forward. Something was happening inside him that I didn't understand. He seemed to be losing control of himself.

"I, uh — At the bridge — Oh, mon Dieu —"

He launched himself at me. I wasn't expecting that, was taken completely by surprise, but it wasn't an attack. He hugged me, eyes shut, turning his head to rest it against my shoulder.

"Merde ... Oh — oh." He couldn't say anything coherent at all now and just sobbed. I was shocked; it seemed completely unlike him to do something like this. But then, I didn't know him at all, did I?

I didn't know what to do so, more or less by default, I held him there, my arms wrapped around his shoulders. After a minute he opened his eyes and turned his face up towards me (I was a head taller) with a sort of eager, hopeful look.

So I kissed him, surprising myself. I didn't think about it; it just seemed like the thing to do. His breath smelled of stale cigarette smoke, but his mouth tasted of licorice. From the pastis, I supposed it was. Pleasant; a little sticky-sweet, perhaps, but nice. It was a conscious choice, a moment later, to drop my right hand to his bottom. Probably shouldn't have done that, but I felt just then like I hadn't touched anyone for a long time. He snuggled up against me. After a bit, I could feel his erection through his pants, up against my thigh. But me ... I felt nothing inside. Too bad.

The kiss ended naturally. He was breathing harder now. I hated to do it, but —

"I'm sorry, Michel," I said, and I let him go, taking a step back. He looked dismayed, almost shattered. "I really am. I mean, I wish — but I don't feel it, the spark, you know?"

"No," he said, and he held his hand out. "Can't we —" but I cut him off.

"Listen," I said, "it's me, all right? My fault. Wrong signal, okay? I can't go through with it. I'm really sorry."

"Oh," he said, and after another moment, "okay."

He really looked destroyed. It hurt me to tell him no, though I hardly knew him, and I almost wanted to change my mind, to have changed my mind, but it was too late now. I put my hand on his shoulder, but he shrugged it off.

"If you need anything —" I said.

"It's okay," he said again, sniffed and wiped his eyes.

Damn. He was crying.

"I'll be fine, I guess. It's just —" he gestured vaguely, all around him.

"Yeah," I said, "the world, right? It's fucked up. I'm sorry."

He walked away without saying another word. I closed the door behind him, sat down, closed my eyes. I wanted the whole world to go away, but it was all still there when I opened my eyes. Wanted to be able to sleep, but wasn't tired at all. Shit. Maybe I should have just gone ahead with it. Couldn't have been that bad. Not as bad as this, anyway.

I tried to pick up Swann's Way again, couldn't read a word. I sat there on my bed for a while, not really thinking about anything. It was 5:30. Hours to kill before it was time to go to the pub. Twice I got up, almost decided to knock on Michel's door, but changed my mind. Somehow the time passed.

•   •   •

At Caernarfon, Nora and Quaid sat by themselves. They weren't saying much but, for once, she wasn't involved in typing away at her laptop, and Quaid was paying more attention to her than I'd ever seen him pay to anything before, like he'd finally come out of his cave after a long hibernation. Usually he'd just sit and drink, rarely speaking. Tonight, though, he seemed animated and lively, and Nora, surprisingly, was responding to him as if she cared what he had to say. The Professor was in her corner, chess pieces deployed. Steiner was bending Rhys's ear when I walked up to the bar.

"Things are changing," said Steiner.

"So?" Rhys shrugged. "Things always change."

"I mean, in a weird way."

"Hm." Rhys made a noncommittal noise. Steiner turned to look at me.

"Take him, for example —" Steiner paused, squinted at me, shook his head.

Rhys nodded at me, started drawing a beer. When he finished filling the glass, he slid it over to me.

"So?" He turned back to Steiner.

"I was going to point something out," said Steiner, "but I guess I can't. He doesn't seem to have changed at all."

"What are you saying?"

"I'm not sure anymore," said Steiner. "I mean, well, Nora and Quaid are obvious. Never would have guessed either of them would ever hook up, much less with each other. Then there's you, Rhys —"

"What about me?"

"Well, your beard."

I looked again at Rhys. Wow. Sure enough, his beard was trimmed neatly. It was a bit of a shock, as I was so used to his previous look. He used to have this enormous wild growth that expanded outward in all directions like an auburn cloud. It was still a full beard but combed out straight, maybe even pomaded, with a clean border and a point at the chin.

"Jesus, Steiner," said Rhys, "I'm allowed to change it, aren't I?"

"Sure," said Steiner, "but it's been, what, four years since I started coming to this place, and you've never trimmed it before. I wouldn't have guessed you'd ever do it. Why today?"

Rhys was silent for a moment.

"I'm not sure," he said at last. "Just felt it was time. What about you? How have you changed?"

Steiner smiled. "On the way over here, it was kind of dark. Some of the streetlights are out, you know? Anything could be hiding in the shadows, right?"

"This is a safe neighborhood," said Rhys.

"Sure. But remember last year, I was creeped out for the better part of a month because of those shadows. Never really got over it, either."

"Yeah," said Rhys, "but you came every night anyway."

"It was tough," said Steiner. "But today, well you know, there's nothing there. Nothing at all, really. I mean, it's pretty dismal out there right now, with no one on the street. But it's silly to be afraid of it. Of course, I knew that all the time. That's how I got through it. But now, I really know it, right? That's what I'm talking about. I changed. Like, overnight. It's like I fixed myself. And there's something more, too —"

"Mutantur omnia nos et mutamur in illis."

The Professor had spoken the line.

Steiner asked, "What is that? Latin?"

"All things change, and we change with them." The Professor got up from her chess set and walked over to us, shot glass in hand. She tipped it back, set it on the bar in front of Rhys, who refilled it. Cutty Sark, neat.

The Professor tapped back the refill in a swallow, nodded sharply and smiled. She put the glass back on the bar in front of her but covered it with her hand when Rhys moved to refill it again.

"I gather you've experienced no unusual personal changes," she said to me.

"I don't think so," I said, distracted by a vision playing itself out behind my eyes that had nothing to do with what we were talking about. It was Michel. I was imagining him looking out the window of his flat, a glass of pastis in hand, a cigarette in his mouth. And now he was holding a steak knife, looking at his wrist, practicing the stroke. Shit. This was ridiculous. So he'd felt a little weak, a little weird earlier, had done something he wouldn't normally have done. He wouldn't kill himself for that, would he? Or just because I turned him away. Surely not ... Maybe I shouldn't have kissed him, but it seemed like the thing to do at the time. And having kissed him, should I have gone ahead and slept with him? If not, why not? Was he even gay at all? Was I? I'd never kissed a man before. I didn't think so, anyway. Confusing.

I shook my head, returned to the moment. More or less. Still a faint image of Michel in my head.

"I'm not even sure," I said. Damn, I was seeing Michel crying now, and walking away. I felt hollow and full of regret all at once. Sleeping with him or not, I shouldn't have left him that way.

The professor said something, but I wasn't listening.

"Sorry, folks," I said. "I've got to go. Left something hanging back home."

The professor surprised me by putting a hand on my shoulder before I left.

"You will return, though? Tomorrow, I hope?"

"Uh, sure, I guess so."

"Good," she said. "It's important. I'll be looking forward to it."

I ran home. The way I figured it there'd be no harm done if it was just a stupid fantasy, but I'd regret it if he really did something to hurt himself. I was out of breath by the time I got to Michel's door, took a few seconds to calm myself down. I put my hand on the painted metal of his front door, took a deep breath, imagined him sitting on his bed now, knife in his hand again. Stupid. I shook my head. As if he'd kill himself over me, of all people, someone he didn't even know.

I raised my hand to knock but didn't do it, felt like a complete fool standing there with my hand in the air. It was like there was an invisible wall in between me and the door, or better yet, an invisible cable holding my hand back. Did I really want to do this? It would be awkward, embarrassing. Fuck it. The wall shattered; the cable snapped. I knocked on the door.

I imagined him looking up sharply, turning toward the door. In my head he put the knife down, got to his feet, took a step toward the door.

"Hey Michel," I called out, "you there? Are you okay?"

I imagined how my voice would sound through the door. Muffled, distant, and weak. Minds-eye Michel took another step forward, paused. Maybe he was running into the same doubts, the same hesitation I had just experienced. At last, he shook his head, turned back to the bed, picked up the knife. It was a horrible moment, but he just walked back to his kitchen counter, opened a drawer, and put the knife away. Then he pulled a tumbler out of a cabinet, made himself a pastis and water, and sat down at his kitchen table to drink it.

Back in reality there was no answer to my knock, but I felt a lot better now, even knowing the whole thing was just my imagination from start to finish. I went back to my own flat, relieved and even a little happy, without the slightest logical justification for it.

I felt tired, even though it was before midnight. Emotional exhaustion, maybe. I went to bed, and if I had any dreams, they weren't nightmares.

•   •   •

I got up the next morning at nine feeling pretty good. Surprising. I usually felt lousy getting up in the morning, but for the last couple of days, not so bad. Turned on the television when I got out of the bathroom, just for the hell of it. More stupid reruns.

It was too early for hamburgers when I was finally ready to leave, so I decided to take a walk, see what was going on in the city. I left my apartment, looked down the hall towards Michel's door. Maybe I'd try him again later.

It was kind of weird walking around town. Everything looked like it was a lot more than two or three days abandoned. No fires, no damage from looting, just everyone gone. Buildings all dusty, their facades pitted and worn, like they'd been standing there for decades. Sure, some of the buildings probably hadn't been cleaned or refurbished in that long, but not all of them. It wasn't right, but I didn't know what it meant, just that it was something I couldn't explain, and it made me uneasy to see the decay.

I took an hour, walked up onto the highway, hiked over to the bridge east out of town. There was the same line of cars from the news a couple of days ago, empty and abandoned now. Looking down at the river, the water looked fake somehow, like one of those old model scenes where they want you to think you're looking at ocean and the camera is really close up to some heavy fluid that's not water at all. And then, across the bridge ... nothing. Well, not nothing, not just a blank space, but I had the sense the town and landscape across the river was like a theatrical flat, like there wasn't anything really there. The idea made me feel sick, though I didn't know why. I turned away from the river prospect before I threw up, headed back down the highway into town, and after a while I started to feel better.

The McDonald's was the only thing at the shopping plaza that still seemed to be in decent shape, the plastic and aluminum of the facade looking as slick and new as ever. Even the supermarket with its plate glass fronting looked as if it had been standing there for years.

"Hello, sir! Welcome to McDonald's!" The clerk was as cheerful as ever.

"Hi there," I said.

"More hamburgers?"

"Yes, please. Two."

She had two blue eyes today, blue-dyed hair worn long and straight, and her nails were the same colour, with a sort of shimmery look to them, like a video special effect.

"Excuse me," I said, "if you don't mind, I don't want to seem creepy, but are you doing okay? In the emergency, I mean."

"Well, yeah," she said, "I guess so." Her sparkling professional facade dropped. "I mean, nothing's all that bad, anyway."

"Are you alone? Or do you have people left for you at home?"

"No one at home," she said, "but really, I kind of prefer it that way. Of course I have Sandeep here. Someone's got to make the burgers."

"Oh, right."

"Hey," she said, "check this out, though."

She flourished her nails, swept her hand out in front of her in a horizontal swipe. Her hand made a sound like five little knives ripping through the air, and she left a blue sparkling trail in the air for a moment.

"Whoa!"

"Yeah," she said, "Cool, huh?"

I wasn't able to say anything for a moment, and she looked disappointed.

"You don't like it?"

"No," I said, "It really is cool. It's just uncanny, if you know what I mean. Do you have any idea where, umm, you got it from?"

"Well, no," she said. "I did my nails last night, but just with regular polish. This morning they were like this. Just like in that anime, you know?"

"Not really," I said, "but it looks good on you, anyway."

"Thanks!"

I was going to say goodbye, but then something occurred to me. Considering the situation in town, I was a little ashamed not to have thought of it before.

"Listen," I said, "there's a few of us who meet in this pub not far from here. If you want, I could show you where it is tonight, after you close up."

"I can bring Sandeep?"

"Of course."

"Good," she said, "he's kind of — well, I guess he could use a change, too. It's a little boring with just Sandeep to talk to, no phone and nothing on TV but those old reruns. Yesterday there were only two customers, including you."

"And the other one was a short guy with a French accent, right?"

"How did you know?"

"My neighbor," I said. "I should bring him along too. I guess I'll stop by after it gets dark, if that's all right."

"Sure," she said, and ducked back into the restaurant, returning with my hamburgers.

"Thanks," I said, "I'll see you later then."

"Hey," she said, "Thank you. And oh, yeah, my name's Mina, by the way."

"Mina? Um, nice to meet you." I was at a loss then. Almost dizzy. Not sure what to say. Then I laughed.

"Call me Ishmael," I said.

She laughed too. "We did Melville in class last year."

I was happy to escape without further damage. Why did I have to make up a name on the spot? I did know my own real name after all. It's just that it seemed like calling myself that would be a lie.

When I got back to my apartment, I found a blonde woman waiting for me in the hall. She was wearing a white sun dress with blue polka dots, white sandals, and (I thought) nothing else.

"Hello," she said.

"Umm, hello."

"Michel told me about you." She took a step forward.

"He did? Is he, ah, doing all right?"

She giggled. "But of course," she said. "It is nice to meet you. I am Michèle."

I heard a difference between the names Michel and Michèle, though I couldn't have said what the difference actually was.

She held out her hand in that formal way that means the person is doing it ironically. Her hand was cool. A moment later, she was in my arms. It was a mutual coming together, unplanned on my part but definitely volitional. I kissed her. Her breath smelled of stale tobacco, and her mouth tasted of licorice.

After a minute, the kiss ended naturally, but I didn't step away.

"Michel," I said, "that is you, isn't it?"

"Oh yes," she said, breathing hard. "But this time, a spark, isn't it?" She put her hand between my legs. I couldn't deny it.

"Yes," I said. "Yes. I'm sorry about last time. I wanted to apologize, but last night you didn't answer the door. I was worried about you."

"You are very sweet," she said. I thought her accent was a little thicker now. "But aren't you going to invite me in?"

"Oh!" I let go of her, fumbled with my keys, opened the door and we went inside.

We kissed again.

"Very nice," she said after a minute. "Come now: "Là-bas." She pointed at the bed.

"Michel, Michèle, I mean, I don't understand. How did —"

She put her finger up against my mouth. "No talking," she said, "at least not this kind. Not now."

Proust went unread. We spent the whole afternoon in bed, taking breaks only for the occasional glass of pastis and water — I thought the way the clear liqueur turned into a milky fluid when mixed with water was an alchemical, almost magical sort of transformation — and to smoke cigarettes, which she had to duck back to her flat to obtain.

"Listen, Michèle," I said. We lay on our backs, holding hands, naked and happy.

She propped herself up on an elbow. "Yes?"

"I have some friends," I said, sitting up in bed to look down at her. "We meet at a pub not far from here. It's where I spend most nights. Apart from you and me and a couple of people at the McDonald's, we might be the only ones left in the city. Will you come with me tonight?"

She looked up at me and sat up in bed. "These friends," she said, "are they fucking friends?"

"Well, no —"

"In that case," she said, "I will go. Do you think I am jealous?"

"Maybe," I said, smiling.

She laughed, put her hand on my thigh. "I tell you," she said, "My whole life, I am a straight guy, n'est-ce pas? I mean, one hundred percent straight, no question. Marseillais, you know, until I come over here for work. I fuck girls all the time, I like it fine, okay? No love, though. Two days ago, you were nothing to me. Just someone to carry the water, you know?"

I nodded. I wanted to hear what she was saying, to understand what had happened to her.

"I was eating hamburgers in my flat yesterday, after you told me about the McDonald's. That's when it hit me. It was like a flash of lightning. I realized there was nothing to me, I was just a shell of a person. Like a balloon, right, just hot air inside? Or a meat-eating machine, a thing for turning hamburgers to shit. I felt like I had nothing left that was me. I lost something along the way maybe, something I needed, I didn't know what it was."

Huh, I thought, *I always feel that way.* But then I realized maybe I was lying to myself. If I didn't feel anything, would I have rushed home last night? Meanwhile, Michèle's eyes had taken on a faraway look. I put my hand on hers as it rested on my thigh. She looked at me and smiled.

She said, "It was, what do you call it? An existential crisis, right? I was trying to think what to do, then I realized like a light turning on, you, you have what I need, okay? I almost choked on the hamburger. Never thought I would want a man like that. But I knew it was true. When you kissed me yesterday, I was in heaven. For a minute you gave me a little bit of myself back."

"Oh," I said. "That makes what I did afterward even worse, then."

She laughed. "It is okay, all right? If you had kissed me two days ago, probably I would have given you a bloody nose. Maybe I would have tried to kill you. My part of Marseilles, someone calls you a faggot, it is not a pretty thing."

"Two days ago," I said, "if you'd asked me to kiss you after I took the water up, I would have run back into my apartment instead."

"Just as well, then." And she ran a finger down the side of my jaw. I almost lost the thread right there, but I still wanted to know what she had managed to do, how she'd changed herself.

"But then," I said, "after I — after I turned you away, what happened after that?"

"Well, I sat around for a while feeling sorry for myself, right? I drank a lot, smoked a lot. I thought about suicide, but I didn't know if I meant it or not."

"You had a knife," I said. "You were thinking about cutting yourself, weren't you?"

"Yes," she said, then looked up at me in amazement. "How —"

"I don't know," I said. "I sensed it somehow last night, when I was at the pub with my friends. I knew it was just my imagination, and I couldn't believe anyone would hurt themselves over me anyway, but still ... I ran home, feeling like a real shit for being so unkind to you earlier, but then I got to your door —"

"I was so happy afterwards," she said. She leaned over, rested her head on my shoulder, and I put my arm around her. "You knocked, and then you called my name. I was so happy, but I was afraid also, and ashamed, so I didn't answer the door. I thought, why even bother answering, he doesn't want me anyway. But I was happy you thought of me. I went to bed happy, too. Very tired all of a sudden. And I slept all through the morning, got up very late. And then, when I woke up —"

"You were a girl."

"With girl clothes in my bureau. Impossible, right? I don't even know how to put some of them on."

I laughed. "I can't help you there. But I still feel bad about this. I guess I'm responsible, somehow? I think I should just have made love to you the first time. That first kiss was pretty nice, really. Maybe you didn't have to change yourself so much."

"But you said it then: no spark. And now ..." She lifted herself up so she was looking in my eyes. I couldn't help myself; I kissed her again.

Later, lying face to face, bodies entwined. "What it is," I said, "I don't think I deserve what you've given me. I feel like I forced you to change your sex without knowing what I was doing, or why. It's not fair."

She said, "You're very sweet. But I am not giving. I'm taking. I said you have something I need. I need it desperately. It's not sex or even love though I like both those things very much. It's something more profound. More strange. I have no words for it, but it's there. You're offering it to me, and I'm taking it."

"I guess that makes me feel better," I said, "but I still wish I knew what was going on. How you were able to change. You seem so different now from the way you were two days ago. I couldn't believe it when you jumped into my arms that first time."

"And now? Maybe it is true, I am playing at being a woman today. It's fun, you know? I admit it, it's a little silly, but I like it. Tiresias was right! But I think two days ago I was playing at being a man. Even more fake and not as much fun."

Michèle kissed me then, and once more: the spark. I couldn't resist her, and I didn't want to.

We finally came to another pause. My endurance had astonished me. It seemed almost uncanny. But maybe it was a natural response to everything else falling apart, the urge to unite and share pleasure. I walked over to the bedroom window and raised the blinds, which took a little trying because they'd been down since I'd moved in. Michèle joined me there. Together we looked down at the city. It looked desolate and lifeless. No people on the street, no birds in the trees, nothing.

"How am I?" she asked, murmuring the question into my ear. "I mean, compared to other girls."

"I can't even —" I broke off, confused. She could feel me tensing up, so she took a step away and we turned to face one another.

"Listen," I said, "I'm serious now, I'm not just saying this. I'm pretty sure I've slept with other girls. But I can't remember any of them now. It's like a dream after you wake up, you know? Everything before the emergency. Or before you. I don't know which it is. But either way, I know this, you — you're the best thing I've ever had."

"Hah," she said, "I make you wake up from the dream of past life. Very nice. Opposite of Proust, right? Marcel is always remembering things. I see you have the book."

"I'm in the middle of it," I said. "You've read it?"

"They make us read it for school," she said. "I hated it then, but now, I think maybe I would like to read it again."

I picked up the book from where I'd left it in my dresser and handed it to her.

"Let's read it together," I said.

"All right," she said. Still standing by the window, Michèle weighed her breasts in her hands and looked down at herself with a critical eye.

"You think I am fully a woman?" she asked. "I mean, not just a man in the shape of a woman, but one hundred percent? Will I have periods? Get pregnant?"

"You look like one to me," I said. "But even if you weren't, would it matter? It wouldn't to me. But what do I know? All I know is the spark, right? I have no idea how you managed to change in the first place."

"You think I do?" She giggled, took my hand and led me back to the bed, pushed me down onto my back, straddled me. "Still time before we go to the pub, right?"

I wanted to sigh, but really I couldn't.

"Right," I said, and I put my hands on her hips. Plenty of time.

We made it out of bed eventually. I have no idea where I got the stamina, but each time was better than the last somehow. I doubt I could have managed it at any other time in my life, not even at thirteen, but today ... well, it was very nice.

We walked together down to the strip mall. All the buildings, and the streets too seemed even more dilapidated than they had been earlier in the day. The process of decay was accelerating. I had the feeling it was irrevocable, that a final collapse couldn't be all that far away. Without Michèle walking next to me, I don't know what I would have done, but knowing she was there kept me going.

At the McDonalds. Mina was at the drive-through window looking like an anime character. Her eyes were solid electric blue now, with no whites or pupils at all, and her blue shimmering hair had a metallic gleam. But she didn't seem to have any trouble with her vision. Instead of her McDonalds uniform, she was dressed in a sort of elastic skin-hugging black jumpsuit with a blue plastic belt low on her hips. The effect was like an athlete or maybe a superhero.

"Oh hi," she said. "Ishmael, right? Is that your neighbor? She's pretty! But I thought he was a guy, the one I served yesterday, you said?"

I introduced Michèle. She said, "You did serve me yesterday. I used to be Michel, now I am Michèle. With an 'e' on the end."

"Oh," said Mina, not showing any surprise at all. "I'm sorry. I should have guessed. Do you like it this way better?"

"Oh yes, very much! But is this look new for you too? It is very cool."

Mina laughed. "Good! I was hoping it would come out that way. She turned to me. "Are we going to your bar now?"

"Yes," I said. "Your friend, Sandeep, is he coming too?"

Her face fell. "He's gone," she said. "I don't know — I think it's my fault. I let him go."

"What do you mean?"

"Well," she said, "after you left, I sort of had to bully him into agreeing to come tonight. He stayed in the kitchen the whole last three days. I think he was afraid to leave. Then I got all excited thinking about going to your bar, and I had to go home and change, you know? So I left Sandeep here, because there weren't any customers coming anyway. I felt nervous the whole way, like I was doing something wrong. And when I got back, he was gone."

"You don't know where he lives?"

She shook her head. "I don't think he's home," she said. "He's gone. You know what I mean, don't you?"

I nodded. "I'm sorry. I guess you wish you could have done something, right?"

"Yeah."

"There's no way it's your fault, though."

"I don't know." She blinked; it looked weird to see those bright blue eyes covered even for a moment. "I have the feeling now, it's crazy okay, but I have the feeling he wouldn't have gone away if I'd stayed here with him."

"Maybe you're right," said Michèle, surprising me and Mina too. "I think maybe — maybe without him," (she patted me on the cheek), "I might be gone too. I was lucky and he came back for me in time. But your Sandeep … it's still not your fault. It's his for not sticking with you. That's what I think."

"He wasn't really my Sandeep," said Mina. "I just worked with him, you know? But I still feel bad."

We were silent for a moment. I couldn't think of anything else to say about Sandeep. Too bad for him I guess, if what happened to everyone in town was bad, anyway. Who knew?

"Do you need to close the shop here?" I asked.

"No," said Mina. "I already cleaned everything up and shut everything down. It's not as if anyone is going to break in and steal the free food. We have like three thousand patties left in the freezer, maybe the same number of buns, that's what takes up most of the storage space, and a couple of barrels of ketchup and sauce left. Lots of pickles and onions left in the fridges. At this rate, it'll last for months. If we have that long."

I didn't want to think about what she meant by that. Mina put one hand on the sill and vaulted out through the drive-through window, not even brushing the window frame with her body. She landed on her feet like a cat. Like she was a gymnast who practiced the move every day. But I bet she'd never done it before.

3

T HE WALK TO CAERNARFON was a little scary in the darkness of a summer evening. The tenements and apartment towers we walked past seemed to be cloaked in age. I had the idea it had been decades or centuries even since anyone had used the buildings. The traffic lights were all turned off now. Most of the streetlights were dead, with only the occasional bulb flickering on and off as we walked by.

Rhys was behind the bar as usual, his beard still neatly trimmed. Tonight he was dressed impeccably, looking almost regal in a conservative gray suit and russet striped tie, an apron at his waist. I'd never seen him in anything more elaborate than a polo shirt and jeans. Still, not a big deal. Anyone can dress up if they want to.

Nora and Quaid, now *they* were different. She used to be slight and bird-like, all bones and nervous energy. Neurasthenic, maybe, if that was still something that people could be. I would have guessed her weight a few days ago at maybe a hundred pounds, tops. But between yesterday and today she'd grown noticeably bigger and stronger, and she looked calmer and more at ease too. And she had tanned to a chestnut brown. Quaid on the other hand had always been big. Yesterday and as long as I'd known him, he'd been tall and portly, a 6'4" endomorph, and he used to move with slow deliberation as if he had to be careful not to break things or knock them over. But now he was almost slender, his motions were more lively, and his darker skin had lightened a few shades. Matching Nora's.

As for Steiner, if he'd changed any further it was nothing visible, anyway. He turned to look as we entered and raised a hand in welcome.

"Hey," he said, "more people."

I made introductions.

"How do you do," said Quaid, and "It's nice to meet you," said Nora. Their voices sounded similar now, like they were brother and sister.

"And that's not creepy at all," said Steiner, nodding at them, but he was kidding.

Quaid and Nora laughed, harmonizing. "We like it," they said together. They stepped forward and each put a hand on one of Steiner's shoulders for a moment, smiling at him, and he blushed.

"What'll you have, folks?" Rhys asked.

"Lagavulin, if you have it," said Michèle, and Mina, who seemed rather shy in the face of these strangers, asked for a ginger ale.

And then I realized someone was missing. Hadn't occurred to me till then. "Where's the Professor?" I asked.

Rhys just blinked. "Who?"

"Come on," I said, "you know who she is."

"Sorry," he said, "I don't. Who do you mean?"

"Steiner," I said, "you know the Professor, right? Nora? Quaid?" Steiner shook his head.

"We don't know any Professor," said Nora, and "It's been fifteen years since I was in college," said Quaid.

I wasn't sure whether to be angry or afraid. She wasn't just in my imagination. I knew that. Didn't I?

Michèle put her hand on my arm. "What's wrong?" she asked.

"There's another regular here," I said, "an older woman. Wears a tweed jacket, always has a chess set. She's here all the time, and every night since the emergency. And now these people say they don't remember her."

"Wait a minute," said Steiner. "An older woman, you said? I almost ..." He trailed off.

Rhys lifted his chin, seemed to be staring into the distance. "Wasn't she — a long time ago —"

"Oh," said Nora and Quaid together. "The Professor!"

Rhys brought his fist down hard on the bar. The sound made us all jump.

"Fuck me," he said, "how could we forget her?"

"I don't know," said Nora, and "I'm scared now," said Quaid.

We looked at each other in silence for a moment, and the door swung open. The sudden motion shocked all of us, I think, and Mina's eyes and nails flashed bright blue. The Professor herself staggered into the pub, looking as bad as I've ever seen anyone in my life. She wasn't injured, but she looked all in: pale, thin and wasted. Her hair was all undone — had it always been white? I thought it was gray — and the expression on her face was chilling. She was gasping, teetering on her feet.

Mina had more presence of mind than the rest of us. She leaped forward and managed to catch the Professor's arm, steadying her, or she probably would have fallen. She helped her to a stool.

Rhys handed the Professor a shot glass of Cutty Sark, and she slammed it back. A little color came back into her face.

"Thank you," she said, wheezing a little.

"Something very odd just happened," said Steiner. "Are you feeling well enough to hear about it?"

"Oh yes," she said, "and I should tell you what happened to me, too."

Steiner explained that the Caernarfon regulars had forgotten her existence.

"I'm sorry," said Rhys, "I feel like I betrayed you, somehow. This is my place, you're my customer. You deserved better of me." Steiner nodded, and Nora and Quaid bowed their heads.

"It's all right," said the Professor, "It was my fault, really. But you say he asked where I was?" She nodded at me.

"Yes. It was very strange," said Rhys. "As if you were someone I had known and forgotten a long time ago. And then you came back into focus, was how it was."

"Aha," she said. "It seems I very nearly made a terrible mistake. But perhaps it's just as well. I think I have at least a sketch of an idea what's going on now."

"What?"

She smiled. "It might take a while to explain. But first, who are these newcomers?"

A new round of introductions. She listened as Michèle explained how she came to be with me, not holding anything back at all. I felt like

I should be a little embarrassed, but everyone looked so pleased at what Michèle had to say that all I felt was the warmth of their regard.

"I see," the Professor said to me, "That's what you were up to last night. Well done. And you were wise to bring this young lady with you." (She nodded at Mina, who blushed; I could tell because her dark cheeks took on a faint bluish shimmer for a moment). "At this point, I suspect there's no one left in the city who is not in this room."

"What?" Rhys was horrified. "No one? How is that even possible?"

"I can't answer that," she said, "but I'd guess that over the course of the first day of this … emergency, around ninety percent of the city vanished. Yesterday, I think it was up to ninety-nine percent. And today it's worse out there. A great deal worse. I want to tell you what I experienced just now."

"I think this probably deserves another round," said Rhys, and he handed out fresh drinks and refills.

"Right," said the Professor, who was now looking much better, "I decided today to investigate the city, to see if I could find anyone left at all outside our little circle here. I thought I'd explore for an hour or two, then head back here. Unwise. I hadn't been walking ten minutes before I got lost."

"Really?" said Nora, and "Lost?" said Quaid. "But it's not that big a city," they finished together.

The Professor looked at them quizzically. "Ah. I see you two are making progress, anyway."

They smiled at her, and she nodded. The two held out their hands and the Professor reached out to them with her own. They held the contact for a moment, and then the Professor blushed and took her hand back.

"Anyway," said the Professor, "I got lost. I turned a corner and found myself at an intersection with no signs, on a road I didn't recognize. It was all apartment buildings. Blank facades. It should have been a block not far from here, but I just couldn't recall ever seeing it before."

"Did you turn back?" Mina asked.

"Oh yes," said the Professor, but then I didn't recognize the street I was returning to, either. It was a nightmarish experience. I felt like I was wandering for hours, and every street was unfamiliar. Of course they were all completely abandoned. Have you noticed how dilapidated everything looks now?"

Rhys shook his head. "To be honest," he said, "I've stayed in this building the whole time. Just looking out the door gives me the creeps." We looked at him and he said, "I have a flat upstairs, you know."

Steiner said, "Probably just as well. But yeah, I've seen it. I live only a block away myself, but on the way here I had the feeling I was walking through a city that's been abandoned for a hundred years. Everything is so fucking desolate."

Quaid and Nora nodded sympathetically. "We try not to look," they said in unison, "while we're on the way here."

"I just concentrate on how Quaid's hand feels while we're walking," said Nora, and Quaid said, "If I just look at her, I feel a lot better than if I look around me."

"I noticed the — the decay too," said Michèle, "but it doesn't upset me so much. Because I'm not a native, is that it?"

The Professor shook her head. "I think there's another explanation. But anyway," she said, "it's as if entropy has been allowed to run wild, isn't it? Things aging around us, things disintegrating, things disappearing."

"But not everything," said Rhys. "Not Caernarfon."

"And not my McDonald's," said Mina. "Just half an hour ago, it looked the same as ever."

"Indeed," said the Professor, "and we should try to understand why this is, why these places seem to be more resistant to the decay than the rest of the city. And why we ourselves seem more resistant than the other people who used to live here. I have a theory. But first let me get myself unlost, if you don't mind the phrase."

Rhys nodded and said, "Go on, then, Professor. We're listening."

"I was wandering around trying to find a landmark, something I recognized, and I felt like I was getting weaker with every step I took. It was like an hour was passing somehow for every minute I was actually lost. I don't think I would have lasted much longer on my own."

"But you found your way back here?" Steiner put his hand on the Professor's arm and she smiled at him.

"Yes," she said. "I turned the corner, and there it was, this street, the pub, Caernarfon, as if it had been there the whole time. I suppose this must have happened just at the point that you all managed to remember my existence."

"You think it's connected?"

The Professor nodded. "Yes. My mistake was going too far from the pub on my own. I nearly lost myself forever out there." The Professor looked at me, "But you saved me, did you not? You were the one to bring me back into everyone's minds here."

I said, "Well, maybe, but I don't know that I actually did anything."

"Yes," she said, "exactly. You didn't do anything special; and you didn't have to."

"Come on Professor," said Steiner. "We're lost here ourselves. Give us some idea what you're talking about."

"Right," said the Professor, "I'm going to have to use some clumsy analogies, metaphors not even as strong as analogies, really, and they're not all going to line up with one another, but it's the only way I can see to explain things. Here we go."

She paused for a moment, then started speaking as if reading poetry, declaiming.

"The world is a watch, and the spring's broken.

"The laws that govern the world have been repealed.

"The world is a computer, and someone just pulled the plug on it."

The Professor looked at us. I think she felt we were in sympathy with her words. Then she spoke up again.

"God has abandoned his creation."

The Professor lowered her head, then tossed back another shot of Cutty Sark.

"Isn't there a poem?" asked Rhys. "Things fall apart; the centre cannot hold; mere anarchy is loosed upon the world ..." he trailed off.

Nora said, "Yes, Yeats. Those lines are apt, but the poem as a whole is perhaps not quite on target." And Quaid said, "Maybe Eliot is more to the point? The city outside is like a waste land, isn't it?" I wouldn't have guessed he read poetry, and maybe he didn't at that.

The Professor nodded. "At any rate, it seems to me the world is pretty much done for at this point; or at least our part of it is. It's possible the rest of the world is all right and it's just us who are in trouble. It's even possible the people who have vanished are living in their own city, wondering where we've gone ... but I prefer to take things at face value. Everyone else is gone, and I think it's everything else that's falling apart."

"Everything?" Michèle was standing beside me, and I could feel her trembling, so I put my arm around her. She nestled into my embrace, and I felt a lot better myself.

"Yes, I believe so," said the Professor. "Or rather, almost everything. What I think has happened is that whatever it is that is required to maintain the existence of things as they are, the ding an sich —, well, whatever it is has run out, or has been removed from our world, or has deliberately abandoned us. Whatever the cause, the world is decaying rapidly, and what's left of it has become … fluid, perhaps is the mot juste."

"Fluid?" Steiner said, "I don't understand."

"Easily changeable," said the Professor, "hence the changes we see in ourselves and in the city at large. Some of these changes are in the way of subconscious or even conscious wish-fulfillment, don't you think?"

I looked carefully at the Professor. When she'd first come in she'd seemed ancient, older by far than the sixty or so I'd had her pegged at. But now … her hair was still white, true, but her face was unlined and young. She looked up at me, seemed aware of my considering gaze, flushed a little.

"Yes," she said, "I've changed, myself. Anyway, all this suggests that our own minds have some power over reality now. Whatever it was that was maintaining the natural law of the universe or of our portion of it is gone, and so everything is changeable. I think what we see around us now is either the last dregs of a rapidly disintegrating former reality, or else is being maintained locally, for the moment at least."

"What do you mean by maintained locally?" asked Mina.

"Ah," said the Professor, "here we come to the really speculative part. On the first day, I had the idea that there might be some fixed points, or standing waves perhaps, places where the process of decay wasn't so rapid."

"Oh," said Steiner. "Like this pub, you mean."

"Yes," said the Professor, "and that notion might not be entirely wrong, but now I think it's not quite right, either. There's precisely one common element to the things that continue to exist without decay, that aren't just shells of themselves like those streets I was lost in."

"Come on," said Steiner. "What is it?"

"Him," she said. And she pointed at me.

"What?" "Are you crazy?" "I don't think —" "Well, maybe —" "Oh! I see …"

Everyone's responses came quickly, and as quickly were cut off, or subsided. And now they were all looking at me.

Michèle squeezed my hand. "See? That's what I was trying to tell you before. I needed you …"

"What do you mean?" I asked. "Are you saying I'm some kind of god or something? That's not true. It can't be. I'm just an ordinary guy, more of a loser than most, even."

"My dear fellow," said the Professor, "I have said nothing of the sort. But you must admit that everything left in the world appears to be connected to you."

"What about the McDonald's? I never ate there before the emergency."

"Oh well," said Mina, "but you came by the first day when things were still sort of normal."

"One way or another," said the Professor, "it seems that the only people and places still remaining with any stability are those you met or visited during that first day. Perhaps you lent a certain coherence to them — to us, I should say. Michèle's experience seems to confirm this directly; she felt such a great need of your, er, essence, shall we say, that she changed very radically indeed on your account."

"I still can't help feeling bad about that," I said, "because I'm still feeling like she changed just for me." I turned to Michèle.

"I don't care," said Michèle. "Perhaps the person I was would have cared, before ... But I know I changed for my own sake, not for yours. And if everything was back to normal, if I didn't need anything from you at all, I would still need you. If you know what I mean."

"Aww," said Nora and Quaid, and they smiled at the two of us.

"You have to admit," said Steiner, "it is kind of nice, the way it worked out for you two."

"Well, what can I say ..." I was embarrassed, but it was hard to stay that way with everyone so pleased for the two of us. I turned back to the Professor. "What does this mean, though? If the whole world is disintegrating except for our little corner, what will be left for us? How long can we keep going on this way?"

"I'm afraid the prospects aren't good," said the Professor. "There's so little left, you see. But I think there is hope, albeit a rather faint one."

We all waited for her to explain. I never knew she liked talking this much or I would have spoken with her more before the emergency. Maybe she really was a teacher, once.

"There's a chance," she said, "that this seeming disintegration is the prelude to some kind of universal transfiguration. Possibly the old reality is being replaced. Something new might emerge, eventually."

"What?" Rhys asked, "Do you mean God might create a new world for us?"

"I suppose that's a possibility," said the Professor. "But I don't mean anything so specific. I'm not saying anything about God, because

I don't know if she exists. It's conceivable that a new reality could form without anyone's deliberate guidance. There might or might not be a place for us there. And also —" she hesitated, but Steiner took up the thread.

"It's possible," he said, "that we could be the ones to create the new world. Is that what you were going to say?"

"It seemed like hubris," she said. "But yes. And if that were to happen, somehow ... I think he would have to be the one to take the lead." She nodded at me.

I wanted to protest some more, but it seemed pointless.

"Let's say you're right," I said. "What would taking the lead involve?"

The Professor bowed her head for a moment.

"There you have me," she said, "I have no idea. Perhaps as the disintegration continues the answer will become clear."

We broke up for a while after that. Quaid and Nora went back to their table, communing silently with each other. Rhys and Steiner started talking about what sort of world they'd make, if they had the chance, and the Professor took Mina aside for a private chat.

"Well," said Michèle, "what do we do now?"

"I don't know," I said. "On a regular night, I'd just hang out, have the occasional drink, and pretty much do nothing at all. I'm not sure we have that kind of time to kill anymore."

She grinned. "I can think of something else we could be doing. The best use of time, don't you think?" She squeezed my bottom, and for all the mutual calisthenics we'd shared already, I wanted her then more than ever. It seemed so unfair to have to lose her after such a short time, if the Professor was right.

I was thinking there must be a lot of spare rooms right here in this building we could use, and I was going to reply, but she flushed, lowered her eyes, and answered herself.

"I'm sorry," she said, "but I think maybe, maybe you shouldn't leave them alone anymore. Your friends here. After what happened to the Professor, you know?"

I was struck by a vision then. I saw Caernarfon decaying before my eyes, all these people withdrawing into themselves, growing distant from one another somehow, their bodies withering, falling apart with the room, the whole place turning gray and barren, and at last fading away completely.

"No!"

I said it out loud, involuntarily, and everyone turned to look.

"Sorry," I said, "but now I'm wondering how much time we really have. I don't know if waiting for the end of everything is such a good idea, after all. I mean, if we fall apart too —"

"We might not have the chance to see what comes next," said Steiner. "I get you."

The Professor stood up from her huddle with Mina.

"Are you suggesting some sort of action?"

"Some sort, yeah. I'm suddenly very afraid of what will happen if we do nothing."

"Hm," she said. "I'm inclined to trust your intuition. Do you have any ideas at all?"

My mind was a blank. I wanted to cry with frustration. "No," I said, "nothing —" and then something did occur to me.

"Listen, Michèle," I said, "you went out driving the last couple of days, didn't you?"

"Not today," she said, "but the days before, yes."

"Where did you go?"

"Well, the first day, I drove to work, you know. A design firm, downtown. But no one is there, so I headed home, turned on the car radio, heard about the emergency. Then I went to the supermarket and got water and groceries. You found me that day when I was parking the car."

"All right," I said, "what about the next day?"

"Ah," she said, "that day, in the morning, before you told me about the McDonald's. I think now I was already feeling like I am losing myself, like I couldn't stay at home anymore. I had to run away. I told myself it was to get away from the city, to find the real world again, but really it was to find what was missing inside me, I think."

She shuddered, turned pale. I had to put my arm around her again, and it seemed like she gathered some strength from me. It was nice to be able to do that for someone.

She patted my arm and continued. "I drove to the bridge first. It's all jammed up with cars stopped and abandoned, and I thought about walking. But something, something is not right there across the river, so I didn't want to even get out of the car. I thought about turning around and going across town south or west, to get out through the suburbs, but somehow I just couldn't do it, I couldn't face the idea of trying again, so I went home. I came back, what a relief that was, you told me about the McDonald's, and the rest of the day you know."

"I'm so sorry," I said, "I know what you're talking about. That would be enough to mess anyone up. I'm sorry even to ask you to remember it. See, I walked to the bridge myself, this morning."

I told them what I'd felt when I went out there, the strangeness of the river, the seeming fakery of the world on the far side.

"I didn't think of it then," I said, "but I felt almost like I was at the edge of the world. It was like the river was a of boundary between our old world and ... well, and something else. I had the idea the view of the landscape across the river wasn't really there, but was some kind of shell. I'm not sure I'm explaining this very well."

"No," said the Professor, "that's very interesting. The bridge is where I wanted to go when I got lost. You say it was like a boundary, the edge of the world? Was the city getting worse and worse as you approached it?"

"I don't think so," I said. "The city up to that point was decaying, for sure, but it seemed about the same near the bridge as elsewhere on the path I walked."

The Professor looked pleased.

"It's not a lot to hang our hats on," she said, "but if beyond the city is only chaos or nothingness, I would have guessed there would be a gradual decay. But with a definite edge ... well, maybe ..."

"Maybe there's something on the other side," said Steiner.

"But how do we get there?" asked Nora and Quaid. "The Professor got lost an hour ago after only a few blocks," said Nora, and "we don't want to get lost ourselves," said Quaid.

"Ishmael went earlier today," said Mina. "Maybe he can go again."

"What," said Rhys, "your name is Ishmael? Since when?"

"Since today," I said. "Long story."

Mina laughed. "You made it up? Well, anyway, if you're the source of, of, whatever it is keeping us here while everything else goes to hell, maybe you can hold us together long enough to get to the river. If we all go, I mean."

"And what do we do when we get there?" Rhys asked.

Nora and Quaid looked at each other and shrugged. "Take a chance," they said.

"You think we should go now?" Steiner asked.

"It's the middle of the night," said Rhys. "I dunno. It's bad enough during the day."

"Yeah, but I get the idea we're running out of time."

The Professor hadn't said anything for a while, but now she spoke up.

"If anyone is wearing a watch, I wonder if you would be so kind as to take it off without looking at it," she said.

"What? Why?" But though he complained, Rhys turned his watch around on his wrist without looking at it, and started fiddling with the clasp. Nora held out her hand, palm up, and Quaid removed her watch as well.

"Well," said the Professor, "it seems to me that we've spent the entire night here talking, do you understand what I'm saying? It's just about sunrise, don't you think?"

"But —" Rhys elbowed Steiner, cutting him off.

"Oh," said Steiner. "Yes, I think you're right."

"Think about the sunrise," said the Professor. "The sun won't be visible from the door here, there's buildings in the way. No tweeting birds around here, but you can imagine how it will look outside, if you close your eyes."

Mina nodded and closed her eyes. The rest of us followed suit. This wasn't going to be easy for me: I hadn't seen a sunrise in a long time.

"Imagine it," said the Professor, "it's still quite dark out, but there's just that hint of brightness in the sky to the east. You know that odd clarity you seem to get at dawn and dusk? The way everything looks sharp and clear, even in the dim light? And every moment the light changes as it gets closer to sunrise. The blackness overhead turns gray, and then a dim blue emerges from the grayness. At last, the sky lightens, and there, the sun's up."

I was seeing it now: the dark streets, the murky sky overhead, and then, that faint change in the air, the sense of something about to be born, and the light gathering in the east …

4

“OPEN YOUR EYES.”
I opened my eyes with the feeling I'd been dreaming, asleep a long time. I was just now waking up refreshed and ready to face a new day.

"Rhys," said the Professor, nodding at the door. "If you would."

"Sure," he said, but he walked a little hesitantly to the door, then threw it open with some force.

"Holy shit!" said Steiner. There was a weak light coming through the door, not from streetlights either.

Michèle laughed. "Why are you surprised? It's morning, isn't it? What did you expect?"

"Ah — Of course," he said. "Sorry, what was I thinking?"

No one wanted to talk about the Professor's little miracle, maybe for fear whatever it was we'd accomplished would collapse. It took a while to get organized but at last we set off, fortified with instant coffee, mimosas (Rhys cracked two bottles of champagne he'd been saving) and microwaved burritos.

Go to the river: not much of a plan, but as we made our way through the empty streets, it became clear that the city didn't have much time left at all. The streets were bare even of loose trash. The buildings looked more like stacks of brick and stone than habitations. Their windows were so scratched and dirty they were completely opaque, and the building facades had developed a sort of gnarly gray-brown surface, like a scab, regardless of their original colors. Automobiles parked along the curb were mere lumps of rust. No traffic of course, and so we walked in silence except for the sound of our own feet. Perhaps the city had never in its existence been so quiet. The pavement of the streets looked all but worn away, the concrete slabs of the sidewalks pitted and spiderwebbed with cracks. The streetlight columns were corroded, and the traffic lights weren't working at all anymore. The sky was a dirty yellow now, a thin overcast illuminated by an as yet invisible sun.

For the most part we walked in a silence of our own. The extent of the devastation was humbling, and none of us had that much to say at first. Perhaps we were mourning the passing of the old world; perhaps we were mourning the passing of our old lives.

Michèle and I held hands as we walked. Her warm grip, the occasional brush of her body against mine, her glance when from time to time she looked at my face to make sure I was okay, it was all a tremendous prop. I had the feeling for a while there I was running on fumes, gas tank almost empty, but then she whispered in my ear, "Maybe we can fuck our way into the next world," and all I wanted to do was stop and take her up on the offer. Who knows, maybe it would have worked.

I supposed Nora and Quaid must have had an even more intimate rapport. I wished I'd had time to talk to them about what they'd gone through, how they'd changed. Was it telepathy, what they had together, or maybe an extreme form of empathy? I wondered what sex was like for them, and with that idle thought it occurred to me maybe they would end up as hermaphrodites, a pair of lovers in perfect physical balance. How would that work out? And just at that moment the two of them looked at me and Michèle and they smiled, and I knew whatever they had it wasn't just between the two of them. Some other time I might have been embarrassed, ashamed even, to be read like that, but now it just made me feel good to be able to share the joke.

Then I wondered how the other four could stand it, being on their own. The Professor had a look of determination on her face, but she seemed to be doing all right. Steiner was tense and withdrawn, but just as I thought I would say something, pat him on the shoulder maybe, he looked up and grinned, showing his teeth. Defiant as ever, but without that core of insecurity he always used to have. Whatever it was he'd done to himself — for himself — had given him some reserves of strength anyway. Mina strode along as if she didn't have a care in the world. It was hard to read her face with her new eyes and all, but she seemed almost to be looking forward to whatever would come. Then Rhys, in his expensive suit and his quiet demeanor. He was walking a little in front of the rest of us as if he was breaking a trail. At that moment he really seemed to me like what an old-time lord or king must have been, back in the days when they mattered, if any of them back then had the dignity and gravitas that Rhys had now, anyway.

At last, the Professor spoke up. "For what it's worth," she said, "your influence appears to be having its effect."

"How do you mean?"

We were heading downtown. Decaying brick apartment towers and ravaged brownstone tenements gave way to pockmarked postmodern office towers and older brutalist skyscrapers whose facades no longer seemed to be plated with gleaming black glass so much as with clouded gray plastic.

"Well," she said, "for one thing we're not lost. If the street signs weren't so corroded, I could tell you exactly where we were. Look, in a few more blocks we should be able to see the bridge."

We paused at the next intersection.

"What the fuck?" Steiner pointed. "Did you see that?"

A flash of white in the distance, then it was gone.

"I saw something," I said. "What was it?"

"I swear," he said, "I thought it was a horse."

"Hm." Rhys squinted, peering down the street. "Well, whatever it was, it's gone now. Maybe we'll see it again when we get to the river."

At the next corner a half a mile off I could just make out the steel towers marking the bridge entrance. We turned east down a street that had just days before been graced by rows of luxurious brownstones. Now they were slabs of scrofulous stone looming four stories to either side, with the withered husks of dead trees lining the curbs.

One block through the ruins of the city, two, and —

"Jesus," said Steiner. "This is horrible."

We emerged from the side street onto the service road for the river highway. The river itself was just a couple of hundred yards away, and to me it looked like it was flowing with ink, not water, or something worse, even. It was hateful to look at, and after a few moments, I turned away.

"It's the river Styx," said Nora, and "the Acheron, maybe," said Quaid, and despite the gravity of the moment, they paused, looked at one another and laughed softly together.

There should have been a strip of green parkland on the far side of the road, with crosswalks for pedestrian access, clusters of trees and the occasional playground, boathouse, or pier. Now there was just a brown blasted stretch of dusty cracked earth. Here and there the fallen corpses of trees could be seen, mere clusters of thin dry sticks.

We walked across the access road up to the highway entrance, under green reflectorized route signs worn away into illegibility hanging from a crossbar above the road. There was no traffic, of course, and the only sound here was the wind, a thin whining scream whipping its way into the city from across the river.

Rhys led us up onto the highway entrance to the bridge, a long sweeping curve of concrete and steel that still had a certain glamorous geometry to it, despite the decay. Until you got all the way up to the bridge, though, you couldn't see much because of the guard walls and the incline of the ramp, so we were spared the impact of the view until then.

And there we were, the beginning of the bridge proper, as far as I'd gotten the day before. From here there was a good view of both the river below and the far side, if that's what it was. The prospect was as daunting as the last time, more so if anything. There was definitely something wrong with the view across the river. There should have been some rolling hills, a cluster of radio and cell towers atop the highest hill, and a town just on the far side of the bridge. All that was there, kind of, but it looked faked up, simulated, if that makes sense. It was more like an artist's conception of what the far side of the river might look like, and not a human artist either, but painted with an alien, inhuman perspective.

"Jesus Christ," said Steiner again. "It's not even close to real, is it? What a horrible sight. And I don't even know why it's so bad. It just is."

Michèle said, "Oh! Oh, it's worse than before." She looked at me, and I thought she wanted me to embrace her again, but then she shook her head. "I should face it," she said, and she turned back to the scene, but she didn't let go of my hand.

Nora and Quaid stood shoulder to shoulder, arms around one another, and they gazed somberly out across the bridge.

"I think it's like a wall," she said, and he said, "Yes, just on the far side of the bridge."

Mina stood there, the wind whipping her long blue hair back behind her like a half-cape, apparently invulnerable to the effects of the scene. I had the feeling that she had a sort of defense in place, like armor or a shield braced in front of her maybe, and the wind was slowly eating away at it, but she seemed all right for now.

Rhys looked at the view and staggered, fell to one knee. I could see him struggling to rise, to right himself, and I was going to move forward to help him, but he looked back at me over his shoulder.

"It's all right," he said, "I can take it. I have to." And he rose to his feet, advanced once more to take the lead. Whatever it was that was affecting us this way, I thought he was taking on more of it than anyone else, was somehow blunting the impact on the rest of us.

What Rhys was doing made me feel bad for a moment, because wasn't I supposed to be the one that was keeping everyone else together? And then I felt it. The connections. I could feel everyone else, all at once: Michèle's warmth, her love and her kindness; Nora and Quaid's mutual focus and the expansive affection they felt for everyone else; Steiner's hidden fire, a burning something he'd lit within himself to replace the old fears; Mina, standing there like a superhero readying herself for battle, a strange power in her hands and eyes; and Rhys, a proud knight carrying his banner in the vanguard, a legionary protecting his eagle, and, oh hell, I was his eagle, wasn't I? And then I sensed my link to the Professor, stepping up from behind me to put her hand on my shoulder; I felt her cool resolve, her wisdom, and her secret hopes for a future beyond all reason and expectation ...

And I was supporting all of them. It wasn't strength, it was that mysterious thing that the Professor had deduced, that Michèle had intuited, that I had available to give for no reason I could say. And I knew that I was doing what I needed to do.

"Very well," said the Professor. "Rhys, if you would be so kind ..."

"Here we go," he said. He strode forward onto the bridge. And we followed him.

Abandoned cars jammed the lanes on the outgoing side of the bridge, but there was plenty of room on the walkway, not to mention the other side of the road. We walked forward, and though there was no physical resistance it felt to me like all of us, Rhys especially, were walking into the face of a strong gale, a hurricane even. A real wind — I think it was real — was keening past our ears, but it was nothing like the ethereal one I thought we were forcing our way through.

It was a struggle, and a mighty one at that, and I doubt any of us could have done it on our own. But in the end the river was only a half mile across, and it couldn't have taken us all that long to walk it, though it felt like an eternity.

At last, Steiner called out, "Hey Rhys, hold up. This is it!"

Rhys staggered, put his hand out reflexively, and then jerked back as he found he had touched something just in front of his face.

"It's a wall," he said. "A wall." There was wonder and awe in his voice. We all looked up. The struggle of making the crossing had distracted us from the scene ahead, but now we could take in the prospect. It really was a wall. At such close range, the view ahead no longer looked the slightest bit like a real landscape. In front of us the view was a smeared-out mess, an expressionist nightmare, a painting ruined by getting far too close to it. Off to the sides, into the distance, there was some semblance of a scene, but it was skewed, elongated, wholly unnatural. And yet it wasn't just a static flat image as might have been painted on a giant fresco. There was some depth to it, some trompe l'oeil sense of three-dimensionality to it, but it just wasn't a very good illusion to begin with, and up close it broke down completely.

Steiner stepped forward. "What does it feel like?" he asked, raising his hand.

"Stop!" cried Rhys, "don't do it!"

But it was too late. Steiner placed his palm flat against whatever it was, not jerking away from it as Rhys had done, but deliberately probing, trying to feel it. And I saw he'd come in contact with something, and then I saw the alarm, the horror on his face. He made a gasping, wheezing sound, a deathly rale. The color drained from him and he froze in place. And I could feel it, a terrible leaching pull, like whatever resource it was I was giving to the others was being drained away through Steiner by a vast insatiable hunger.

Rhys tried to knock Steiner's arm away, but it seemed he was stuck; Steiner fell to his knees, but his hand remained in place, above his head.

I rushed forward myself, raised my hand to try to pull him away.

"No!" Steiner gasped it out. "Don't do it. Let me go! You'll only lose yourself too!"

And indeed, he seemed to be dwindling before my eyes, not in height, or in the mass of his body, but in some other way, as some sort of underlying form or structure was being drained out of him.

"Don't be an idiot," I said, and I grabbed his forearm. It was stiff, unnatural, almost seemed like it wasn't a human arm at all anymore, but strange chalky stuff. And I felt it, the pull, the hunger of whatever this thing was, redoubled now that I was in actual contact with him. It was dreadful, and I think if I had been alone, it would have broken me right there, but the connections ... Rhys, and Nora and Quaid, Mina, the Professor, and a desperate surge from Michèle —

The two of us, working together, could do nothing to free Steiner. I could feel him, though, the wall draining his essence, his form, his life.

"Get back," said Rhys, and I took a step away. "Mina. Your nails. Can you — can you cut him away from the wall?"

"What?"

It only took Mina a second to understand what was being asked of her, and another second to muster the determination to do it. She flourished her nails, and they began to emit a blue laser-light glow.

"Oh," said Steiner then, whispering, "that's it — It's pulling me through ..." His voice cut off with an unpleasant clacking noise, and his face turned an unnatural gray.

Mina swept her hand down in a flash of blue. She left a glowing trail in the air behind her, and her nails cut through Steiner's wrist with a dry click, just as if it was chalk.

There was a pause, just a heartbeat, and Steiner's body disintegrated, turning to a fine dust along with his clothes. All of us stood back in shock. For an instant his hand remained, adhering to the strange devouring wall, but then it too fell apart. The cloud of dust was taken by the wind, and a moment later there was nothing left of him at all.

"Oh," said Mina, "oh no." The glow from her nails went out, and she raised her hands to her face.

We stood there for a moment, paralyzed. At last Rhys put his hand on Mina's shoulder, and she flinched.

"It's all right," he said. "You did your best."

She looked up at him, shook her head.

"I don't understand," she said. "How could something like this happen?"

"I don't know," said Rhys, "but the seven of us are still here, and he said — Steiner said he was going through. Maybe, maybe ..."

"You think he's been pulled through?" asked Nora, and Quaid said, "but his body fell apart. He's gone."

"Yes," said Michèle, and she moved up next to me again. "But still, maybe part of him ... I don't know."

"That's the problem," said the Professor. "We don't know. But if the world is lacking this resource, whatever it is, this order, or essence, or organizing force, whatever you want to call it, maybe that's a kind of hunger? Or a kind of debt, perhaps might be a better way to put it. That might be what happened here to poor Steiner. Maybe something similar happened to everyone else in the city, even without having to touch the wall."

"Is that what's behind this shell?" asked Nora, and "That's it? An enormous hunger, a debt?" asked Quaid. They looked at one another. "Then is there anything left for us, if that's true?"

The Professor shook her head. She looked tired all of a sudden, and older than before. "I don't know," she said. "I just don't know."

"No," said Michèle. "That's not it."

"What?" The Professor asked, "What is it, Michèle?"

"Listen," said Michèle, "we are looking for a new world, yes? If you can touch it, here and now, while we are on the bridge, that means it is no new world. You say it's the debt of the old world, trying to be repaid. So this wall, this shell, it is still our world. The edge, yes, but the edge of the old world. Not the new one. There is still hope."

The Professor looked up. She smiled. "Thank you," she said. "That's plausible. More than that, it's sound reasoning. I should have realized it myself."

"All right," said Rhys, "but what then? We can't even touch the damn thing. What are we supposed to do with it."

Mina laughed. "That's easy," she said. "You say it's a shell? All right. I say it's an eggshell. The eggshell of the old world we don't need anymore. We're like the chick, right? In the egg? So what do we do? We break out!"

And she stepped forward, raising her own right hand. Her fingernails gleamed a brilliant blue like a video special effect, like five lasers, and her eyes flared like xenon lamps, enormously bright. I think we all wanted to stop her, but she was too quick for us, too decisive. She pulled back her hand and leaped forward, striking at the strange surface, a brilliant arc of five blue lines trailing behind her in a sweeping curve as her hand lashed forward.

Her nails hit the wall. There was a whining sound. A screaming sound. A brightness grew from the point of contact.

Mina was poised in a long low lunge, one hand on the ground forming a tripod with her legs, the other hand pushing forward against the wall. Her body was like frozen lightning, her stance conveying all her strength and power forward, through her hand, through those five strange nails. What was happening there was unclear. It was too bright to look at now, but I didn't feel that horrible draining, that terrible hunger as I had with Steiner's contact.

I don't know how long she stayed like that, but it must have been at least a minute. We watched her, in awe I think, as the brightness grew from the point of contact, as her eyes grew brighter and brighter, until she seemed like some sort of elemental creature, someone who had transcended all human boundaries.

And then she collapsed. Her eyes guttered out, and her hand dropped away from the wall, fingernails now only gleaming like telltale LEDs, not the cosmic weapons she'd just been wielding. Her strength failed in her left arm, and she toppled over to her left, fortunately away from the wall. The spot in the wall where she'd been trying to break through retained a curious glow, a gentle sort of lingering radiation like newly blown glass almost cooled down to a dim orange heat, but I saw it was slowly dying away.

Rhys rushed forward, raised Mina up, held her in an embrace.

"Not enough," she gasped. "I'm sorry!"

Rhys shook his head. "No," he said, "I'm sorry. We were damn fools to let you try that by yourself." He looked up over Mina's shoulder at us. "You know what I'm saying?"

"Oh!" said Nora, and "Yes," said Quaid.

Michèle said, "I'm sorry, Mina, we should have known better."

The Professor nodded too, turned to me, "You understand, do you not? What happened?"

And I knew it too.

"Yeah," I said. "I'm an idiot. Whatever it is Mina has given herself with those nails, whatever strength she's gotten from her own change, it's from that — that organizing force, right, that essence. And we're all connected, we all have some of it now, and maybe I have more. And we stood around like fools watching, when we should have been helping. Right?"

"Exactly," said the Professor. She turned back to Mina, "I'm sorry too, my dear. I should have known better what was going on."

"Jeez," said Mina, and she wriggled out from Rhys' embrace. She kissed him on the cheek, though, and it was cute to watch him blush.

"Okay," she said, "so we messed up. My fault too, for not giving you guys a chance to help. So why not just try again?"

So we tried again. What the hell, right?

It's not easy to fit six people into a tight formation around just one, especially when the one is trying to do something athletic, and it's even harder when the six have to avoid touching a soul-eating wall right in front of their faces. But we decided that physical contact would be better than imaginary moral support, so we managed it eventually. I'm sure if anyone was watching it must have looked goddamn silly, but after all if there was anyone to watch we wouldn't have been in this situation in the first place.

"Ready?" asked Rhys.

"Ready," said Mina.

"All right," said Rhys, "now it's going to work this time. And the reason it's going to work is it can't not work, because we're the only ones here, and we all want it to happen. So all of you except Mina, close your eyes, okay? And you can see it now, can't you? It's a star, a six-pointed star, and Mina is in the center. And all the points of the star, that's me and that's you guys, you're all feeding the center, right? You're sending in everything you have for her to use. You can feel it, can't you? I know I can. And okay now, Mina, you can feel it too. So whenever you want, you go for it, okay?"

And I felt it too, and I saw it. I had one hand stretched out to the small of Mina's back, and I had my other arm around Michèle. She had one hand on Mina's left shoulder, and the other around me, squeezing my bottom, for pity's sake. Nora and Quaid were on Mina's other side in much the same position, though I don't know if there was any bottom-squeezing going on. The Professor was wedged between me and Nora, crouching a little, her hands on Mina's waist, and Rhys stood just behind her, his greater height allowing him to loom over top of the Professor, his hands gripping Mina's shoulders closer to her neck. And when I closed my eyes, there it was, a six-pointed star, lines of energy connecting us all, and it looked a lot prettier than the contorted position we'd formed for the task.

"I can feel it," said Mina, "so here I go!"

She didn't lunge this time, there wasn't room, but she thrust forward as hard as she could, braced against our own bodies, our own strengths.

I heard a keening sound rising in pitch into a demonic screaming, like a buzz-saw trying to cut through a steel vault door. Even through my closed eyes I could see the brightness of whatever was happening between Mina's hand and the wall.

And then it stopped. I opened my eyes. Mina had lowered her hand. Michèle and I took a step back, and so did the Professor, staggering a little as she tripped over Nora and Quaid. Rhys disengaged himself, and Steiner stood there and looked up at the wall.

"What's that?"

There was no more glow from the wall. But what there was was a tiny black pinprick, like a missing pixel in a television screen.

"Is that it? That's all we got?" Rhys was disappointed.

Mina laughed. "You don't see it?" She reached out, not with her nails, but with the back of her hand, and rapped sharply at the spot with her knuckle. Just like knocking at a door. Or perhaps it was more like rapping an eggshell ...

There was a cracking sound. I think it was a sound, anyway. Jagged black lines, infinitesimally thin, spread outward from the spot, like an ultra-slow-motion video of a pane of glass struck by a bullet. The lines moved slowly at first, but accelerated as they spread outward, and as they moved through the wall, the lines branched, and branched again, intersecting, racing onward, forming a vast tessellation of the backdrop shell, a crazy-quilt mosaic stretching up to the sky and outward to right and left as far as I could see.

After a minute, the cracking sound, or whatever it was, stopped.

"Talk about an extended metaphor," said Nora, and Quaid said, "Nice job with that eggshell, Mina."

"Thanks! But what do we do now? Smash our way out?"

"Wait," said Rhys, "something's happening. It's not over yet."

I saw it too. The network of black lines was changing. I wasn't sure what it was at first, then I realized light was shining through. It looked like a white light, another sun perhaps, was shining through the cracks. The light grew brighter, and it was hard to see the tiled backdrop now, all I could see was the glow of the jagged cracks. And then it grew brighter still, so bright that the tiles themselves seemed to be shrinking, the cracks of light widening to form rivers, then lakes, then vast seas of brightness.

No one spoke while the process went forward. We were all too awed by it. At last, after a minute or so there was nothing but white light in front of us. Nothing at all that we could see, anyway, and bright as it was the light wasn't blinding at all. I looked over my shoulder. The city was washed out by all this light, seemed to be fading away. The ground beneath my feet, the structure of the bridge, was almost translucent now, and I thought I could even see the river below us through the surface. It wouldn't be long now before everything we knew was gone forever.

I thought I heard impacts behind me. Hoofbeats, shattering in their intensity. A neighing horse. Impossible, but … I turned. Buildings across the river, back in town, collapsing, falling apart, smoke rising up around them, but all of it impossibly quiet like an old silent film.

"All right," said Rhys, suddenly tentative. "What do we do now?"

Michèle laughed. "What do you think? We go forward."

And so we did. Into the light.

BOOK TWO

OUTSIDE THE SHELL

5

T HE TRANSITION FROM THE BRIDGE into the white light was abrupt. All at once I was completely bodiless, floating through a realm of whiteness. A moment before I had Michèle's hand in mine, and I still felt as if she was right there beside me.

Even without a body I could still see, just not with my eyes. I was suspended in a pellucid white medium shot through with myriad tiny glittering points. Most of these points were off in the distance, but I knew the six close by were my friends, my companions who'd entered the light with me. I could sense them, sense the connections between us.

We were moving. The other sparkling points off in the distance ... they were dancing, gyrating, oscillating, orbiting one another, but not going anywhere in particular, forming a vast glittering matrix by which I could measure our progress. The other points of light streamed by us. It was like driving through a snow flurry at night, the swirling crystals glowing in the headlights.

I don't know how much time passed in the light, or if time was passing at all, really, but I think we must have gotten someplace because at last we came to an end of the vast starfield and still we kept going. As we moved onward, leaving the glowing points behind, I got the idea we weren't just moving through a field of light but through a fluid medium. The quality of our motion, a sort of undulating glide, felt like movement through water or maybe an even thicker liquid.

Without warning we were caught up in a powerful current. Our group was carried off in a grand sweeping curve, accelerating, the curve tightening ... there was nothing I could do but ride it out. And then we hit some kind of conflux, a maelstrom perhaps, and the violence of the currents tore us apart from one another. I couldn't do anything to hold on to her, and Michèle and I were separated. The medium here was no longer almost transparent, and all I could see now was white stuff flowing around me, no more sparkling points of light. I couldn't sense Michèle nearby, nor any of the others. And I was feeling an increasing sense of pressure, of submersion. Before this I was only sort of conceptually underwater, with none of the real sensations of swimming or diving. But now it felt like I was actually down there, full fathom five below the surface.

I started to take a breath, choked, and I realized I had a body again, a real human body, and I was fully immersed in liquid. For a panicked moment I was unable to breathe, isolated, totally disoriented. There was fluid in my nose and in my windpipe, and I wanted desperately to inhale and cough it out, but I knew I couldn't. It was probably only a couple of panicked seconds and then I surged out of the fluid like a breaching whale, splashed back heavily, and wound up lying on a black sandy beach with gentle white ripples lapping all around me.

At first, I was paralyzed, completely unable to do anything but gasp and choke. After that I tried to stand up, but for a minute or so I felt like my limbs were palsied, too weak to support me. It was almost like I'd forgotten how to use them. But at last I managed it, forced myself to all fours, and then rose shakily to my feet.

A couple of other figures lay nearby, sodden and pale against the black sand, and a third was a little way down the beach. All three of them were looking like beached sea-creatures writhing around naked on the sand. We'd all lost our clothes somewhere along the way. The first was Michèle, and I rushed over to her side. She was coughing, but she seemed all right to me. I crouched down to put my hand on her shoulder and she looked up at me and smiled: my heart missed a beat. A little further away I saw Rhys, unmistakable with his auburn beard, pulling a woman who had to be the Professor further out of the white waves.

Now I had a moment to look around, and I gazed out at the strange sea. Vast slow swells of white ocean were moving in the distance offshore, but only small ripples rolled up on the beach here. I tasted a warm flat sweetness in my mouth. Smooth and unctuous with just a hint of the sour, and familiar too. At last, I figured it out. It was an ocean of milk.

I turned away from those impossible white waves. The shore ran in both directions into the distance. Inland there were dunes of black sand, many rising a good ten feet or more, so it was hard to see any distance in that direction. Overhead the sky was pale yellow, brightest at the zenith. I wasn't sure if that was the normal appearance of the sky here, or whether there was a high hazy overcast concealing the sun around noontime. It was warm, a comfortable temperature in which to go naked, and there was a light breeze wafting in from the sea of milk.

I shook my head. Droplets ran down my face and I blinked them away. No one seemed to be in any immediate danger. The Professor was getting to her feet now, so I stayed with Michèle, who was sitting up.

"Are you okay?"

My voice sounded strange in my ears, like I'd never spoken before, and maybe I hadn't, not in this body. But the body was familiar enough. All the parts still there, the way I remembered them.

Michèle looked up at me, blinking and bedraggled, hair sodden with milk, a dusting of fine black sand adhering to her back, legs and bottom. I don't think I've ever seen anything as beautiful as her in that moment.

"Oh," she said, and she moved one hand to her groin, not in shame, but (I guessed) to confirm she was still female. "I think so." Then she laughed. It was a joyous sound. Maybe the first laughter ever heard in this world.

"Dis donc," she said, "I mean look, we're still alive!"

I laughed too. I couldn't help it. The whole thing seemed so improbable.

"You're right," I said. "Who'd have thought it?"

Michèle started getting to her feet, so I gave her my hand, pulled her up. She took an extra step, put her arms around me, and we wound up kissing. One thing might have led to another, except for a cough from behind us. We broke apart, me blushing and Michèle giggling.

"Get a dune, folks," said Rhys. Even naked he gave the impression of being fully dressed. Half of it was his natural dignity, half of it was being pretty much covered in body hair. He gestured. "There's plenty to choose from."

Michèle shook her head, and white droplets ran down her neck from her hair. "The fuck is this anyway?" she asked, wiping it off. "Milk?"

"So it appears," said the Professor, who'd walked over to us with Rhys. Three days ago, I'd thought she was an old woman, or late middle-aged anyway, and now she looked to be about sixteen. Her hair was still white, though. "I'm trying to remember," she said. "Something … something mythological, religious maybe. There was a sea of milk …"

"Milk and honey?" Michèle asked.

"No, that's not it. Damnation. I've gotten too used to the Internet, can't remember anything anymore."

Rhys scratched his chin. "So, no ideas where we are or what happened to us? I mean, apart from washed up from an ocean of milk on a beach somewhere?"

"Sorry, no," said the Professor. "But it's obvious this isn't our world, anyway, not the one we came from."

"All right," said Rhys. "What about the others? Can any of you, well, sense them? Before the end, back there on the bridge, I could sort of connect up with you guys, like some kind of telepathy. When we helped Mina to break through the wall."

"Yes," said Michèle, "I remember. But …" she closed her eyes for a moment. "Not now, though. It's too bad, you know? I liked that."

The Professor shook her head. "No," she said. "You're right. A pity. But I suppose we'd better look for them. Which way? Should we split up?"

The shore went in both directions, but to my left, facing the sea of milk, it turned inland after a half mile or so, and my view of it was cut off by the dunes. To my right it went on into the distance, all the way to the horizon. There was nothing dangerous or scary about the prospect, but it looked unwelcoming to me. Like this was a place I wasn't supposed to be. Didn't feel good.

"Fuck no," said Michèle. "Let's stay together. It's bad enough losing the others."

"Agreed," said Rhys. "Who knows what this place is like. There could be anything here. So let's go that way." He pointed left. "We can see they're not the other way, at least not within a couple of miles. First let's go up one of these dunes, maybe get a better view."

It wasn't easy to get to the top. The sand had a dust-like quality to it, softer than you'd expect from the pumice look of the stuff. But after causing a few miniature avalanches I managed to scramble to the top of the tallest nearby dune, and from there was able to hand everyone else up.

The black sand went inland a long way, though it was hard to say exactly how far. A lot deeper than a mere beach, though.

"Is that a strip of something else back there, near the horizon?" The Professor pointed inland over the dunes.

Maybe it was a line of green? But it could have just been a mirage or some other effect of the horizon. It was too hazy to be sure. I looked left, at the way we were planning to go, and I could see the white sea in the distance, but I couldn't see the strip of sand where the little milky waves were rolling in: too many dunes in the way.

"Maybe," said Rhys. "But there's nothing else nearby. Let's head on up the beach. For an hour, say."

"And how long is an hour?" Michèle asked.

"Oh." Rhys glanced at his bare wrist where he'd once worn a watch, and shook his head. "Right. Just have to guess at it. I don't feel very clever right now. Let me know if you think of something smart to do, all right?"

The Professor surprised me by giggling, a girlish sound at odds with her usual manner of speech.

"We've just barely survived the disintegration of our world, been washed ashore from a sea of milk, and now we're four naked people alone on a sand dune, and you want us to be smart?" She reached out and patted Rhys' cheek. "Good luck with that," she said.

Rhys blinked. "Well, you have a point, but I don't want to lose anyone else."

"Of course," said the Professor. "I don't mean to make light of that. It's just that all this —" she gestured all around, "— it's not very realistic, is it?"

"What?"

"I mean there's a sea of milk out there. Cow's milk, too, no question." Apart from her white hair, she looked like a teenager, a naked one too, but the Professor's demeanor was such I felt I was in class, listening to a lecture. It was charming, but I didn't want to tell her that, in case I offended. But she was still talking.

"Not that it would matter if it was some other kind of milk. And if in our world someone filled a pool with milk from a tanker, how long would it take to turn nasty? For that matter, shouldn't we all be sticky and feel like we need a shower? But I feel clean. This whole situation doesn't make sense in the terms we're used to, so I'm not sure we can be all that smart about it."

"All right then," said Rhys. "Smart or not we've still got to do something. Let's go."

We scrambled back down the dune, made our way back to the milk-wet strand, and set off down the beach. Rhys and the Professor walked together, Michèle and I trailing a little behind.

"She has a nice ass," said Michèle. "Don't you think?"

"If you like that sort of thing," I replied, trying to keep my voice down.

"I think maybe I do," she said, "and Rhys has a nice one too." But then she patted me on my own bottom. "But I like yours better still."

"Michèle," I said in a low voice, trying to keep from growling, "if you keep this up, they're going to have to wait for us."

"Oh! Oh! Quel dommage!"

I was going to say something, but she smiled and put her hand on my arm for a moment. "I know. Not now. I'll be good. It's just that I really thought that was the end, back there on the bridge. And after what happened to your poor friend Steiner, well ... I don't want to wait too long. Who knows if this place will last, even. It's like a dream, isn't it?"

"I'm not sure I agree," said the Professor over her shoulder. Shit. Did she hear any of the rest of what we were saying?

"It's true," she continued, "this is all very surreal. But it doesn't feel like a dream. You know that point near the end of some dreams, when it finally occurs to you that you might be dreaming? Then you realize how disjointed, how crazy your dream was, and how weak your powers of imagination. But this isn't like that at all. It's too consistent. Look." She turned and pointed behind us.

We stopped and looked. I couldn't see what she was pointing at. We'd been walking for a half a mile or so, were coming up on the point where the shore turned sharply, but there wasn't anything behind us but the tracks we were leaving in the sand.

"What?"

"That looks like it should, doesn't it? See, our tracks. And that's the big dune we climbed over there, partly collapsed from our climbing it. If this was a dream it would probably all be gone, be something else by now. And in a dream, we'd feel the loss, we'd wonder what happened to the things we remembered, but we probably wouldn't even think of the possibility we were dreaming. Not till waking up, anyway."

"Sure," said Rhys, "but does this help, somehow? I mean, no offense to either of you, I agree it's not a dream. But so what?"

The Professor nodded. "It's not much help," she said, "but the point is, the burden of keeping everything around us more or less consistent isn't on us. It's not our own minds having to remember every little detail and not quite being able to do it. This world is impossible by our standards, so maybe it really is a construct, an illusion of some sort. But if that's the case, it's someone else's illusion. You see what I mean?"

"Oh!" said Michèle. "I do, now. Someone made this world. For us?"

"That's the question," said the Professor. "You put your finger on it. Rem acu tetigisti, as Wodehouse liked to have Jeeves say. A sea of milk, after all. Speaking of which."

She walked down to the water-line — milk-line — bent over exposing the feature Michèle had commented on and reached down with her hands cupped. She raised her hands and took a drink, swallowed, and licked her lips.

"Not bad," she said turning back to us, "but it would be nicer if it was colder. Oh, and thanks, by the way." This last said to Michèle.

"What?" asked Michèle.

"For the compliment before. You know ..."

"Ah, fuck! You heard!"

An hour later, more or less anyway, we were atop another dune. The shore was fairly straight here, and we could see the beach stretching all the way to the horizon. No other features except for that hazy line inland we'd seen before. No sign of Quaid, Nora, or Mina, or anyone or anything else for that matter. No milk-crabs, no milk-gulls, and no milk-clamshells in the sand.

"This place is sterile, isn't it?" I didn't like the way my voice sounded. Sort of dull and monotone.

"Yeah," said Rhys, "it's like we're the only living things. Except for the cow, I guess."

No one laughed.

"The others could be all right, still," said Michèle. "The coast keeps going."

"Yes," said the Professor. "They could be anywhere if that current carried them off. Or they could be still in the sea, bodiless. Maybe they will be coming up soon. There's no way to tell."

"All right," said Rhys. "Three choices. No, four. Keep going. Or we could go back to where we started. We could head inland, see if there's really something there on the horizon. Or stay here building sandcastles."

I looked up at the sky. Was it possible the bright area was now a little displaced from the zenith?

"Let's say we're having real days here," I said, "and the sky is just overcast. Looks to me like just past noon. So maybe we have six or seven hours till it gets dark. How far off is the horizon, or that line we saw?"

"Four miles," said the Professor, "considering we saw it from up on a dune. No way to be certain. That guess assumes we're on a planet with Earth's diameter."

Michèle laughed. "You think we're in space? Aliens took us?"

The Professor shook her head. "I only wish. I'm afraid the situation we're in is a lot stranger than that. Still, I suppose we might as well assume the horizon works the way it used to."

"Well anyway," I said, "inland seems doable. Even if the sand slows us down, I think we can be back at the beach by dark if there's nothing there."

"Suppose the others show up while we're away?" asked Michèle.

"I was thinking about that," I said. "Either it's high tide now, or there are no tides here. You can tell because there's no high-milk-line. The tracks we left on the beach should be pretty obvious until the wind or waves clears them away, but there's not much wind, is there? They should last at least a day, don't you think?"

"I agree," said the Professor. "If our companions show up, our tracks ought to lead them to us."

Rhys didn't say anything for a time. Then he turned to me. "Listen," he said, I just want to talk to you for a minute in private, okay?"

"Sure," I said, and he took me by the arm and led me down off the dune. We walked for a good hundred feet or so in silence around the sides of a few more dunes, me wondering what was going on. It was just the two of us here, surrounded by black sand dunes, a hazy yellow sky overhead, and the only sound the flat wet lapping of little milk waves washing up on the shore.

"All right," he said then, turning to face me. He was looking in my eyes, trying to find something there, I guess. "You want me to call you Ishmael, now?"

"That was just a joke. I guess I should explain it. See, I can remember the last year pretty well. Since I started going to Caernarfon, right?"

Rhys nodded. I groped for words. I'd been thinking about this over the last few days, in the back of my mind, but only now was it coming out.

"But before then … It doesn't seem real to me. Since all this started, I've been wondering if I really existed at all back then. I wasn't much of a person, if I did. I mean, there was nothing to me at all. But I feel like I woke up a little over the last year. Do you know what I mean?"

Rhys shook his head. "Not really," he said. "But you seemed okay when you started coming to my pub."

"Thanks. I think I was maybe only half human for most of that time, though. Maybe being there filled me out some, though. But I think what it really was that made me more of a person was Michèle. She made me care about her when she was still Michel. That might have been the first time I really ever cared about anyone. Two days ago, when I went home to make sure she — he, I mean, was okay. That's what did it."

"I see," said Rhys. "Or maybe I should say, I understand what you're saying. I think you're underplaying your hand a little though. I can't tell you about how you were before last year, but I don't think you were just half human then."

"Well, thanks again. I have to tell you, Rhys, I think that maybe without Caernarfon, I mean, without you being there to host it, I would have fallen apart long before the emergency, the crisis, whatever it was that ended the world. So I feel like I owe you, is what I'm saying."

He was silent for a moment.

"I'm happy you feel that way," he said, "though I don't know if I deserve it. But this has to do with what I wanted to say. You remember when I — when we lost the Professor? None of us could even remember she existed, and she was fading away out there, lost in the city."

I nodded. "Yeah. That was a bad moment for me. It was like being in a nightmare for a minute, where no one understands what you're saying."

He shook his head, closed his eyes. I think he was living it over again.

"It was worse for me, though, when you finally made us remember. It was like I'd failed her. I felt like you were all my people, that I should have done better. Forgetting her like that, it was a betrayal."

I didn't tell him I'd been thinking of Rhys like he was an old-time lord or a king even. But it was true. He was feeling responsible for all of us.

"Well, no harm was done," I said.

He shook his head again. "But there was. We lost Steiner."

Rhys cut me off before I could reply. "Yeah, I know," he said, "it wasn't anyone's fault. But I don't want to lose anyone else, you understand me?"

"Yes. I don't want to lose anyone else either."

"Good," he said. "See, back then, it was you who saved the Professor. I'm sure of it. You helped us all to remember her, and she came back, just like that. And then, later on, it was you who kept us going while the city was falling apart, and it was you who helped us power up Mina to get through that damned wall."

"I guess it's possible I had more of that ... what did the Professor call it? Organizing energy? Essence? Enough to keep us all going through the disintegration. But there's no virtue in it, is what I'm trying to say. I didn't do anything to deserve it, and I didn't do much to help you guys with it. I can't even feel it, if it's even there at all."

"Okay," said Rhys, "I'll accept that if you say so, though I'm not sure you're right about not doing anything. But the thing is, it could be that it's you who has the ability to save the others. Quaid and Nora and Mina. And maybe Steiner too. He said he was being pulled through before his body was destroyed. Maybe he's here too, somehow."

He grabbed my arm, but his attitude seemed almost supplicating, pleading even.

"Don't forget them," he said. "Maybe you can't do anything, well, active, but we both want all four of them back, right? So if anything occurs to you, if you can think of anything at all that will help them — just tell us, okay?"

"Sure, Rhys. If I can. This is about heading inland, isn't it?"

"Yeah," said Rhys. "It makes sense, right? We can't stay on this dead beach forever, drinking milk and playing in the sand. But I feel like I'm giving up on the others if we go, even just for a few hours."

"The idea of the tracks doesn't make you happy, I guess."

"It makes sense, sure," he said. "But I still can't shake the feeling, all right? Maybe you, or us okay, maybe us being on the beach will make it easier for them to — to emerge? And —" he cut himself off. "But I guess there's no point to what-ifs. We're going to go and see if there's something there past the dunes. That's just common sense. I just wanted to say what I was feeling, to get you to understand."

"I do," I said. "I can't promise you much, but I promise not to forget the others. And if there's anything I can do, anything you think I can do, I'll try it. Just tell me."

"Okay," he said. "Thanks."

6

W E RETURNED TO MICHÈLE and the Professor, who were still sitting atop their dune, talking.

"While you were gone," said Michèle, "I remembered something that we should try."

"Yes," said the Professor. "Stupid of me not to think of it myself. Remember, our last night together at Caernarfon?"

"Oh, yeah," said Rhys, "when we made it be morning."

"Yes," said the Professor. "Of course, the world was coming apart at the seams then. Still, I have to admit I was a little surprised we could do it, change night into day by pretending. This world is different, but it might still work. It might be subject to our desires."

"Sure," said Rhys. "What do we do?"

"Let's just sit down here. Maybe we should hold hands, just for the connection?"

So we did it, we sat down cross-legged, knee-to-knee at the base of the dune and held hands. I had Michèle's and Rhys's hands, and the Professor did too, on the opposite side.

"Michèle? This was your idea, so perhaps you should guide us," said the Professor.

"Okay," said Michèle. "Now we haven't ever looked behind that dune over there. So we don't know what's there. There could be anything, right? Wouldn't it be nice if there was one of those beach safety flags left lying there? You know, the ones that say it's safe to swim, there's a lifeguard on duty, or whatever. Because if there was one, we could plant it at the top of the dune, and it would be a good landmark, and if our friends saw it they would come to it."

"A cooler of beer would be nice too," said Rhys.

"One thing at a time," I said. "I'm not sure I can believe in this, but let's try it. I guess we should agree what it probably looks like, right? I haven't been to the beach in a while. I mean a real beach. With water waves. You know what I mean."

"All right," said Michèle. "It's just a simple thing, okay? For good weather and safe swimming, it's a green flag. That flat kind of washed-out green, you know, between forest and khaki, it might have been brighter once, but it's been out in the sun a long time. So maybe it's about a square meter, maybe a little less. That strong heavy-duty nylon stuff, yes? It's got a sort of sleeve that fits over a pole, with some string or something to tie it on. And the pole, that's just metal, right? An aluminum pole, let's say it's three meters long, it has to go deep into the sand to stay up when the wind blows. It's got a little cap at the top to keep the flag from sliding off."

"Okay," I said, "I think I got it."

"Good," she said. "Now it's right back there, okay? It's a place like this one where we're sitting now. Between the dunes. It's just laying there on top of the sand. Can you see it? In your mind's eye?"

I closed my eyes, tried to imagine it. The metal rod, the green square, the sleeve on one side, with a kind of lanyard to tie it on, but it would be sort of half-furled, lying on the ground. The rod with a little bow to it from resisting the breeze for a long time, maybe some corrosion from being out in the weather. Right. As for the dunes, that should be easy, just like here ... But I couldn't quite picture the mound of black sand, despite the fact I was sitting beside one and had been looking at them on and off for over an hour now. Instead, my mind insisted on giving me a rolling hillside covered in grass. I fought with it for a bit, then gave up and opened my eyes. Black sand dune, right in front of my face. Closed my eyes. Grassy hillside. Frustrating.

"Okay," said Michèle at last, a little tentatively. I opened my eyes, and we all let go each other's hands.

Rhys scratched his chin through his beard. "I dunno," he said.

The Professor stood up. "We might as well look."

Yeah. There was nothing there.

"I didn't think so," said Michèle. "I'm sorry for wasting everyone's time."

"Funny," said Rhys, "but I really thought I had the look of the flag down, too. It's just ..."

"Don't tell me," said the Professor. "You couldn't get the setting."

"What? Oh, yeah, I couldn't imagine it beside a dune."

"I said, "I couldn't either. All I could see was a grassy hillside instead of a sand dune."

"Très bizarre!" said Michèle. "Me too. That line on the horizon? I thought maybe it's green, you know? Could it be grass?"

Rhys stood up. "Let's go see."

The path of least resistance led us single file over the tops of broad shallow dunes and around the sides of the taller less stable ones. The sand was so soft it didn't give good traction, but we were all in decent walking shape, so it wasn't too bad. The black dunes gave the feeling of walking through a harsh volcanic landscape, and I had that feeling of rejection, of not being welcome again, like I was in the wrong place for me. But my attention was continually distracted because I was walking behind Michèle. I wanted to tell her she was wrong about the nicest bottom in our group, but yeah, this wasn't the time or the place.

After a while, maybe another hour, we stopped for a break, and scrambled to the top of another tall dune to take our bearings. It was reassuring to see our track back to the shore, a more or less straight line. From here we could see a band of white in the distance that was the sea of milk. The land was rising gradually as we went inland, so there wasn't much of a better view from here than from back at the shore. Still, there was a distinct line of green in the distance now, a definite end to this region of sandy dunes.

"I've been thinking about what we've experienced since we left our world," said the Professor. She sat down in the sand, picked up a handful of the stuff and let it fall away between her fingers. It was a perfect feathered stream, like the fine sand in an hourglass, nothing like what you'd expect from a beach or a desert.

"The field of stars," said Rhys. "Or whatever you want to call it."

"Yes," said the Professor. "And the sea. And this place. I'm certain none of it could arise naturally. This is all someone's design."

"God, you mean?" asked Michèle.

The Professor hesitated. "I wish I could say otherwise," she said, "but I can't rule out the possibility. But speaking philosophically, no matter what miracles we're presented with there's still no way to prove any of this is actually the work of a transcendent deity. All this could be an illusion, or if it's real it could be the product of superior power and intellect that's not divine. But ..." She trailed off, lowered her eyes.

"Come," said Michèle, "be brave. We want to hear your thoughts. You know more about these things than we do."

The Professor looked up, smiled, and then lost her smile. "I know nothing at all. That's the problem. You shouldn't put too much faith in what I have to say. I may be wrong about everything, wrong even about the way I describe our situation."

There was something very vulnerable about her just then, and I had the feeling for a moment she really was a shy and inexperienced young person, not the mature, masterful individual she usually seemed to be. Rhys was sitting next to her, and he put a hand on her shoulder, I think feeling the same as me, and Michèle reached across to pat her hand.

"We trust you," said Michèle. "But you don't have to be right all the time."

I thought the Professor might cry there for a moment, but she mastered herself. She put her hand on Rhys' and bowed her head for a few seconds before answering.

"Thank you. That means a great deal to me. But you're right that I was afraid to speak. I'm sorry. I have to trust you all too. I was going to say that on the one hand what we see here is attention to the human scale. The region of souls. The sea of milk, this very land. The fact that we have received new bodies, that we're in a place that we can comprehend at all with human senses. All that suggests someone or something has us in mind, or has people like us in mind, anyway."

Michèle nodded. "I see. That makes sense."

"But there's another hand, you see," said the Professor. "It's possible some or all of this could be the product of our own minds, our own expectations, subconscious maybe, a consensus that we've come up with for want of anything better. The way we're not all sticky with drying milk. Probably we should be more anxious and upset, too. I mean, I think I would have been a few days ago, anyway."

She brushed her hair back, and I saw it was looking like she'd shampooed it. Surely it should still have been damp. And yeah, I felt normal, neutral, without any discomfort at all. It was a little odd. I could see we were all taking inventory of ourselves.

The professor nodded, recognizing what we were doing.

"That's what I was hesitating to say out loud," she said, "Back in the city we all changed in different ways, apparently according to our desires. Suppose that this place is something we created? Not something given to us, but something we made? That's why I hesitate. Even suggesting that feels … impious, and I'm ashamed to worry about such a thing because I've always been an atheist. So that's why I balked before, and why I'm nattering on now. I just don't know."

"I have mixed feelings," I said. "Everything you say makes sense. And I think we're all too comfortable, more than we should be if we'd taken a milk bath without a shower afterwards, and then walked for hours through a dry sandy desert. So maybe we've been sort of altering ourselves here. But I don't feel like this is my place, you know? I feel like it's someone else's. if you know what I mean."

"Yeah," said Rhys, "it kind of creeps me out. But we've only been in this world for a few hours." He turned. "Listen, Professor, you've already made a bunch of things clear I might never have worked out on my own. But whether someone else made this place, or we did it for ourselves, we're going to have to figure it out."

As we passed through the black dune desert it became clear that greenery lay up ahead. It looked like the dunes rose toward a broad hillside or bluff that was topped with turf. It was too high to see over the top to find out what was actually up there, but there were places where the slope looked climbable, and as we approached, we made for one of these cuts.

By the time we got to the base of the hillside, I thought it was around four or so in the afternoon. The overcast hadn't changed at all during our hike, but the bright spot had moved down toward the horizon. The climb wasn't too bad. Mostly it was just a calf-aching walk up the slope, with a couple of all-fours scrambles. The feeling of stress on my legs was oddly reassuring, like it confirmed I really did have a body, and not just the dream of one. The black sand gave way to packed earth as we ascended the hundred feet or so of the grade to the top of the bluff. Clambering over the top was something else, though.

"Holy shit," said Rhys, "it's Windows."

"What?"

"You know, that big lawn they used to use for the background image, years ago?"

It really was that, too, or close to it anyway. Shallow rolling hills covered with a perfect lawn of grass so green it was almost intoxicating. And above us, an achingly pure blue sky with a few puffy clouds of an exquisite pristine white. A cheerful yellow sun, familiar but somehow less harsh than the one I knew, at just the same angle as the brightness behind the overcast over the beach. A gentle breeze blew all around us, feeling like a caress on my naked skin.

"It's like a new world," said Michèle. She took a few steps onto the lawn.

"Hmm," said the Professor looking up at the sky. "It is at that." Then she paused, gasped. "Look!" She pointed.

I hadn't noticed it at first glance because the green of the flag blended in with the grass. But there it was on the ground. A beach safety flag, the one we'd visualized before. It was exactly the same as the thing I'd seen in my mind's eye.

Rhys was there in a moment, picked the thing up, brought it back and handed it over to me; sure enough, a long, slightly warped metal rod, a sleeved nylon flag, even the metal cap and the little lanyard I'd imagined before. An ordinary enough object, just completely impossible. I passed it to the Professor who hefted it, touched the fabric of the flag, and then gave it to Michèle. She sank the shaft quivering into the ground, and we all looked up at the flag in silence for a moment.

I felt a little sick, then, just thinking about it, realizing what it meant. I guess I knew it before, but now it hit home. Sure, I understood this was a new world, and the Professor had made it clear enough we were in a place where the old rules didn't necessarily apply. But even so, even after all the changes we'd been through, even after all the strangeness we'd seen already, the idea that it was possible just to will something into existence like that … If that was possible, what wasn't?

Suddenly I was woozy, weak in the knees, and I sat down heavily on the soft grass, surprising myself; I hadn't meant to do it. Michèle was there in a moment, kneeling beside me, arm around my shoulders, her breasts pressing into my back. I had to hold back tears, and I didn't even know why.

"Are you all right?" she asked.

"Yes," I said. "Yes, it's just —"

"What is that thing doing here?" Rhys squatted next to me. "Right? That's it, isn't it? Did we create that flag? I didn't really believe it would work, before. But that's it, for sure, what we tried for back at the beach. What does it mean that it's here?"

"I'm ... not sure," said the Professor. "But we'd better find out, hadn't we? Let's try something."

She said, "Chateaubriand," and snapped her fingers, pointing at the ground. Nothing. It was almost a relief.

"That was without actually trying to visualize it," she said. "It was just a sort of request for a steak, really. And maybe it didn't appear because I tried to place it right here, and actually materializing something right in front of us wouldn't normally seem possible." She smiled. "But of course, just like before, it's possible there's something on the other side of the hill, something we just can't see. Forgive me, I just can't resist the temptation ..."

The Professor closed her eyes, and at first I saw a look of concentration on her face, but after a moment she relaxed her expression, seemed to be at peace, as if meditating instead of concentrating.

I heard a low growl from around the curve of the nearest hillside.

Pacing around the hillside, a tiger. Eight feet long, not counting the lashing tail. It was a big Bengal: tawny orange, black and white.

"Holy shit!" Michèle sprang to her feet, took a few steps back, and Rhys also jumped up, but he stepped forward, raising his hands. For my own part I'd looked into the beast's golden eyes and I couldn't move or act at all.

"Don't worry," said the Professor, and the tiger padded toward us, walking gently considering how heavy it must have been. He walked right up to the Professor and pressed his forehead against her side. She put her hand on his head.

"Oh," she said, "it's real!" She sank to the ground, sitting down on the grass, and the tiger lay down as well, putting his head in her lap. It rested there, almost motionless, his huge torso heaving slowly with his breaths, a deep rumbling purr rising up from his body.

"Is — is that yours?" Rhys breathed the question. "Did you ... summon it?"

"I'm so sorry," said the Professor. "I should have warned you, but I didn't believe it would come. I've always loved them, you know, tigers. And Borges. I think I have his piece memorized. Please, this is important, I'll recite it."

She closed her eyes for a moment, lips moving silently in recollection, and then she spoke, declaiming:

And so, as I sleep, some dream beguiles me, and suddenly I know I am dreaming. Then I think: this is a dream, a pure diversion of my will; and now that I have unlimited power, I am going to cause a tiger.

Oh, incompetence! Never can my dreams engender the wild beast I long for. The tiger indeed appears, but stuffed or flimsy, or with impure variations of shape, or of an implausible size, or all too fleeting, or with a touch of the dog or the bird.

"But this tiger is real," said Rhys. "He's flawless. I can even smell his scent."

The Professor nodded, and her eyes were full of tears now. She buried her face in the soft fur of the tiger's neck for a few moments and then looked up, smiling.

Michèle asked, "May I touch him?"

"Please do," said the Professor. "This is my own dream tiger. I summoned the beast of my own childhood dreams, who would never harm me or any of my friends."

Michèle moved over to the Professor, knelt down and hesitated, then put her hands on the tiger's shoulders as he lay there. He turned his head and yawned at her, gaping his jaws hugely, but there was no threat to the gesture. After stroking the animal's back for a moment, Michèle stepped away from him.

"Quelle merveille!" She came back to me, put her hand on my shoulder. "I can't believe it," she said.

"Me neither," I said, "but I'm frightened now. Not of the tiger, I mean, but of the fact of the tiger. Does that make sense?"

Michèle shook her head, but Rhys said, "Yes. I understand."

The Professor bent her head down to her tiger, and he turned his own head to gaze into her eyes. "Thank you," she said, and he rose to his feet. With one enormous leap he bounded back around the hillside from which he had emerged. And just like that he was gone, though I could still see the impression left in the grass where he had lain.

"Oh," I said, "you didn't have to get rid of him."

"It's all right," said the Professor. "He's not gone forever. He'll be there if I need him."

"Listen, Professor," said Rhys. "I don't even know what to think anymore. I mean, after all this, you throw in a friendly tiger on top of it all and you'd think it wouldn't be a big deal, but I have to tell you I'm at a loss. What does it mean if you can make something like that appear and disappear? Are you a god now? Am I?"

The Professor took a moment before answering. She drew up her knees to her chest and wrapped her arms around them, defensively.

"I said before that I don't know what's going on. But I can't help but speculate. Whether all this is real or an illusion, I'm pretty sure there's someone or something that made that tiger for me, that it wasn't me acting on my own."

"Why do you say that?" asked Michèle.

"My mind's not powerful enough to visualize a tiger properly," said the Professor, "much less to materialize one that can move around. That's part of what Borges was complaining about in that quote. Think about it. When you imagine something, you're summoning the idea of it more than anything else. I'm not going to get into platonic forms, because I don't even agree with that whole line of philosophy. But that's the idea, that I just sort of have the symbol and some superficial sense data for a tiger in my head, not the fully fleshed out understanding of what a tiger really is."

"But what about dreams? Don't we see all kinds of things in dreams?"

"Well, yes," said the Professor. "But I think we are mostly deluding ourselves that we really see them. It's debatable though, so let's say we do see things fully in dreams. Let's say that my mind really can completely visualize what a tiger should look like. I still don't know anything about a tiger's anatomy. There's no way I could get the skeleton and musculature right. Even if I could sort of imagine the visuals of a tiger, it wouldn't look and feel realistic up close.

"But you all saw it, and Michèle you even petted it. That tiger was real. There were all kinds of little details I didn't recall about tigers, like those amazing eyes, how its whiskers were arranged, what its teeth and mouth looked like when it yawned. Its smell, even. I can still smell it a little, can't you? There was no distinguishing that tiger from the real thing."

"Okay," said Michèle, "it was real. Like my body is real now, even though it was different three days ago. Like you, too, Mademoiselle Teenager. But what does it mean to be real? In a place like this, anyway."

"In a place like this," said the Professor, "well I don't know, to be honest. But to make something like that for real, to materialize it ... Suppose someone gave you the raw power to materialize things using just your mind, back in the world we used to know. You still couldn't make a tiger, even with another one standing right there to use as a model. I'm talking about getting the internal details right. You'd have to be able to visualize its complete biology, its cellular structure, all the complexity of a real body, all its chemistry. You might even have to visualize all the atoms. All the computers in the world couldn't even store the data. It's inconceivable that I could do something like that, and in fact I didn't. All I did was imagine the tiger of my dreams coming from around the hillside."

"I don't understand," said Rhys. "You say you couldn't do it, but you did it."

"I'm sorry," said the Professor. "I meant to say that someone or something else did it for me, or with me. Someone or something recognized my intention to summon the tiger I used to fantasize about when I was a child. Someone or something knows what a tiger is, how to make one from scratch. It knows what I'm thinking and feeling, and it gave me one when I asked for it. That's what I'm saying."

"Oh," said Michèle.

We were all silent for a moment. I noticed that Rhys had assumed the same sitting position as the Professor, and I wondered if he'd done it consciously or not.

"All right," I said, "If you folks don't mind, I'm going to try something a little less existentially distressing."

"Sure," said Rhys, "why not? What are you going to do?"

But I already had my eyes closed. I was thinking about the look and feel of the white cardboard, the cheap red printing, that one chef that somehow every place in the whole country used to use on their boxes, the heat you'd feel when picking it up, the smell of it. Yeah. The Professor had mentioned chateaubriand, but I didn't even know what it tasted like. She'd have to show us some other time.

I opened my eyes, rose to my feet.

"Let's see if it worked."

I took a few steps around the curve of the hill. Shit, there they were, two pizza boxes, the white cardboard just like I imagined. "You tried the rest, now try the best." I flipped the lids, just checking. Sure enough: one with peppers and onions; the other a meat-lovers special.

I brought the boxes back.

"My hero," said Michèle. "I wonder how it will taste?"

"Okay Rhys," I said, "you might as well supply the drinks. It's your job, after all."

He laughed, and I felt a little relief at the honest sound of it. I'd been worried about him the last little while, since he took me aside, and especially now, with the Professor's tiger.

"What the hell," he said. "Beer okay for everyone? Or do you want Cutty, Prof?"

"Diet Pepsi, please," said the Professor.

We all looked at her.

"What? I don't drink whiskey all the time," she said.

"It's not that," said Rhys. "Diet Pepsi? Seriously?"

She shrugged. "I'm used to it."

"Oh well," he said, "let's see if I can do this too."

He closed his eyes, then opened them and walked around that same hillside. A minute later he came back lugging a plastic cooler. He set it down on the grass and opened it to reveal a dozen bottles of Pilsner Urquell nestled in ice, along with a couple of larger bottles of something called Brains Bitters. And a six-pack of Diet Pepsi.

I hadn't been hungry or thirsty since coming to this world, hadn't consumed anything if you didn't count a few drops of milk. The idea of the pizza was due to prompting from the Professor and her steak. But I flipped open the pizza boxes and was ravenous. I think everyone else had the same reaction, because no one spoke for a good half hour. It was good pizza, too; really good, actually, better than anything you could get from the strip-mall pizzeria near my old apartment building.

At last, we all sat back, four naked people with very slightly swollen bellies, rubbing our fingers on the lawn to wipe off the grease. If it had occurred to me, I'd have included wet-naps in my order — that's how I thought of it, a delivery order — but I was hesitant to use the power or whatever it was for something so trivial.

"All gone," said Michèle: a little mournfully, I thought.

"There's more where that came from," said Rhys. "Though I'm not sure where that might be."

The Professor looked distracted for a moment, then she held out her hands, closed up into fists. She opened her fists to reveal two handfuls of those pastel-colored chalky mints, the kind they keep in glass bowls in Greek diners. So much for triviality. All of us took a mint. She closed her fists again, and flared out her fingers, as if doing a magic trick. The remaining mints were gone, except for one that she popped in her mouth.

"There," she said, "that was easy enough."

Then she looked at the pizza boxes, frowned.

"I can't get rid of the boxes," she said. "Maybe that's because the rest of you assume they should still be there? Or maybe it's because you were the one to summon them." She nodded at me.

I tried it, closed my eyes, imagined the boxes being gone, just the lawn still there beneath them. Opened my eyes.

"Nope," I said, "still there. I'll try carrying them around the hill again."

And that worked. I dropped them off where no one but me could see them, closed my eyes and tried again, and when I opened my eyes, the boxes were gone.

"So is that it, then?" asked Rhys when I returned. "We're gods now, pretty much, even if it's someone else actually providing the after-dinner mints. Same thing, isn't it, if you can get anything you want?"

"Perhaps," said the Professor. "I suppose we'll have to experiment. There must be limits to this thing."

"Limits?" asked Michèle.

"Yes," said the Professor, "and dangers, too. I was foolish to call that tiger into existence, not knowing if it would be in all respects what I imagined it to be. Suppose it was just an ordinary tiger? If you think about it you could easily kill yourself with this power, or worse."

"What does that mean? Or worse?"

"Well," said the Professor, "if really large scale creation is possible, we could destroy everything just by accident. But putting that aside there are other distressing possibilities. Suppose I tried to make a person? What would it mean if I succeeded?"

"Jesus," said Rhys. "Can we summon Steiner back? Or Mina, Nora, and Quaid?"

"It might work," said the Professor. "We might even try it as a last resort. But supposing just wishing for them to appear doesn't bring that particular person back from wherever they are, if they are in a place at all? Suppose it really creates them from scratch? Suppose the person created is only what I remember of them, not really a full person in their own right? There are all kinds of horrible outcomes."

"Oh," said Rhys, "I see."

"Anyway," said the Professor, "seeing as I foolishly tried a dangerous experiment of my own without consulting all of you, I really have no right to ask that we be careful. But if any of you would like to try something … innovative, perhaps you could let us know, so that we can either help you, or at least observe the results?"

"I'm willing," I said. "Frankly this power scares me almost as much as it, well, draws me into trying it out. One thing does occur to me right away, though. How about a book? It's just a harmless object, right?"

The Professor laughed. "I suppose I should say something clever about how words have killed more people than bullets, but yes, it seems safe enough. What book do you want?"

"Well," I said, "there's two, actually. The first is, ah, let's call it 'Where You Are and Why, and What You Should Be Doing'."

Michèle giggled. "You mean, 'Godhood for the Complete Idiot'?"

"Yeah," I said, "that will do. A little while ago the Professor said that maybe someone is making this all happen for us. This is someone's chance to tell us something, if for some reason they don't feel like just coming out and talking to us."

"Huh," said Rhys. "I guess it's worth a shot."

"What's the second book?" asked the Professor.

"Oh," I said, "I was halfway through Swann's Way when the world ended, and I want to finish it. I suppose a lot of people have died in between starting it and finishing, but maybe I'll be the last to read it at all."

The Professor smiled. "And that too will be an interesting experiment. Can you summon a book whose ending you don't know? That will tell us where it's coming from, in a way, if you wind up with a complete text."

"But how will we know?" asked Rhys.

"Oh, I read it long ago," said the Professor.

"They made us read it in school," said Michèle.

I nodded. "I'm sure none of us remembers every word, though. So if it's fragmented or doesn't make much sense, then it may be because it's coming entirely out of our mutual memories. But if it's complete and it all seems to make sense, well then …"

"Then God or whoever is remembering the book for us?" asked Rhys.

"Perhaps," said the Professor. "Or the collective unconscious maybe. Perhaps Marcel Proust himself is one of those sparkling points floating beneath the sea, and he will be the one remembering for us. Let's find out."

Over the next couple of minutes, I tried to recall the details of the edition of Swann's Way I'd left behind. I'd read the first page so many times in failed attempts to finish the book I think I had it memorized, but of course that would be no help in restoring even the half of the book I'd managed to get through in the last few days, so I concentrated on the remembered look and feel, not on the actual text. Started with the words "Swann's Way" and the original French title in smaller print on the cover, which was worn and creased with age. It was an old Penguin edition printed in the 1960s, the penguin logo on the right side. No cover illustration, just vertical red stripes defining the title space, with thin horizontal black bars at top and bottom. Originally sold in the UK and then, I suppose, resold by a used bookstore there before eventually showing up in the US for me to buy at a book exchange shop, there was a sticker with the more recent British price ... yes: 6/-. It was only $1.95 by the time I picked it up, though.

There. I thought I'd done it, so before looking behind me (where I'd imagined the book showing up) I tried again with the book I had mentally retitled An Explanation. What would it look like? Let's say an ornate leather tome, suitably ancient. Embossed and now almost completely worn away gold print for the title on the spine, with no author, of course. The irregular edges of pages that had been cut open instead of chopped off by some factory machine. A faint smell of rot coming from it too, if you brought it close to your nose.

I gave a sort of mental push, turned around to find two books nestled in the grass behind me. Sure enough. One was the old Penguin edition of Swann's Way, just as I remembered. I flipped it open to the first page:

For a long time I used to go to bed early ...

The opening I was sure of: it was the real text, as translated anyway. Then I turned to the end, almost dreading what I'd find there. The last page was a single solid paragraph. But that wasn't uncharacteristic. I was almost expecting to read gibberish. The final lines read:

The places that we have known belong now only to the little world of space on which we map them for our own convenience. None of them was ever more than a thin slice, held between the contiguous impressions that composed our life at that time; remembrance of a particular form is but regret for a particular moment; and houses, roads, avenues are as fugitive, alas, as the years.

Sure as hell sounded like Proust, anyway. The aptness of the text was almost painful. Could it be a coincidence? A series of chills ran down my spine. I handed the book to Michèle. She opened it, paused.

"Fuck," she said, "How should I know? I only read it in French. But … yes, yes, this seems right. Something like this, anyway. He dreams a woman into existence on page one. I remember wishing I could do that when I was in school. So strange, isn't it? In the end I dreamed myself a woman."

She gave the book to the Professor who started skimming through the text.

Meanwhile I was looking at the second book. It was just as I had visualized it, old brown leather with black stripes on the spine, the faded gold-embossed title, the irregular cut pages, even the smell.

I handed it to Rhys. "I'm afraid to look," I said.

"So am I." But he opened the book anyway, fanned the pages, chuckled and handed it back. "I'm almost relieved," he said.

I looked. The pages were covered with paragraphed blocks of little open rectangles, like the boxes you get on some phone and computer displays when your app doesn't have the right font to display the characters.

We tried a few more experiments and found that if a book had ever been read or even glanced at by any of us, we could create a complete copy with apparently correct text. Imaginary and completely unknown works were out of reach, though: they came out blank, or full of random letters or just patterns of symbols like mine. The Professor's attempt to create a tablet computer was a failure too. It looked plausible and would even turn on, but the only thing that happened after that was the screen turned white, like all it had was the flashlight app.

At last Michèle said, "Uh, I have something maybe, maybe I want to make, but I'll unmake it if you don't want me to."

"What is it?" Rhys wanted to know.

"I'll show you," she said, and she disappeared behind the hillside for a moment. When she returned, she was wearing the same white sundress with blue polka-dots she'd had on before the world ended.

"Oh," said the Professor. "Clothes. Stupid of me not to think of them earlier. But why should we want you not to wear them?"

"It's — well, it's because you didn't think of them yourself," said Michèle. "Do you see what I mean? I can't explain it too well. Eden, you know?"

"Oh," said Rhys, "I think I understand."

"Yes," said the Professor. "It didn't hurt any of us to go naked for a day. I was uncomfortable for the first thirty seconds, maybe. But whether it's this place or the company or both, I don't feel like I need clothes the way I used to." She nodded at Michèle. "It was fun, even, when we were walking on the beach, and I heard you say you liked my ass, so I bent over to show it off. I would never have done anything like that in the old world, not when I was grown up and certainly not when I was young, either."

"So that's why —" Michèle started, but the Professor interrupted.

"That's why you're uneasy? Don't worry about it. I'm fine either way. Three days ago, well, I didn't know you then, Michèle, but I knew Rhys and — and Ishmael here, and Quaid and Nora too. But we never shared much of anything but our presence at Caernarfon. I'd never have talked this way with any of you, and I'd have been terribly ashamed if you somehow saw me naked. Now, though, after going through those three days with you all — Well, I feel like there's nothing left for me to hide. But I don't think if you wear clothes you're hiding anything from me. I trust you, all of you, is what I'm trying to say, I suppose."

"Aww," said Rhys.

"That's very sweet," said Michèle, "and I know you all only for two days, but I trust you too, hein? And for now, anyway, I will take it off, all right?"

And she shrugged out of the dress. I'd been watching naked flesh all day, including of course hers, and now I got half an erection. I think there was a time I would have been mortified too, but not today; it gave me pause for just a moment, and then I just ignored it. There'd be plenty of time for it later.

So after a moment I nodded and said, "Thank you, Professor. But I don't really want to be called Ishmael. That was just a joke with Mina, yesterday. Or whenever it was. You can use my real name if you want. I mean, I think it's my real name. It doesn't feel quite right to me, but there's nothing better. It's Jay, all right? Jay Grant."

"Thank you, Jay," said the Professor. "I had the notion from the little I've heard from you over the last year that you were unhappy with your name, so I never used it with you before. Of course I've never told any of you my real name, either. I like my nickname, you understand, so it's fine as it is. But I always used to hate my real name when I was a girl, though I thought it was vain to change it. So I just never used it. That's why I'm sensitive to your preference," and she nodded at me, without saying my name a second time. "But it seems silly to hate my name now, for some reason. My real name is Harriet."

I said, "Hi, Harriet", and she caught my eye and smiled.

"Enchanté," said Michèle.

Rhys stood up, bowed, and sat down. Funny, even naked it was an entirely dignified gesture.

"So," he said, "what next? It looks like night is coming. I think it would be safe enough to walk back to the beach, but much as I want to meet up with the others, I don't think it will be easy to find anyone in the dark."

"Listen, Rhys," I said, "what you just said is probably right; but you've got to know I want to find them too, and even if I didn't, I'm always going to be at your service anyway. Just tell me what you want me to do."

The Professor nodded. "Yes, I feel the same way."

Michèle said, "I don't know you very well, Monsieur Bartender. One day at the end of the old world, and one day at the beginning of the new one. But I know the Professor just as long, and Mina and Quaid and Nora too, the same time. And I know, ah, Jay only a little longer."

I realized then I never did tell her my name before. I'd have been ashamed except I knew it didn't matter.

"But I like you all," said Michèle, and then she shook her head. "No, I love you all, all right? After the bridge, you know. After what we did together. So tell us what to do, and we do it, okay?"

Rhys bowed his head for a moment. "You're going to make me cry," he said. "But thanks. I'm feeling this obligation, you know? To the others. I really want to make sure they're all right. And if they're not here yet, I want to, to welcome them to this world, you know? But I don't know how to do it. Going back to the beach, in the dark, it seems like a waste of time. It feels wrong to drag you all there just to make me feel a little better. Maybe in the morning when we can see further it will make more sense, we can look for some sign of them then."

We talked it out a little more but didn't get anywhere useful, so we eventually decided to sleep out here in the grassy hills of the interior.

7

T HE SUNSET WAS GORGEOUS, orange shading to crimson with pink streamers radiating across the darkening sky. We watched it together, with drinks courtesy of our newfound creative power. Rhys quaffed his Welsh bitter from a stein, the Professor sipped from a tumbler of whiskey, while Michèle and I had flutes of dry champagne. She sat next to me as the sun disappeared beneath the horizon, and I couldn't help but put my arm around her. I was aching for her, and I could tell she felt the same way, but the both of us wanted to see in the night in company with the others. Rhys was either entirely oblivious or entirely discreet, but at one point I noticed the Professor glancing at us; she smiled, and it felt nice to have her approval.

At last, it got dark, and a glittering panoply of stars appeared overhead. Michèle and I walked far enough over the crest of the hill to have some privacy. I could tell she was as eager as I was to test out lovemaking in this new world, but starting the moment we separated from Rhys and the Professor I became more and more uneasy. I felt naked for the first time since showing up in the world, naked like I was being spied on, like I was exposed to the sky up on this hill, like the stars themselves were looking down on me maliciously. Nothing had changed, and everything. It was getting worse, too. From unease it turned into a feeling of impending doom, something horrible about to happen. But all I could see was grassy hills and the starry sky, same as before, so it was a shameful, reasonless fear, one I didn't want to admit to.

Michèle looked at me. She asked, uncertainly, "Do you feel it too? Like ... like you're a target?"

I was relieved that it wasn't just me, but also alarmed. "Yeah. We'd better get back with the others."

It was a long minute, scrambling over the top of the hill. I had the sense of something chasing us and lying in wait for us at the same time, but still, nothing was visible. When we got there, the Professor was sitting huddled on the ground, her arms around her knees, and Rhys was gazing intently in the direction of the beach. He whirled around when he heard us coming, like we might have been a threat, but then he relaxed when he saw it was us.

"Shit," he said, "I was afraid —"

He cut himself off, as if struck by a thought, and the Professor looked up sharply. For a moment I saw that same apprehension on her face, the same thing I'd been feeling myself, but then she visibly girded herself up, and even smiled at us.

"That's it," she said, getting to her feet. "Afraid, but of what?"

"Nothing, yeah." Rhys shook his head. "There's nothing here to be afraid of. Which means, I guess — what?"

"Maybe it's not really our fear," said Michèle.

"I don't understand."

"Maybe it's someone else's. Maybe they're afraid of us."

"And we're picking up on it? Telepathically somehow? I don't know —"

It was like someone hit me in the stomach. Pure loathing, and I was pretty sure it was us who were being loathed. Someone or something wanted us gone, no, not just gone, eradicated. Expunged.

"Ugh. Yeah. That's pretty fucking clear," said Rhys. "Something's out there. And it doesn't like us at all."

I was going to say something, maybe ask who it could possibly be, when I noticed movement down the slope of our hill, in the direction of the beach.

"What's that?" I pointed. The shimmering starlit grass near the base of the hill was shuddering, not rippling in the wind, but showing a disturbance. For a moment I had the wild thought that the grass was reacting to these emotions we were feeling, but then I realized that wasn't it. The motion was more deliberate and it had a direction. Like invisible things were walking toward us.

And like that the fear took us again. It was panic, it was terror, and it didn't have to make sense.

We started retreating from the motion in the grass, heading over the top of the hill to the far side, first at a sort of half-hearted trot, then faster as we acknowledged what we were doing. Rhys, out in front by a few meters, came to a sudden stop shortly after we crested the hill. We could all see the movement down below in that direction too. It seemed that whatever it was had us surrounded.

We backed together into a huddle of four naked people, all of us fearful, intimidated, watching the rippling grass closing in. None of us said a word, we didn't even meet each other's gazes or reach out for a touch, it was that bad. Time passed, it seemed like an eternity, but maybe it was only a minute. The ring of movement surrounding us was only a hundred meters away now, and still we couldn't see what it might be. If there'd been a direction to run, we'd be running, but there was nothing we could do, and soon, soon — Seventy-five meters away, now, then fifty, and I couldn't even bear to look at the encroaching movement anymore, so I closed my eyes —

The Professor stammered, "Is it ... slowing down?"

The sound of her voice was oddly reassuring after all this silent panic. I felt myself still wrapped up in fear, in a blanket or a straitjacket of the stuff, maybe, but her voice was a reminder that I hadn't always been afraid. It had only been a few minutes, really —

"I think so," said Rhys. His voice was nervous and hesitant as the Professor's had been, but it too was like a lifeline for me, a reminder that there was another way to be besides panic-stricken.

I opened my eyes. Indeed, though the ring of rippling grass was only twenty meters away, its pace had sensibly diminished.

"Like it's afraid of us," said Michèle. "Having second thoughts maybe?"

Her voice was what really brought me back to life. It wasn't that I should be protecting her or anything stupid like that, it was that we all of us should be protecting each other, and in the grip of this strange fear, we'd forgotten.

"Yes!" I said, "That's it. It wants us to be afraid, because it's afraid too." I had no idea who or what I was talking about, but it seemed right when I said it anyway.

At that moment, as if in response to my voice, dozens of enormous cobras reared up out of the grass in a ring around us.

I was impressed, I have to admit. Each of them must have been at least ten meters long, as thick around as pythons, and their heads loomed well above my height. I'd never been around any kind of big snake and I felt like I would be at the mercy of even one of them if it struck at me, much less the fifty or more that had come at us, apparently from nowhere. Which led to an obvious thought, one that maybe we all should have had a while ago, but whatever.

"Someone's created these things," I said.

"Yes," said the Professor. "Or sent them to menace us, at least."

She strode forward toward one of the cobras, which impressed me even more than the cobras did themselves. I didn't think I could have done it.

"Listen you," she said, sounding like a school head addressing a particularly refractory student. The particular cobra she'd approached reared back, but uncomfortably, not with hostile intent. "We're not here by choice. Whoever you are, we don't mean you any harm. But we won't be bullied. Not like this."

The sound was halfway between a cough and a roar. It came from behind me. I glanced back and the Professor's tiger bounded forward from wherever she'd summoned him. He landed amid the cobras but didn't claw or bite any of them. Still, the tiger was obviously poised for violence. And yeah, maybe tigers weren't immune to venom, but I wouldn't have wanted to be one of the cobras making the attempt, either. The cobras seemed to think so too, because all around him, they began to draw back, hissing but not attacking. Then, all at once, they collapsed back into the obscuring grass and began to withdraw. A minute later they were gone completely, not even ripples in the grass betraying their existence, and maybe they were no longer in existence, either.

None of us said anything as they withdrew, like it might break the spell or something, but as soon as it seemed the snakes were gone completely, Michèle started clapping.

"Professor," she said, "you're my hero!"

"Yeah," said Rhys. "I'm ashamed now, like I should have come up with something. But I was totally paralyzed. And I think you really did save us, too. Those snakes, or whoever sent them, maybe they were just trying to scare us. But I think whoever sent them wanted us dead, it's just they were scared too, and your tiger freaked them out. If you hadn't done something, I bet the snakes would have attacked us eventually."

The Professor looked embarrassed. "Oh. Well, it was just luck I recovered first, perhaps. But I was thinking, you know, 'Snakes, why did it have to be snakes', and after that I couldn't be frightened anymore."

Rhys and Michèle both laughed like she'd said something funny, but it went over my head. Maybe something from a book? Definitely not Proust, anyway.

"I do hope whoever sent those things could hear and understand me. I hope they're willing to talk. Because of course we're lost here. We need answers. And if they're listening now ..."

"I don't like the idea of that," said Rhys. "That we're being spied on."

"Neither do I," said the Professor. "It's just that those cobras behaved as if they were being controlled by someone who could see us. But if they really have been watching us, they should realize we mean no harm."

"Yeah. But now I really want to find our friends, right away. If they're here, maybe they've got snakes to deal with too, or something worse."

Rhys turned to me. "What do you think? You've been pretty quiet."

"I agree," I said. "Before I figured if they were here somewhere, they'd probably be in good shape, and not in any great danger, so there was no urgency. But now — I just wish I had some idea how to find them. If this place is an island, it's a pretty big one."

"I guess we're just going to have to wait till morning to even have a hope of finding them. But it's going to be a long wait. And I don't think we should sleep apart, either. We're going to need to keep watch."

"Hey," said Michèle. "What's that?"

I looked and saw a narrow column of light apparently straight up from the ground, maybe a few kilometers away, inland, not toward the beach we'd come from. It was hard to tell the distance, but it had to be the better part of a kilometer high, brighter near the ground, and fading out at the top.

"Huh," said Rhys, "something new from the snake guy, maybe?"

The Professor was silent for a moment, but then she started to laugh. We waited for her to wind down.

At last, she said, "Well, so much for being smart. Something like that should have occurred to us, too. Don't you recognize it? It's a searchlight."

It was obvious in retrospect, but neither Michèle nor I had considered the possibility the light could be something technological.

"Probably one or more of our lost lambs created it," said the Professor. "Though I suppose from their point of view we're the lost ones. I wonder if they made a generator to power it?"

"So what do we do?" asked Michèle. "Make our own light? Go to them?"

"It seems to me," said the Professor, "we might as well go to them. I know Rhys is anxious to go as soon as possible. And after those cobras, I don't see why staying here should be any safer than traveling at night. The stars give us enough light to see by, and the terrain here is very gentle. Does anyone feel too tired to travel?"

I looked at Michèle and she shook her head.

"I'm okay," I said. "Seems like I should be tired after today, but I don't feel it."

"Huh," said Rhys, "since you mention it, I'm not tired either. So let's do it. Let's go."

If it weren't for worrying about the mysterious stranger and about our friends, it would have been a pleasant sojourn through the rolling green hills. The night was just a shade cooler than the day, still quite comfortable for an unclothed walk. As the Professor had said, the terrain was so gentle we had no fear of running into anything, so the going was easy.

As we walked, I developed an eerie feeling of being watched, but not by any person stalking us. I didn't want to say anything because it was such a crazy notion, but I felt like something was staring down at me from the sky, and something not very happy with me either. But above us there was only sky and stars. Stars like a million eyes, maybe. Not a pleasant thought, so I tried to shrug it off, without much success.

After a while, Rhys called a halt. The width of the beam in the distance had grown a little, so we were making progress, but we still had a long way to go. There was nothing special about this particular low grassy hillside on which he'd chosen to stop.

"Are you all okay?" he asked.

"Yes," said Michèle, but she sounded a little tentative to me.

"I suppose so," said the Professor. "Why do you ask?"

"It's — well ..."

"You feel like there's something out there," I said.

"Yeah," said Rhys. "Snake guy again, you think?"

"Maybe," I said. "I mean, it's just a feeling. But if there's one ... person here, there could be more too. And who knows what they're like."

"Aw, shit," said Michèle, "I feel it too, now."

"Come on," said Rhys, and he raised his voice, "Come on out if you're there! Show yourself!"

But there was no response.

"Damn it," he said, "it can't be nothing."

Nothing, I thought. Why not?

And just like that, the feeling of being watched, of a menacing sky overhead, it all vanished.

Michèle recovered first.

"Okay," she said, "what was that?"

The Professor said, "I felt like — like a mouse is supposed to, with a snake looming over it."

"Oh yeah," said Rhys, "Just like with the cobras. I went from just being a little uneasy to being outright afraid without even noticing, and then, then it was gone."

"Was it even there at all? Or did we imagine it ourselves this time?" I asked.

"That's the question," said the Professor. "Did something do that to us? Or did we do it to ourselves?"

"To ourselves?" asked Rhys. "How could we —"

"Oh!" Michèle exclaimed, "Like in the movie *Forbidden Planet*, right?"

Another reference over my head.

"Ha," said Rhys. "Okay. I remember that. Monsters of the id."

"Yes," said the Professor. "That's what I meant. Maybe we somehow amplified our own fears. I don't know. Because if we didn't ..."

"Yeah," said Rhys, "It made me feel like I wanted clothes, and a weapon too. I was just about ready to create a gun to discover over the next hillside. That's what I was thinking I should have done when the cobras showed up, come up with a gun. A machine gun, something like that."

He paused, put a hand to his eyes for a moment, then looked at us all.

He said, "It's, well, I feel embarrassed now. I've felt embarrassed a lot in the last few days, but for silly stuff, you know? I mean, nakedness, right? Intimacy. Sharing. I'm not used to it. But that was nothing, really. There was no reason to be ashamed. But now I'm wondering if I came close to failing, somehow."

"Failing?" When I said it the word just hung out there by itself, like someone else had said it.

"Yeah," said Rhys, "like failing a test, you know? I was in the army when I was younger, when I was even stupider than I am now. I know how to shoot a gun. I was that close to making a set of fatigues and a rifle to go with it. But what would that have done to you guys? Would you all have wanted weapons too? And clothes? Maybe it would have made us more and more afraid of stuff we haven't even seen yet."

"Oh," said Michèle. "Do you think that I — that I failed when I made clothes before?"

"Of course not," said the Professor. "Don't be silly."

"Oh no," said Rhys hastily. "I'm sorry I used the word. A little thing like that couldn't do any harm, even if it was wrong, and I'm sure it's not. And probably making guns and clothes now wouldn't do any harm either. I mean, they're just things, after all. It was just the way I felt, right? But the idea we're being tested, well ..."

"It could be," said the Professor. "I wish it were true, even, because I'd rather there wasn't some frightened person out there trying to hurt us. But there's no evidence of anything. It's too early yet to come to that kind of a conclusion."

"All right," said Rhys, "but anyway I feel better now. Shall we go?"

We walked onward. And though that nagging sense of being watched didn't entirely vanish, it didn't occupy my mind anymore either. Michèle was walking beside me now.

"Listen," she said, "I don't want to sound too fragile, you know? But that talk of failing hit me right here." She patted her belly. "I thought to myself right before the cobras came, we are in a little paradise now, okay? Anything we want we can have, but really all I want is to be with friends, and to have time together with you. And that's what I have already. No need to try anymore. So I was relaxing, right? Having fun."

I took her hand. "And if this is a test, if it's something we can fail, it's not fun anymore, right? And maybe it's dangerous too. You can't get something for nothing, is that it?"

"Yes," she said, "and more than that. If I was here, in this place I mean, as the guy I used to be, I think I would be all excited about it being a test. I'd want to push my way through it, get it over with. Beat it, you know? And now I'm wondering if I'm too much pretending to be a girl now, if it's fake, all this feeling stuff, if I'm just putting it on."

I raised her hand and kissed it, which is not as easy as it sounds while walking.

"Yesterday," I said, "or maybe a million years ago, I don't know, I think you said something very wise. You said that for all your life you'd been playing at being a man, and now you were playing at being a woman."

"Yes, I remember. You don't think that was trite?"

"I suppose it's commonplace to say that we choose the faces we show other people. But most of us never had the chance to choose our bodies. It's a wonderful freedom. But I really do think that there's nothing fake about what you are now. Honestly, I've felt fake all my life, and maybe it's only since I met you that I've become real. It's all right to play, is what I'm saying, okay?"

She squeezed my hand.

"All right," she said. "I'll keep playing, then."

8

W E WALKED FOR A WHILE without saying anything more. With no insects, no birds or frogs or anything like that, the night was almost completely silent, the faint sounds of our feet on the grass the only noise. Even the breeze had mostly died away. So it was something of a shock to hear a rustling coming towards us from not all that far off.

We stopped short. I saw Rhys trying to peer through the darkness to see whatever it was. A dark blot came whizzing towards us out of the sky, and I think we all flinched, even Rhys, who raised his hands defensively as it came toward him. It approached rapidly with a loud flapping of wings, and then I realized belatedly it was just a bird, and not a very big one either.

The thing flew around our heads once and cawed loudly, like a crow. I thought it had dark plumage like a crow, too. And then it started to speak.

"I am Mina's myna," it said, "and this is my message. Come to the light."

"Oh!" Rhys lowered his hands, and Michèle laughed, a note of relief in her voice.

"Can you talk," asked the Professor, "or is that just a memorized message?" She held out her left arm, and after a moment the bird fluttered down to her and alit on her wrist. It hopped up her arm to her shoulder and pecked once at her hair.

"No," said the bird, "I can't talk. Sorry. Mina was afraid to make something that could."

I couldn't help laughing, and Michèle snickered too.

"Oh for pity's sake," said the Professor. "I suppose you'd better come with us."

"Thanks," said the bird. "It was a pain not having anything to perch on while I was flying around looking for you guys. I keep thinking there should be things like that, but there's only hills and it's scary walking around on the ground."

"Hello, Monsieur Bird," said Michèle. "Or should it be Mademoiselle Bird?"

"Hm," said the bird. It tried to look between its legs and almost fell off the Professor's shoulder. "I think it's Mr. Not sure, though."

"Oh well," said Michèle, "I suppose it doesn't matter very much anymore," and she giggled. "But I should introduce us. My name's Michèle, this is Rhys, the Professor, and Jay."

"Pleased," said the bird. "I don't have a name, though."

"Do you want one?" I asked.

The bird cocked its head to one side. "I don't know. I'm not sure I'll be around long enough to need one."

"What does that mean?" asked Michèle.

"I was just made an hour ago. Now that I've found you, I've done my job. There's no more need for me."

Michèle made an O with her mouth. "But don't you want to live?"

The bird shrugged with its wings, a gesture I thought looked rather unavian.

"I suppose so," it said, "but I have no purpose now."

"Mina created you?" asked the Professor, turning her head to look at the bird. It gazed at her for a moment, and its whole body twitched once, violently.

"Wow," said the bird, "I totally overcame the urge to peck you on the nose there. I mean, yes, she made me, and she told me to go and find you, and she gave me the message to say to you when I did."

"But she doesn't know you're self-aware? I mean, that you can speak on your own?"

"Yeah," said the bird, "I didn't say anything while she was telling me what to do."

"Why not?"

"You don't understand," said the bird. "That was — that was Mina. She's my — She *made* me. And she said to those other two that she made a bird because she didn't want to accidentally make a person."

"Other two? Good. That must be Nora and Quaid." The Professor placed her index finger on the bird's head and brought it slowly down its neck.

The bird shuddered and raised its head.

"Oh," it said after a moment, "you have no idea."

"I'm sure avian existential philosophy is fascinating for some of us —" (here Rhys looked at the Professor and smiled) "— but let's get moving and we can hold the colloquium when we get there, all right? How far do we have to go?"

The bird made a kind of choked squawking noise and after a moment I realized it was laughing.

"Well," it said, "as I fly, it was pretty quick, but I guess it will take longer for you people."

We got moving again, and it wasn't all that long before we found the source of the searchlight beam. It was on top of a hill, a squat steel cylinder a good meter across mounted in a gimballed cradle, a heavy power cable snaking out of the mounting and piercing the earth.

"Well that answers the electricity question," said the Professor. "Kind of."

"Mina and the other two are down below, next hill over," said the bird. We looked, and there they were, seated around a little campfire in the valley. The three of them were as naked as us, so if they'd had the idea of clothes, they likewise hadn't acted on it. Rhys called out, and we all scrambled down toward them, the bird fluttering aloft and circling for a bit before alighting on Mina's arm.

I was a little uneasy on the way down the hillside. I didn't know why at the time, but in retrospect I think I was worried that we might have lost whatever unity we'd had back on the bridge. Maybe it was just a few hours we'd been separated, but another way of looking at it was an eternity. Would we still feel the same connection, all seven of us? Suppose they'd come to different conclusions about this place? Anyway, wherever it came from, the anxiety turned out not to be grounded in anything real.

As we descended the hill, they started running up it. We met in the middle. Quaid and Nora were waving and whooping, and Mina launched herself at me like a missile, almost knocking me down, the bird squawking and fluttering into the air just in time to avoid being crushed.

We spent a good five minutes hugging each other and laughing. It was especially pleasing to watch the three of them, Quaid, Nora, and Mina, wrapping Rhys up in a gang-tackle of an embrace.

I was curious if any of the three of them had changed since last we met, took a moment off from the scrum to look them over.

The last time I saw Mina, she'd given herself gleaming blue hair and nails and metallic blue eyes like some sort of anime dream of an android. I saw now that she'd dialed it back a little here in this new world, keeping the blue color scheme, but now with more natural-looking eyes with actual whites to them, and hair that now looked like it had been dyed blue instead of actually spun from blued steel. Quaid and Nora still looked very similar, though they were recognizably different even now.

At last, we sat down in a circle around the campfire. I suppose they'd conjured up the wood as well as the fire itself, but it looked natural as it was now. The bird perched on Mina's shoulder. He was just a bird, after all; but I wondered about him. Did Mina realize what she'd done?

"We were worried about you guys," said Quaid, and "We didn't know what was going on for a while," said Nora.

Mina laughed. "Like we do now?"

"When did you figure out that you could make stuff?" asked Rhys.

"It was Mina," said Nora. "She reminded us about what we did to make it morning the other day."

Quaid nodded. "What we did to change ourselves."

"Just a couple of hours ago," said Nora.

"So she thought we might be able to change the world, too."

"Hence the searchlight," said the Professor. "A wonderful idea."

"And the bird found you too," said Mina. "It did a good job." The bird shuddered, just as he had done when the Professor stroked his head.

"Right," I said. "About that bird —"

The bird cawed. I thought it sounded like a warning.

"Sorry," I said, nodding to the bird. "I've got to tell her. It'll be all right."

"Tell me what?" asked Mina.

"He's real," I said. "I mean, he's not just a thing, not even just a bird."

"What?"

"You'd better tell her yourself," I said.

The bird hopped off Mina's shoulder, fluttered to the ground in front of her.

"I'm sorry," he said, misery unmistakable in his voice. "I didn't mean it. I didn't mean to be able to talk."

Mina goggled at him, speechless, and Quaid and Nora were nearly as nonplussed.

"It's all right," said the bird. "Get rid of me. I don't mind."

"Holy shit," said Mina, "I made ... a person?"

"Yes," said Michèle, smiling, "and he's a cute one, too. Very sweet."

"Please don't be upset," said the bird. "Get rid of me now if you like. It's fine with me."

Mina bent over to lower her head to the bird's height.

"Not in a million years, you," she said, waving a blue-nailed finger. "I didn't mean to make you a person, but if you are one there's no way I'm getting rid of you. I don't know much about what's going on, but I know you're my responsibility now. Okay?"

The bird took a tentative step toward her, and they looked in each other's eyes for a time, not saying anything. I wondered how I would feel if I was in his place. Looking into my creator's eyes.

"Okay," he said at last, and we all could hear the emotion in his voice. Whatever he was, he was more than a bird.

"You tell me if you need anything," said Mina. "If you want anything. Got it?" She held out her arm and the bird hopped up on her wrist.

"I do want something," said the bird.

"Oh?"

"I want to do more things for you. If you have any more messages, maybe? I liked that."

"Sure," said Mina, and the bird made its way to her shoulder, perched there like a guardian spirit, which maybe he was.

"I hate to say it," said Rhys, "but —"

"Yeah," said Mina, "I know. This worked out okay, maybe. But it could have been bad. Suppose he came back without finding you? Suppose he didn't say anything? Suppose I didn't care how cute he is? I got it."

"Good," said the Professor. "You understand. There's more to say about this, but let's catch each other up first."

It took about an hour. Their story was the same as ours at first: they washed up on the shore, wandered around for a while, and eventually turned inland, where they discovered they had the power to cause things to come into existence. Like us, they'd all at once felt a baseless fear of what might be out there, just at the same time we'd noticed it ourselves, but I got the idea it hadn't peaked in a crisis so much for them. And they hadn't had any confrontation with cobras, either. When we talked about the episode now, no more than an hour later, it seemed to me like it hadn't ever happened, like maybe I'd read about it happening to someone else. A memory of a memory is all it was. I couldn't recall how it had actually felt at all anymore.

"Of course with Mina here, we had nothing to worry about," said Quaid. "You have no idea how reassuring it was to have her with us," said Nora.

"Come on guys," said Mina, "I'm not all that. Three days ago I was just a regular person working at McDonalds."

"And now you're our champion," said the Professor. "Classic origin story."

Mina laughed and the Professor said, "I hate to make you uncomfortable, Mr. Bird, but I do want to talk about you for a minute."

The bird cocked his head to the side. "Be my guest," he said.

"I also created a living thing," said the Professor, "before I understood that it might be dangerous. But wonderful and amazing as it was, it wasn't a person. I'm sure of it. More like an extension of my desire, really. So I can't help but wonder where our friend here came from, really."

"What do you mean by that?" asked Mina.

The Professor explained her notion that something else, something external, was actually performing the act of creation for us, on our behalf.

"Oh," said Mina, "I wanted the bird to do more than an animal would normally be able to. So whatever it is, this creation-helper thing, you're saying it had to make the bird be a person to do what I wanted?"

"Maybe," said the Professor. "That might be part of it. But this bird, you know, he's very smart. A lot smarter than he needed to be to follow your instructions. I'm sorry even to talk about him like that, when he's right here listening to us."

The bird clicked his beak once and made a sort of chirruping sound. I thought he was pleased.

"So I was wondering whether he might not have been created at all. Not even by the — the instrumentality responsible for all these acts of creation we've attempted."

"Not created? What does that mean?"

"Oh," said Michèle. "I know. The stars, right? The ones we flew past coming through the light."

"Very good," said the Professor. "I'm happy you had the same idea. Now this is just speculation but that's pretty much all we've got right now. Suppose those stars or points of light really are people. Souls, let's call them. Survivors of our world, perhaps. If you were a god with a small g, and someone asked you for an intelligent bird, maybe you'd find it easier to use an intelligence that was right at hand."

"But the bird doesn't remember being anyone else. Does he? I mean, do you?"

The bird flapped his wings once. "I don't even know what you're talking about," he said. "Remember being someone else? I hardly even remember being myself. I'm only a couple of hours old, you know."

"Sure," said Michèle, "but when you get reincarnated, you're not supposed to remember your past life, are you? If you're not a lama, anyway."

"What was that you just said?" asked the Professor.

"If you're not a lama," said Michèle.

"Yes and before that you said 'reincarnated'. Damn!"

"What?"

"When we first got here," said the Professor, "I thought I'd heard something somewhere about a sea of milk. It's a Hindu belief. I still don't recall the details, but it has something to do with eternal life. Karma and reincarnation. And cobras too. They're all through Hindu and Buddhist mythology. If only I had Wikipedia to look it up!"

"Wow," said Nora, "She's really come into her own, hasn't she?"

Quaid just nodded at the Professor, and smiled at her when she blushed.

"Yeah," said Rhys, "we'd probably be floundering around at the shore still if it wasn't for her." He turned to the Professor. "But let me understand something here. I don't think you're saying Hinduism is the true religion, are you?"

"Well, no," said the Professor. "To be honest, I'd find it hard to say that even if elephant-headed Ganesha himself was on the beach to welcome us with garlands of flowers. But that sea of milk is so very odd. It's at least possible some other aspects of Hindu cosmology and even theology may be relevant here too."

"What other aspects?" asked Mina.

"And that's where I let you down," said the Professor. "I just don't know much. The names of some of the gods. Probably the same idea of karma and resurrection that most of you have. Not my field, you understand. I don't suppose anyone else knows anything about it?"

No one answered.

"Oh well," said the Professor. "I suppose it's still possible we'll meet someone who wants to talk to us and has some idea what's going on here. In the meantime, I suppose we should set our priorities."

Rhys sat up. He'd been quiet for a while, letting us all talk.

"Right," he said, "Seems like we've got the usual survival basics granted us by magic. But I'm feeling a responsibility, you know. I just wish I knew what to do about it."

"Steiner," said Nora and Quaid together.

"Yeah," said Rhys. "Finding you all has been a huge load off my mind. But him ..."

"I'm sorry," said Mina, "I don't mean to be cruel. But are you thinking he's maybe alive here someplace? Or that he's floating in the middle of all those stars, maybe?"

"I don't know," said Rhys. "But I was thinking that what happened to Steiner might have been something like what happened to everyone else in the world. And if there's something left of him, if there's a way to resurrect people ..."

"You think we can just, like summon him? Make him appear here?"

"Maybe," said Rhys. "If nothing else works. But we talked about this before. Suppose we screw it up somehow. There's all kinds of horrible things we could do by accident, not knowing how this stuff really works. What I really want to do is be sure I know that he exists now, somewhere, and rescue him from wherever he is."

"Gotcha," said Mina.

"All right then," said the Professor. "Are we agreed? We want Steiner back. We can worry about all these deep questions when we've got that done."

"For sure," I said.

Nora and Quaid put their hands on Rhys's shoulder as if it was a choreographed maneuver. "We like him a lot too," said Quaid, and "I don't have anyone to tear into without him around," said Nora. "The rest of you are way too nice, or way too dignified."

Michèle nodded. "I don't know this Steiner much at all. Not like most of you. I only met him the day he — the last day. But even if I don't like him at all from our time together, and I do, I like him a lot, still I say he's the most important thing. Right, Mina?"

"Oh yes," she said, "What you said is just the same for me. There's no question. And what happened to him was so horrible — sorry, but if there's anything we can do for him, we've got to try."

"Good," said the Professor. "Next steps in the morning, then. There's still a chance he's heading toward the light tonight, so we might as well wait till then."

No attempt to force a new morning this time. We separated by ones and twos, in a sort of accelerated version of what might have taken all night at a party back in our old world, though I don't suppose most parties used to work out so neatly for everyone.

"Oh well," said Mina, "I guess it's time to turn in."

Mina gave Rhys a hand, hoisted him to his feet as if he was weightless, and led him a few steps away from the fire where the two of them exchanged a few words, both of them glancing at the Professor, who seemed oblivious to the conversation. Mina walked over to her and held out her hand, but instead of merely helping the Professor to her feet, she picked her up bodily in her arms like an infant. For a moment I thought she might protest, but then she shook her head and smiled at us all.

"Who am I to disagree," she said, and putting her arm around Mina's neck, kissed her on the lips from her suspended position.

Nora and Quaid made "*woo-woo*" noises at them as Mina let the Professor down and the two of them walked off together to find a spot to spend the night, the bird fluttering off behind them.

"See," whispered Michèle in my ear, "I was right!"

Rhys sat back down by the fire, but he was interrupted by Quaid and Nora, who each put a hand on one of his shoulders. He rose to his feet; they shared a brief colloquy, and then the two each kissed one of his hands before departing themselves.

Michèle looked at me. "Should we?" she asked.

"Why not," I said, "everyone else has," and she giggled.

We both squatted next to Rhys at the fire, which by now had almost died away into embers.

"Hey," I said.

"I don't suppose —" said Michèle, but Rhys laughed, cutting her off. "You guys too?"

"Yeah," said Michèle. "We were going to ask you after dinner if you and the Professor didn't — but now you've sent her off with Mina, so ..."

Rhys looked at her seriously for a moment. "I'm flattered," he said. "I mean, I really am. Any of you, literally any of you asking me just last week would have blown my mind. I hope I would have said yes, too, and I'll say yes soon, but not tonight, okay? I'm, ah, preoccupied."

"Oh," I said, "you're that worried about Steiner?"

"Yeah," he said. "I'm thinking about him being all alone somewhere. Remember how he used to get, right? The phobias. I was kind of proud of him on the last day, you know? He overcame it all to go with us. Makes me angry, what happened to him, what he might be suffering now."

"I didn't realize," said Michèle, "he seemed okay that one day I knew him. A little tense maybe, but who wouldn't be with the world ending?"

"But he used to be pretty much a mess most of the time," said Rhys. "Wasn't just one thing. Every week or two, he'd come up with some new phobia or anxiety. He knew it was all bullshit, though, fought his way through whatever it was that week just to get to my pub. I'm thinking that was probably his only way of connecting with other people, at Caernarfon. That's why he struggled so hard to get there every night."

"Yeah, that I understand," I said. "You had something there for us. I still don't know what it was, not in words, but it was important. But I'm thinking he might have got rid of those phobias for good. You know, the way we all changed in those three days, inside or outside."

Rhys nodded. "I hope that's true, but he used to have a few days in between, you know, when he was okay, except for worrying about what the next damn thing was going to be. And if anything was going to throw him off course, it would be being left alone like that. And after such a horrible thing happened to him, too."

"Poor guy," said Michèle. "I had no idea. You're incredibly sweet, though, for caring so much about him."

"Yeah, well," said Rhys, "it's keeping me from relaxing right now, all right? That thing with the Professor, I don't know, I still feel like I did something wrong there."

"What? You think she didn't want you? You think she was just being kind, or something?"

"I know better than that," said Rhys. "But not all of me does. I mean, I'm not sure I completely believe it. And I know she's interested in Mina. And she's hardly more than half my age, but I get the feeling she's more grown up than I am, you know?"

I laughed, thinking about her. "She's pretty special. I was lucky to run into her at that McDonalds. I guess we all were, come to think of it."

"Ha," said Rhys. "That we were. Anyway, I need a little time to ease into all this group-love stuff, okay? I've never even slept with a guy, just for one."

"Neither have I," I said. "Though I should have, a couple of days ago, when I had the opportunity. Fortunately Michèle gave me a second chance, but I was stupid to let her go. To let him go, back then."

"You know I like it better this way," she said. "But you too are very sweet. It's a good thing I like candy."

"I got you," said Rhys. "Got you both. That was really just an excuse, I think. There was a time the whole idea of this kind of thing would have made me bounce completely off it. But now, I kind of like the idea. I mean, of all of you. It just, well, takes time, I guess. Call me slow. Does that make sense?"

"Sure," said Michèle. "When this all started, I'd have punched you in the nose if you told me I'd be kissing a guy the next day. And I'd have laughed myself sick if you told me what I'd be doing the day after that. But you have a point about being alone."

"What?"

"I mean, romance and fucking and all that is very, very nice, but this place is so strange … Remember how we all got frightened for no reason before? It's good Mina isn't by herself tonight. And I think it's not good for you to be alone either. So why not just sleep with us? I mean just sleep? I could be in the middle, if it makes a difference."

He laughed, a little shakily. "Now you're making me ashamed of myself." He frowned, and then his face cleared. "But you know? That sounds very nice. I was sort of preparing myself to be alone, psyching myself up for it. But why should I do that to myself? I don't know. And maybe we don't need that much sleep here, maybe it's not all that long till morning, but it still seems like a good idea."

"All right then!"

She took us both by the hand.

9

I RECALL LYING DOWN, spooning with Michèle comfortably up against my chest, Rhys facing her on the opposite side, as she'd suggested. Not sure how it was I woke up in Rhys's arms, with Michèle nowhere to be seen. Or rather, considering the problem, it was pretty obvious. Michèle hadn't promised to stay in the middle.

Anyway, Rhys woke a moment later. *Just before dawn,* I thought. *Still dark out.* Probably something about my movement on waking woke him as well. He was a little shorter than me, so his head was tucked into my neck, his arm draped over my side. He looked up at me, stiffened for a moment, then smiled.

"Morning," he whispered.

Now Rhys is not the type you would ever call winsome; but just at that moment there was something extremely appealing about his expression. So I kissed him. Just like I kissed Michel a couple of days before. No licorice flavor or tobacco scent this time, and it took him a moment to respond, but when he did it was for real, it was very nice indeed, and it lasted quite a while.

That was all we did, though. I could tell Rhys was holding back a little, and I wasn't entirely sure how I felt about it either, about actually having sex with him. I think if he'd been completely enthusiastic, I would have been too, but, as it was, I hesitated. When I considered he was preoccupied with Steiner I felt like I didn't want to push him. So eventually we broke apart from one another and sat up.

He said softly to me, "She set us up, didn't she?"

"Not my idea," I said. "But yeah, I think she did. Are you sorry?"

"No. It's just — well, yeah, I'm slow sometimes. Slow to figure myself out. But I think I've figured something out, anyway. Steiner, you know. It never would have occurred to me back in our old world."

"You've fallen for him?"

"Yeah. Did you all know?"

"Michèle said so. And then I realized it too."

"Wow. Maybe she knew before I did. Anyway, I know it's not like I'm betraying him, not like he even has a clue, assuming he's even alive or that we can call him back or whatever. But ..." He trailed off.

"I understand," I said. "Well, actually I don't really understand what's happening here at all, between all of us, but it's been pretty nice so far. A few days ago I would have told you I was straight, but now I don't know what that even means anymore. I don't think it's all that important, either, so long as we get along."

"Yeah," he said. "But I do like you, you know, and I think I really would like to try it. Just ... not today is all. I want to find him, Steiner, I mean, and work out what that means if I do. So another time, okay?"

He held out his hand. It was a ridiculous situation, but what the hell. I shook hands with him. Just two naked guys after the end of the world, shaking hands after sleeping in each other's arms, agreeing to have sex sometime, like we might have agreed to do lunch.

"Hey," he said, "do you smell something?"

"Coffee. Eggs. And Jesus, I think that's bacon."

We followed our noses around a couple of hillsides and discovered Michèle had created one of those big multi-tiered room-service dollies, laden with a dozen silver platters and trays, a huge coffee pot and samovar on their own wheelie cart off to the side. A low octagonal table held china service for eight with an array of gold flatware, including one setting that was just a plate of birdseed and fruit with a wooden perch emerging from the table in front of the plate.

Michèle was standing by the coffeepot, a little white cap on her head and a frilly white apron around her waist, like a comic pornographer's conception of a maid.

"Did you sleep well, gentlemen? Time for un petit-déjeuner."

Rhys laughed. "You know we did. But that was all three of us."

Michèle smiled, but with a little trepidation behind it, I saw. "It's all right?"

"Oh yeah," said Rhys, "but you know how it is when you're a little kid and someone makes you try some new kind of food? And it turns out to be good? You don't necessarily want to admit it."

"Oh, oh," she said. "Next time I want to watch."

"You'll do more than watch, next time," I said.

I'm not sure where that would have gone, but the aroma had already summoned the rest of our company.

"Watch what?" asked Mina, walking hand in hand with the Professor, the bird in his place on her shoulder.

"Oh, nothing," said Michèle. "But breakfast is served."

"Wow," said Mina, "I was thinking I'd make a sack of McMuffins, but this spread is for real. How long did it take you to make it?"

"A long time," said Michèle. "I think I'm not that good at it. I had to imagine each dish by itself, and then by the time I was done half of it was cold and I had to do it over."

"Well it looks great! Hey, is this stuff gold?" Mina picked up a knife and fork. "It's heavy!"

"Yes," said Michèle. "I think it is anyway. That's what I tried to make. But since you say it, it makes me feel funny now. Like it's showing off, you know?"

"Not to worry," said the Professor. "I have the feeling that one way or another we'll have to do something a lot more ostentatious than serving breakfast soon enough."

She sat down cross-legged at the table. "Are those omelets? Is there ketchup?"

"Ketchup? With Provençal? Barbaric!" said Michèle. "But I suppose there might be some under this linen ... She frowned for a moment, pulled out a bottle of Heinz, passed it over. I noticed it was marked with a big ornate 1 instead of the usual 57. "That's it," she said, "the last bottle of ketchup in the world."

"Hey," said the bird, "a place for me." He fluttered over to the perch, and Michèle poured him a thimble-sized cup of orange juice.

Quaid and Nora arrived a moment later.

"Good morning," they said in chorus, and sat down at the two remaining places as if it was a routine occurrence.

Michèle served out coffee, tea, and cocoa, and then sat down to eat with us. It was another glorious meal, certainly the best breakfast I'd ever had, and there wasn't a lot of time for talking while we were eating.

"Right," said the Professor, when she'd finished her last croissant. "There's all kinds of deep philosophy we probably need to talk over, but there will be plenty of time for that later. First comes Steiner, are we agreed?"

No one demurred, and even the bird looked serious, though I suppose he had no idea who we were talking about.

"My plan's pretty simple," said the Professor. "We go down to the beach, we imagine him coming to us, we visualize him coming up through the waves to the beach. Just like we did ourselves."

"Makes sense to me," said Rhys.

"Yes," said Nora, and "Let's go then," said Quaid.

So we did. It took us a while to get back to the shore, but it wasn't long past midday when we were walking again on the milk-wet black sand. It was almost the same as yesterday, the same hazy yellow sky, the same black beach, the same thick white waves rippling up onto the sand.

But not quite the same.

"Jesus," said Rhys. "This is dire, isn't it?"

That feeling of dread from last night had returned just as we got to the shore. Without seeing any evidence of it, I had the sense of something lurking beneath the waves.

"You wouldn't think an ocean of milk could be so fucking ominous," said Mina. "But you know, I think I'm not very scared at all. Are you guys?"

"No," said the Professor. "It's too blatant. And I know it's not real. Like a warning, maybe."

Mina said, "I think it's more like a challenge."

"Agreed. How should we proceed?"

"Let's ignore it," said Quaid.

"Yes," said Nora, "unless we see something, let's just follow the plan."

"All right," said Rhys, "I like it too. Michèle, would you lead us? Like the way you had us make that beach flag."

The Professor frowned for a moment but didn't say anything.

"Okay," said Michèle. "Let's try it this way. You all sit around me, right? So we are all touching. Maybe if we try, we can get that rapport back again." She sat down on the beach a couple of yards above the waterline. I followed and sat down just behind her, and everyone else formed a close circle. It was kind of cramped, but no contortion was required. I had my knees touching Michèle's hips at 6 o'clock in the circle, and I was able to reach out with my hands to support her back. Nora and Quaid sat to either side of me at 4 and 8; reaching out they were able to put their hands on her thighs. The Professor and Rhys were able to sit close enough to her at 2 and 10 on the clock that her knees were touching theirs, and Mina sat in front at 12, her hands on Michèle's crossed ankles, the bird on her shoulder shifting from foot to foot. I thought he had a gleam in his eyes I hadn't seen before, but he said nothing as we got ourselves sorted out.

"Here we go," said Michèle. "Tell me if you feel something happening that's not right, but if it's going okay, we'll take it to the end."

"Understood," said Rhys, and we all added our various agreements.

"Remember that field of stars," said Michèle. "I think it was beyond the ocean of milk, not within it. So maybe it's a sort of ocean of something else. Ether, maybe. It's far away, but we can still see it from here. That big field of millions, billions of bright little stars. And each one of them is a soul. All we need to do is find the right one. Steiner. We all remember Steiner. He wasn't that big. Wiry, though, like I used to be when I was Michel. I bet he worked out. And his face. That dark hair, right? That five o'clock shadow. The glasses. The sound of his voice, you know the way he spoke: fast, a little tense. Okay. Take a minute, remember him."

She paused. I tried to recall Steiner for myself, but it was strangely difficult to do. I kept getting these little fragmentary glimpses of him, like a bit of his face, a few of his words, but then I'd lose him, I'd lose focus, and I'd have nothing at all. Shit; I'd seen him probably two hundred times at least in the last year, talked to him probably more than anyone else at Caernarfon except Rhys. He was always talking. How could I not remember him now? And then I had the thought, maybe something is getting in my way? Getting in our way? That fear, that sense of unease had been out there in the waves.

So rather than trying to imagine Steiner in his own person, I thought about the sea of milk, the idea that the sea of souls lay beyond it somehow, with something in the middle blocking our reach. I imagined our collective desire to pull Steiner out of the sea as a long ethereal arm, with an outstretched hand, as it said somewhere in the bible. Oh yeah: Exodus, the hand of God. Well, the Professor did say what we were trying to do was hubris. I figured Rhys and the other regulars had all the memories of Steiner they needed. Michèle was organizing us, directing the effort, but Mina, she didn't know Steiner all that well.

"Something's blocking us," I said in a low voice. "Mina, can you push us past it? I think it's out there in the ocean. If the rest of you guys keep trying for Steiner, Mina, maybe you and I can get through whatever it is?"

"Oh yeah," she said, "I feel it now. It's in our way. Gotcha."

Even with my eyes closed, I saw her now, sitting just across from me, on the other side of Michèle. Her eyes had resumed that glow they'd had when we were trying to break through the wall of the old world, and her nails were glowing too. I could almost hear a tone now, like a vast synthesized power chord: slowly rising, a complex note backed with harmonics up and down the scale, like a rocket engine firing just before liftoff, getting more and more powerful, louder, higher. And with all that build-up, the resistance was rising too, I could feel it solidifying, not so much a wall as it was in the old world, but an active force pushing back against our efforts ... I didn't know what I was doing, really, but I tried to back Mina up, to lift her somehow, to give some kind of push to that rising chord.

A silent explosion and the resistance collapsed. We punched through it, and I could feel the force recoiling, giving way, spiraling off to the sides, our arm rushing onwards.

"All right," I said, "I think we did it. Michèle, you can take over again."

"Yes! We're in the sea of stars now, right? You all can see it? We're there, and one of those stars is Steiner. Look carefully, you can see him, like he's inside the star, right? See his face, hear his voice. It's that star. That one right there. The one that's trying to come towards us on its own now. All we have to do is help him. Just pull him back to us ..."

I could see Steiner clearly now. Like he was standing at the bar, talking to Rhys, taking a little heat from Nora maybe, or else bending my ear and Quaid's on whatever his topic of the day might have been. And then I saw him as he was while we were crossing the bridge, with some secret fire he'd found burning inside him, keeping him going in the face of all his fears. Yeah, that one star out of all those billions. That was the one. Our hand was reaching for him. Grasping him firmly, pulling him out.

"We've got him now," said Michèle. "That's it! He's coming toward us and nothing is holding him back. Soon we'll be out of the field of stars."

The vast array of glittering points was rushing away from us as we pulled him back, my point of view moving with Steiner's own point of light. And the medium we were moving through was growing thicker, more like fluid than ether, and I thought it was almost time —

"Now," said Michèle, "as we enter the ocean of milk, he's getting his body back. Just a sort of ghostly body to begin with, right? We don't want him to drown or anything. But you can see him, right? Sort of transparent, moving through the white milk, through the currents."

And I saw him just like that, that shimmering soul star expanding into a ghostly form shooting through the milky depths like a torpedo and at the same time rising rapidly toward the surface high above.

"He's almost back," said Michèle, "and as we bring him up to the surface, he's right there, his body is getting to be more real, more solid. He's just a hundred meters away now, he's a tarpon on a line, we've got him, he's coming closer, he's breaking through —"

I heard a splashing from close by, nothing like the sounds of the tiny milk waves lapping at the shore. Couldn't resist opening my eyes, and there he was, a milk-sodden body half immersed. Steiner in the flesh, gasping for air, shaking his head, trying to lever himself up.

We all surged forward, but Rhys was there first, hoisting Steiner onto his feet as if he was weightless, and then hugging him. Seeing the fierceness of his embrace it was clear Rhys was showing more than just a noble sense of duty. I almost laughed out loud, wondered if Steiner realized it, too. And then it occurred to me: Rhys and Steiner, the Professor and Mina, Quaid and Nora, and Michèle and me: four couples, even if we weren't exactly exclusive. Very neat. Symmetrical, even, considering genders. Almost suspicious.

But then we mobbed them like a baseball team after winning a championship, and I stopped working my conspiracy theory.

"Hey man," said Mina when we finally stepped back, "it's good to have you back."

"I guess I'm supposed to say it's good to be back," said Steiner, wiping milk drops off his face. And then he laughed. "But damn if it isn't."

We went through a jumble of disconnected chatter for a minute or two, trying to tell what had happened to us at the same time as asking what had happened to him, but at last it settled down.

"But what was it like?" Mina asked.

"On the one hand it was pretty goddamn horrible," said Steiner, "but on the other not so bad." He shook his head, closed his eyes, remembering.

"Yeah, when that wall, that thing grabbed me like that, I was shocked, right? And it was devouring me from the inside, is what it felt like. Like everything I had was being taken from me. That was pretty nasty. And losing you guys, yeah. I didn't like that."

Rhys bowed his head. "I'm so sorry," he said, "it all happened so fast, there was nothing we could do. It's been eating at me since it happened."

"All of us felt that way," said Quaid, and "Yeah, surviving the end of the world wasn't as sweet as it should have been, without you," said Nora.

"Damn," said Steiner. "Sorry to do that to you, then. But afterwards, after it was done eating me, it was like there was a tiny bit of me left, you know? And I felt like that last bit of me was being swallowed, but not in a bad way. I know that doesn't make much sense, but ... You know those pneumatic tubes they used to use in some old office buildings? For message delivery?"

"Yes," said the Professor, "I remember those things. Some hospitals and other businesses still use them. I mean they used to."

"Well it was like that little bit of me was sucked into one of those tubes. I could feel myself shooting off someplace, but I couldn't see anything, couldn't tell where I was going until I got there. And then ..."

"The sea of stars," said Michèle.

"Yeah. Hey, who's telling this? But that's right. I was just sort of floating there in the middle of a zillion of these shiny little stars. I was kind of confused, but this is the part that wasn't that bad. It wasn't that I didn't remember what had happened to me, it was more like it didn't matter anymore. I could feel a sort of dismay all that time, I guess, because I wanted you guys back, but it wasn't nearly as bad as it sounds. Just sort of floating there, nothing to worry about, right? And after a while I got the idea that I was one of those stars myself, since I could tell I had no body anymore. I couldn't talk to anyone, couldn't even sense the slightest bit of response from anyone else, but seeing all those maybe-people around me made it a little better. But really I guess it was just limbo. And on my way out of the sea, I started to feel like a person again. But what happened to you guys? How did you wind up here?"

Together we gave a patchwork explanation of how Mina broke through the wall that had devoured Steiner, our passage through the ocean of milk, and our day and night here on the island.

"You can make stuff just appear?" asked Steiner. "That's pretty cool. And a talking bird? Oh, hey there, sorry. Didn't notice you."

"Hi," said the bird. "Nice to meet you."

"The same," said Steiner. "Sorry if I'm a little confused still. This is kind of hard for me to swallow, all at once, you know?"

"No problem." He flapped his wings once and clicked his beak.

"Hey," said Steiner, "anyone want to demonstrate that making-stuff power? I get that you pulled me out of the sea with it, but I want to see it with my own eyes."

"Sure," said Rhys. "Stella Artois, right?"

"Yeah."

"Okay, I'm sure there's a bottle right behind me ..." Rhys frowned, turned to look. "It's not working," he said.

I could tell from people's expressions several of us were also trying, and not succeeding.

"Oh," said the Professor. "Of course. Remember the flag?"

"We couldn't make it here," said Michèle. "It showed up on the grass. And everything else we made was there."

"What?" asked Rhys. "It only works inland? But then how did it work to, ah, rescue Steiner here?"

"Well, at least to begin with we were working far away, beyond the ocean of milk," said the Professor. "And for that matter, it felt like something was trying to stop us. Mina had to break through the resistance. Perhaps whatever is opposing us is trying to stop us from doing things right here. And maybe if we all tried to break through to make something here, we could. But something doesn't want us to."

I felt it right then, that nameless fear. It must have faded while we worked to recover Steiner. Maybe at the moment we broke through the resistance. But it was back now. Felt localized, too: not far offshore. We all turned and looked out to sea. The white swells seemed ominous now, not merely strange or even ridiculous as they had before.

10

“**Y**OU KNOW WHAT?” said Mina. “I was going to say we can figure all this stuff out another day. Time to go back inland, rest up, have a dinner that can't be beat, right? But this thing is pissing me off.”

“Yeah,” said Quaid, “this is no coincidence. This is deliberate. Wonder if it realizes how blatant it's being. I'm angry too.”

“It's trying to get us to back off,” said Nora. “And I don't much like it either. Stupid thing won't even talk to us.”

“Okay,” said Rhys, “but what do we do about it?”

“How about the same thing as with Steiner,” said the Professor. “Work as a group. Try to find it out there, see if we can pull it up to the surface.”

“Then what?”

“Then we proceed appropriately,” said the Professor.

Rhys laughed. “Yeah, right. 'So that's your plan?' But okay. I'm happy with it. Anyone have any objections?”

Everyone was looking at me.

“No,” I said, “I want to find out what's going on here. And it seems to me, if there's something out there, we'd better find out what it is.”

“Good. Michèle? You did a good job with Steiner. Want to try again?”

"D'accord. This time, maybe we should all be looking out there, instead of in a circle, so we can see what happens if it works. Okay?"

We stood there at the milk-line, arrayed in a loose arc focused on the place we felt the fear coming from. I figured it was around 200 meters out there, just around the point the swell gave way to low heavy waves of milk that diminished to ripples as they lapped at the black sand beach.

"All right," said Michèle, "it's out there. Hiding under the milk. But it's afraid to let us see it. Maybe that's the fear we feel? But it's got no business fucking with us, either, if it won't show itself. So we're just going to make it come up. That's all, okay."

She raised her voice.

"Listen to me," she called out. "You there, out there in the sea. We're too strong for you, aren't we? And now … you're coming up!"

And the fear grew. Before this, when we realized that it was something fake, something imposed from the outside, it was easy to ignore. But now it was gaining strength. The fact that I knew it was external didn't matter anymore. There was something there, something horrible, something I didn't even want to think about. If I'd been alone, I wouldn't have persisted. But everyone else was there, and whatever they were feeling, they were still there, still trying, so I had to try too.

It was a terrible struggle to keep my focus, to keep looking out there at the placid white sea. I was thinking about something rising up from the depths, something emerging from those rolling milk swells, and I could tell the rest of us were concentrating on the place, doing the same thing. It was resisting, I felt its rage, and the fear flared up in a spike of emotion so intense I almost broke and ran. It was worse than any nightmare. But Rhys was there, standing firm, and Mina, her nails flashing blue, was holding her ground. Even Steiner was facing it down, Steiner who had no idea what was what yet, Steiner, who'd lived a life beset by phobias, by anxiety attacks. Steiner whose body had been horribly consumed at the bridge, and he was standing fast. The Professor raised her hand to her eyes for a moment, lowered her hand, clenched her fist, screamed something, but it wasn't fear, it was anger. Quaid and Nora clung together, arms around each other's waist and shoulders, not budging. And there was Michèle, at the center of our group. I could tell she'd been affected, could see a tremor run right through her body, saw her stagger, saw her sudden gasp for air. I had to stay there for her, if for no one else. When I realized that, my own fear didn't matter. It didn't go away; it just wasn't important anymore. I took a step forward, put my arm around her, propped her up for a moment, and I could feel her gather her strength as she stood up straight again.

Michèle held out her hand as if to grab something, fingers clutching, clenched her fist, jerked her arm sharply upward.

"Come on," she said, "come on you salaud!"

And it came. I heard a soundless cry, not sure how, but something was down there, something angry, and I knew it was afraid, too. The swell broke up into a turbulent maelstrom of milk a good one hundred meters in diameter, and I could sense something emerging from the depths, something very big. After a few seconds, the chaotic splashing and bubbling cauldron of milk resolved itself into a whirlpool, like a huge drain-plug had been pulled somewhere deep down below. Something was coming, for sure ... more than one thing, I could see now, five, six, no seven vast forms circling as they emerged from the sea of milk. There was a last awful wave of fear, and the terrible feeling tore apart like gossamer, vanished into mere wisps of frayed memory like a nightmare after waking.

For a moment I couldn't grasp what I was seeing. Seven huge, elongated bodies, like snakes or tentacles with bulges at the tips were rising out of the milk, arcing high into the air. At first, I couldn't tell what they were at all, but then as they shed cascades of milk, I could see they really were snakes, cobras, their hooded heads the bulges I'd seen before. Huge cobras, their bodies curving absurdly high above the waves.

"Sacre merde," said Michèle, whispering. In the tumult of the cascading waves, I only heard her because I was standing right there beside her.

All seven heads opened their mouths and spoke at once, their voices hissing and shrieking in a terrible, harsh chorus.

"Mortals! How dare you try to bind Ananta Sesha!"

There was an awkward silence, the violence of the maelstrom dying away now into placidity as the snake heads ceased to move about in the swell.

"Ananta?" The Professor stood there looking up at the nearest head, still quite a distance away. Her voice was calm, but it carried well.

"Hm," she said. "Sounds vaguely familiar, but I can't place it. Sorry."

"Ignorant fool! I am the endless, the infinite! I am the remnant, the sole survivor of the age of ages."

The seven heads approached us. They didn't move through the milk, but instead their snake bodies arced further up from where they emerged from the swell and shot towards us, extending improbably as they curved through the air. They paused perhaps ten meters from our group and twenty five or so above our heads, their hugely elongated bodies like suspension bridges of iridescent scales. The cobra hoods, heads, and the dorsal surfaces of their bodies were a purple so dark it was almost black, but their bellies were a nacreous white with faint rainbow traceries shimmering moistly on each enormous scale like the swirls in soap bubbles.

"Wow," said Mina, "you're really something. But it doesn't feel like it's time for the end, yet. Maybe a mid-boss?"

The head closest to her pulled back, and I was afraid it was going to strike. Mina's nails glowed bright blue, and she dropped into a defensive martial-arts stance, the bird fluttering off her shoulder and rising into the air like a hawk, though I doubted the creature would even notice his attack. But before anything else could happen Rhys spoke up, and the rearing head paused to look at him.

"Hold on," he said, "we don't want to fight you. We just want some idea what's going on here."

"I am not here for your edification, mortals," said the chorus.

"Well then," said Rhys equably, "what are you here for?"

"I guard Vaikuntha between creations. Trimurti has withdrawn from the world. There is no need for the Preserver to reign here in the hiatus between cycles, and so I am free."

"Come on," said Rhys, "we don't know these words you're using. Vaikuntha? Tri-what-y?"

"It is not required of me that I repair your ignorance," it said primly.

"Okay, fine," said Rhys, "but why have you been lurking around here? You were watching us last night, weren't you? And why get in our way now? We've got nothing to do with you."

"Vile mortals," it hissed, "you defile the sacred land with your mere presence. Disgusting feculent creatures."

Rhys laughed; it wasn't bravado, it was humor.

"Seriously?" he asked. "You think we're disgusting? You, a pack of giant venomous snakes?"

A head approached him, stood poised over Rhys's head.

"Enough!" it shrieked. "How dare you even address me? You should be quaking in fear, writhing on the ground like worms before me. I should wipe you from the holy face of Svetadvipa here and now."

"Writhing on the ground?" asked Rhys, "You mean, like a snake, right? But come on now, you can't expect us to be all that scared. Not when you're so frightened of us."

It screamed again, all seven heads at once, a horrible discordant sound.

"I am the ultimate steed! I am the guardian of the ages! I am Ananta the infinite, Sesha the sole remnant of destruction! I will not be spoken to as if I was nothing but — merely —"

It choked off its speech, apparently so enraged it was unable to continue.

"Calm down," said Rhys, "we don't know much about what you're talking about. If you'd just explain —"

"Enough!"

The head closest to Rhys reared back to strike, and Mina leaped in front of him, her arms held up, hands angled slightly inward. Her nails flashed and ten blades of brilliant blue light came forth, three meters long, crossing above her head to form a large X pattern. Ananta's head struck downwards like a hammer blow, but despite its awesome size and speed, when it hit Mina's defense it crashed to a stop, the light flaring blazingly bright for a moment, and a loud piercing chord sounding, like ten giant tuning forks all struck at once.

The flash was enough to blind me for a second and, when I blinked away the purple spot in my vision, I saw that Mina had scored the serpent head with her nails, giving the head the appearance of having been roasted on a grill. The head pulled back, ten new scars gouged into its face. One of the eyes ruptured, and a stream of smoke rose from the burned-out socket.

Mina staggered then, and fell to her knees, her brilliant nails extinguished. I think she would have fallen all the way to the sand, but Rhys was there to hold her up. The bird flew down toward her, and alighted on her shoulder. I think it was saying something to her, but I couldn't hear the words.

"Aaaaaaa!" The six undamaged heads screamed again, the damaged seventh curving back towards the milk. I supposed it would soothe the pain of a burn pretty well at that.

"You *monsters*! I'll destroy you all! The poison of Kshirasagara will consume you!"

The pearly white necks of the remaining six heads were stained with blue, the tinge rising out of the sea towards the heads. For a moment I wondered if it was something Mina had done, but it wasn't the piercing azure brilliance of her nails but a sort of murky cyanotic hue, like an infection working its way along those improbably long necks.

All six heads reared back. Their hoods distended, the dark purple scales turning that same murky blue, and a sort of miasma of roiling vapor formed around their mouths and nostrils. None of us had any way to respond to this; we couldn't even reach them, poised as they were high above us. It looked like Mina had used up whatever reserves she had in defending Rhys from that first strike.

And then the bird fluttered into the air once more, beating his wings strongly and spiraling upward. I was surprised to see the six heads retreating somewhat as if they were afraid of him, though any one of them could have swallowed the bird and a dozen more like him in a single gulp.

Rhys bent his head down to hear something Mina was saying, and then he turned to look at the rest of us.

"She says to support the bird!" he called out.

Steiner hadn't said anything this whole time, had been goggling at the giant cobra-thing since it appeared. But now he shook his head.

"What does that mean?"

"Come on, doofus," said Nora, "you must know by now. It's what we did to fetch you just now."

"Yeah," said Quaid, "try to connect with him. Give him your strength, if you can. The thing is afraid of him."

"Oh," said Steiner, "I see. I do see."

The Professor advanced now, helping Mina to her feet; I could see she was still a little shaky, but she looked to be unharmed, anyway. Rhys took a step back, next to Steiner, and Quaid and Nora stood together as before, not huddled, but with arms outstretched, reaching up to the bird. Michèle put her arm around my waist; no, she was squeezing my bottom, and for a half a second, right there in the middle of the crisis, I wanted more than anything else just to kiss her again.

She laughed then, and called out, "All right, let's do it!"

Okay, fine, I thought, and looked up at the bird, but I felt no connection at all, none of the easy linkage we'd been able to achieve just a few minutes before to rescue Steiner. Maybe it was too far away. The bird was up at the level of the serpents' heads and flying higher, still spiraling upwards. The cobras were now entirely colored that ugly murky blue, and their heads were bloated up too, distended with whatever stuff it was that had climbed up their necks from the ocean of milk.

Ananta's six-fold voice was garbled now, and the bubbling, gurgling sound could have arisen from a chorus of the drowned.

"Surrender," it said, "or be destroyed."

And the miasma began pouring forth from its gaping mouths, swirling together to form a large bluish cloud up there, a cloud that completely surrounded the bird and began to drop grotesque bulging streamers towards us on the ground.

Well, hell, I thought, he could have asked us to surrender to begin with.

It was a thin piercing sound, and really I shouldn't have been able to hear it at all from a hundred meters up in the air, but somehow it reached us down on the ground. The bird was laughing. I knew he was just a dull black myna, but up there I saw a flash of gold.

And there it was, the connection I was looking for. I still had no idea what it was I was doing, but I had something to offer, anyway. I poured it into that little golden speck up there, and I could feel my friends doing the same.

"Surrender," said the bird, a hundred meters above my head, "Surrender to a rotten little snake like you?"

I could hear a trace of Mina's strength in the bird's voice.

"I am Ananta, the infinite ... Sesha, the final remnant ... In this place I am all-powerful! I must be! I — I am —"

"You're a snake, a worm. You're less than nothing. I once wore you on my smallest toenail, but it seems you've forgotten your lesson. You'd better back off, or I'll twist you into something even worse this time. An earring maybe? But I haven't got an ear in this form. Perhaps one of my friends can wear you."

Nora's sharpness; Quaid's solidity: both were present a hundred meters overhead.

"What? What? The poison of Halahala will burn you! It must! It must!"

The bird laughed again. It was an incredibly loud sound, considering the tiny little throat it was coming from. But then again, maybe he wasn't so little at that. Within that swirling blue cloud I could still see the flash of gold, but it seemed much larger now. A lot bigger than a little black mynah bird.

"You fool," said the bird, and its voice was as piercing as an eagle's cry, "I cannot be burned. Agni's fire lives in my breast."

"Oh yeah," muttered Steiner, far below, "fire. I understand now." And I could sense him committing himself to the conflict, sending his own fire up high to join with that of the bird's; a moment later I felt Rhys's presence as well, supporting Steiner's effort.

"What? What? Who are you?"

"There are five kinds of fire," said the bird's voice, speaking conversationally now, "if you didn't know. Perhaps I should show you one of them. Jnana-agni is the fire of knowledge."

"Indeed," said the Professor. "I believe I remember some of this now from an undergraduate class on comparative mythology. Very apt, I must say." I could feel the connection between her and the bird now, too, with a renewed stream of energy from Mina.

There was a brilliant flash from above. The poison cloud writhed. Violent turbulence was tearing it apart. All at once it dissipated entirely, coming apart in a roil of a million little burning vortices, and revealed there was an enormous bird big enough to hold elephants in its talons. The bird's feathers were many colors but with gold predominating. It had a long curling tail like a bird of paradise, vast metallic wings, and a fiery crest.

"Nooooo ..." The six serpent heads screamed, but this time it was a scream of fear and horror, not rage.

"I am Garuda," said the enormous bird, "and all serpents are my rightful prey. I am sworn to the destruction of the naga race. And you, my little cobra's nest, you *are* a naga, are you not?"

"Garuda!" The six-fold scream was panicked.

"Now," said the mighty voice of the bird, and

"Now," I said, and

"Now!" said Michèle.

Whatever it was we had, we gave it all to the bird, and there was a bright light in the sky, a flash of fire and something more than fire. It was blinding, and accompanied by a deafening thunderous blast, a rolling crashing sound that went on and on, loud almost past the point of endurance.

Eventually it came to an end. There was no sign of Ananta anywhere, though the sea of milk was still turbulent and chaotic. In the sky high above us the Garuda bird hovered, but his fiery aura had faded and his feathers were dull. His body was shrunken too, hardly bigger than an elephant now.

Down below, we weren't in much better shape. None of us had actually fallen, but it was a near-run thing. Mina was supporting the Professor, and Steiner had one of Rhys's arms slung across his shoulders. Quaid and Nora were leaning on one another, and I became aware that I was draped over Michèle's back. weighing her down. I managed to lurch back onto my feet, and she gave a whuff of relief.

"Man, you're heavy," she said.

I was going to say something, but there was a cry from overhead, thin, desolate and piercing. We all looked up.

"Jesus," said Steiner, "he's coming down. Look out!"

We scrambled and stumbled away from the point of impact. The bird fell straight down, not even making an attempt to stay aloft, and he hit the milk-wet sand with a terrible crunching sound. The great bird's torso collapsed, deformed out of shape from the impact, and one of its wings was broken and twisted back on itself. The bird's enormous head was flat on the ground, and he showed no signs of life at all.

"Oh hell," said Mina, and she ran over to the bird, and tried to embrace it, but its neck was too big around. "Thank you," she said, and buried her face against the feathers at the base of the bird's head. "Thank you," she whispered again.

And then as the rest of us stood there dumbly the enormous body shuddered and began to fade away, dissolving like a wisp of steam, and in its place a nude human form, prone on the ground, Mina almost fell on top of him, but she managed to stumble back just in time. It was a slender young man with black hair and light brown skin. His body didn't appear to be damaged, but there was something strange about it.

Mina knelt beside him, looked at his face, and gasped.

"Sandeep? My god, is that you?"

He turned his head, opened his eyes.

"Oh, hey Mina," he whispered, "I'm so glad you're okay."

"Sandeep! You were the bird all this time? Are you all right?"

"Sorry," he said softly, "not so much. Went a little too far, I think, with that Garuda thing. I was pretty cool, though, wasn't I?"

"Shit! Hold on! We'll try to heal you!" She turned her head, "Come on, let's do it! Imagine him being okay."

Michèle squeezed my hand, and I knew she was going to help. I closed my eyes, tried to connect with the form on the sand, tried to visualize him stronger, healthier, tried to give him whatever I'd been giving the bird before. But it was no good. It was like he wasn't there at all, or worse than that, it was like there was a hole there instead of a person, and I was just pouring whatever I had into an abyss.

I opened my eyes, saw that his body had become transparent, ghostly. He was losing his form.

"Sandeep!" Mina tried to embrace him, but her hand moved through his body like it wasn't there.

"It's okay," he whispered, and the words were so faint I could barely make them out. Maybe they weren't sounds at all. "I was happy to be of service."

"Come on," said Mina, crying now, "don't go! I let you go once; it was my fault! I'm so sorry, Sandeep!"

"Not your fault ... But it really is okay. Maybe ... in the next world, we'll meet ag —" He faded away completely in mid-sentence. There was no trace of him left at all. It was as if he'd never existed, not even a depression left in the sand where he'd lain.

"Shit! Oh shit, Sandeep! God damn it!"

Mina sat down heavily on the sand, and put her face in her hands. The Professor knelt by her side and held her tight. For the last couple of days she'd looked like a fresh-faced teenaged girl, younger if anything than Mina, but just then Mina seemed like a child in her arms.

The Professor glanced our way and nodded her head, and the rest of us retreated a short distance down the strand to allow Mina some time to recover.

"Umm, so who is Sandeep?" asked Steiner. I could tell the others wanted to know as well.

I told them what little I knew. That he'd been Mina's coworker at the McDonalds, that she'd meant to have him accompany her to Caernarfon on the last day of the old world. But not realizing what was happening to the people of the city she'd gone home to change, and, when she returned, he was gone, vanished like everyone else in the world. Everyone but us eight survivors.

"I never actually got to see him before today," I said, "but Mina was pretty broken up over it. She thought if only she'd stayed with him that last day he wouldn't have ... gotten lost."

"Oh man," said Steiner. "That really sucks, Do you think we can get him back somehow? Like you got me back?"

"We can try," I said, but I heard the uncertainty in my voice as I spoke the words.

"You don't think we can, do you?" asked Nora, and Quaid shook his head. "I don't have a good feeling about this," he said.

"It was like he wasn't even there when we tried to help him at the end," said Michèle. "But maybe he's back in the field of stars?"

Rhys said, "We'll try for sure. But I hate to say it, I don't feel confident about it either."

"And just to beat that stupid snake, too," said Michèle, shaking her head. "So very sad."

"He did say it was okay, though. That's something."

Mina's voice. We looked up to see that she and the Professor had returned. She looked better now, but there was something in the way she held herself now. She was angry, holding it in, and I wouldn't have wanted to be the one to stand in her way just then.

"I'm so sorry about Sandeep," said Michèle. "He was a hero, though, wasn't he? He saved us from that thing."

"Yeah," said Mina, "I'm pretty sure that haha poison stuff or whatever was going to be bad news. But he blew it all away, and those damn snakes, too."

"Apart from everything else, I bet he could have explained all this Hindu mythology to us," said the Professor. "I do remember a couple of things from that old course, though."

"Yeah?" Steiner scratched himself. "Might as well tell us now."

"It's not much," said the Professor. "But the cobras, the naga, I suppose it was, mentioned the Kali Yuga, and that made me remember. The Hindus have the concept of a cosmic cycle of four yugas, ages of the world. I forget what the others are called, but it starts with a sort of golden age where everyone is close to the godhead, and it deteriorates from there by stages over a few billion years. Finally, the Kali Yuga is an age of decadence and destruction, where people abandon all virtue and society falls apart. At the end of the yuga the world is destroyed, and then the cycle starts again with a new world in another golden age. We were supposed to be living in the Kali Yuga."

"Okay," said Rhys, "that sounds like us. Decadent society, things falling apart. Our world came apart at the seams, pretty much."

"Maybe," said the Professor, "but I'm not sure I agree. Certainly our old world had problems, and we had problems too — the eight of us, I mean. But we were getting along, weren't we? Maybe things were getting worse, climate change and billionaires and all that, but maybe they were getting better in some ways, too. It's hard to say. If the world ended because some god somewhere decided it was time, it wasn't fair at all."

"Does that make a difference," I asked, "if it's fair or not?"

"Not if it was some natural process that ended our world," said the Professor. "But if someone is responsible for all this — and from the way this place works, it looks more and more like someone is — then they're going to have to answer for it. That's the way I feel about it, anyway."

"Oh," I said, "I see what you mean. Half of what's happened to us since the beginning seems almost like it's part of a plan. But the other half, well —"

"It's fucked up," said Mina. "This whole thing is messed up. All those people just blown away like that. All that everyone was ever working for, all that everyone ever did, dead or alive, it's all gone. All that's left is whatever we remember, and that's like almost none of it. Billions of people we don't know. All those books and movies and things that people made. All gone. Even if all those people are in limbo or whatever, now, it's still a bad job, and it's someone's goddamn fault."

We were all silent for a minute thinking it over. At last Rhys spoke up.

"About that cobra thing. The naga, I mean, Ananta. He's the only, um, representative of whoever set this place up that we've found. From what he said he seemed like a sort of caretaker. He at least sounded like he knew what was going on. Do you think Garuda-Sandeep actually blew him away completely, or is he still out there someplace?"

"Huh," said Mina. "We can find out, can't we? We can reach through the ocean of milk. We did it already to get Steiner back, and we got past Ananta's resistance that time too. I bet we can just ... summon him if we want to. If he's still alive."

"Right," said Rhys. "And we need to try to find Sandeep too. He could be out there someplace."

"Yeah," said Mina. "I don't think so. I think he's gone somewhere further than that. But it would be stupid not to try. I guess, the naga first? To get him out of the way, right?"

Nora and Quaid spoke up together. They were looking out to sea. "Uh guys, I think we might not have to summon him."

We all turned. There was an unnatural swell moving in the milk sea, a soliton wave coming our way.

"All right," said Mina. "This time I'm ready for it. I've thought of some more stuff to do. Last time I didn't have a chance to come up with anything."

The moving wave erupted in milky froth as Ananta's head emerged from the sea. It was the one head that Mina had scored with her nails on its first strike, the one that had recoiled back into the sea before the confrontation with Garuda-Sandeep. One of his eyes was just a blank crater now, and his coloration was back to normal except for the red gouges Mina had burned into his face.

"No," he said, "please don't. I come at your summons. I submit to your power." He made a pathetic noise, halfway between a sigh and a sob. "I am defeated."

BOOK THREE

PICKING UP THE PIECES

11

SO THERE WE WERE, the eight of us, the sole survivors of planet Earth and maybe of all of creation. Sitting there on the shore of the ocean of milk with the one surviving head of Ananta Sesha, supreme ruler of all the nagas. We'd tried to locate Sandeep for an hour or so, the same way we used the power to find and restore Steiner, but with no success. Either he hadn't returned to the sea of souls or else our power was insufficient to locate him. So we turned our attention back to the naga.

"Who commands you?" asked the Professor. "You claim to be a servant."

"I obey the Preserver," he said thickly, hissing a little on the sibilants.

The creature looked to be in considerable pain, blood trickling from ten deep gouges in his huge serpentine head under a purple cobra's cowl, one eye ruptured and leaking ichor.

"You mean Vishnu?" asked the Professor. "Or Krishna?" She was obviously recalling more from her long-lost undergrad class in comparative theology. I'd heard of Krishna, as in the Hare Krishnas, but didn't know much about him.

"The Preserver," he repeated, "whose name I am unworthy to speak."

"Depending on the sect," the Professor said to us, "Vishnu is either one of the top Hindu deities, or else he's the supreme, the transcendent Godhead itself. Krishna is an avatar of Vishnu; but some sects address their devotion to Krishna as the primary personage of the deity."

She was sitting next to Mina on the fine black sand of the beach, just by the milk-line.

"Whatever," said Mina, a little roughly, but she smiled at the Professor when she did.

"You're going to tell us everything you know," Mina said to the naga. "And I don't have to tell you 'or else', do I?"

Ananta flinched, though even with a single head remaining out of the seven he'd started with he was at least a dozen times her size, and probably more than that as his body and head were arching up out of the ocean of milk; no telling how much length he had down beneath the heaving white swell. Mina had hurt him badly enough for that to be a reasonable response on his part, but I think he'd gotten the idea that Sandeep-Garuda was her particular friend, and he was obviously afraid she would lose her temper with him. I wouldn't have blamed her if she *had* killed him, but I thought she was playing the bad-cop role here, and it made me smile a little to hear the hard bluster in her voice.

"I ... wish to live," said Ananta. "Before today I did not realize there was an alternative."

"Evidently you were mistaken in your assumptions," said the Professor. "You say you're the caretaker who survives between one age of the world and the next. Tell us of the end of the last world, and the beginning of the next one."

"As you wish," said the huge creature. "May I assume a form suitable for conversation?"

"Very well."

The vast scarred head withdrew into the sea of milk. I wondered for a minute if he would be coming back at all, but then I saw a form emerge from the ripples of milk lapping at the black sand beach. The milk streamed away from his body as he arose, revealing a slender young man with dark purple skin the same shade as Ananta's cobra hood, striated with faint scaly patterns in cobalt blue. The man was hairless, and one of his eyes was nothing more than a ruined and empty socket. He had a shimmering sphere like a pearl set in his forehead. Like a pearl, but if nacre was metallic gold, not white. Faint rainbow shimmers played on the surface of the thing.

He sat down cross-legged before us, graceful as a snake.

"Shall I answer your question?" he asked.

"Proceed," said the Professor.

"I do not know what transpired at the end of the last age," said Ananta. "My only concern is for Vaikuntha, and for my master's commands. But I presume your world fell into decadence and decay, the gods withdrew their gaze, and at the last the Destroyer annihilated the wreckage."

"What of the myriad stars we saw in the whiteness beyond the ocean of milk?"

"Souls awaiting purification," said Ananta. "They will be reborn in the next world."

"This is not the next world?"

"I told you before," he said, "this is Vaikuntha. This is the Preserver's seat during the ages of his reign. It is immutable and eternal, and it lies far beyond the walls of your world."

"But the Preserver is not present?" I wasn't sure what the Professor was getting at, but it was interesting to listen to her line of questioning.

Ananta shifted a little. He looked uncomfortable.

"Not in person," he said "The Preserver has withdrawn until the next age begins. I, his humble servant, the remnant, the endless one, am all that remains."

"So who shall create the next world?"

"The Preserver will nominate a new Creator. The appearance of the Creator will mark the first moment of the new age."

"The Creator is inferior to the Preserver?"

"Of course. The Creator's deeds are ephemeral, as are those of the Destroyer. The Preserver is responsible not only for the world over time, but for the eternal recurrence of worlds within worlds and ages after ages."

"And what of us?"

"Pardon me?"

The Professor smiled. "According to your view of the world we should not be here, should we? Mere mortals in your Vaikuntha. And having somehow made our way here, we should not have had the power to disturb you, much less to defeat you in a confrontation."

"I —" Ananta was speechless for a time. At last, he said, "I was defeated by the Garuda bird, my ancient enemy, the Preserver's steed. I did not know he was still in existence. That dreadful creature is my cousin, and was always my superior in strength."

"No," said Mina sharply. "That was Sandeep. My friend. From our world. I called him to this place, not even knowing what I was doing. He was a soul awaiting rebirth. He recognized you as a naga and took on Garuda's form to cow you. It was my own power that burned your face, and it was all our power together with Sandeep's sacrifice that defeated you."

"Then — then you must be asuras, demons, escaped from some prison beyond the stars, monsters come to wreck the Preserver's throne from sheer spite."

"No," said Mina. "You see us before you. We are human beings. Nothing more."

"This cannot be. Somehow I have failed in my duties. This must be some kind of punishment. Mortals could never do such a thing. Perhaps one of you is a god in hiding."

"What's that in your head?" asked Michèle.

Ananta looked up, surprised. Michèle hadn't said much lately, and her question knocked him out of his little rant. He put his fingers to his forehead, tapped the golden stone.

"This? This is my nagamani. It shows my spiritual development."

"It's special? Something a mortal couldn't have, I suppose?"

"Certainly not!"

Michèle stuck her hand into a hillock of the fine black sand on which she was sitting, frowned for a moment.

"Like this then?" She withdrew her hand, producing an identical golden sphere. She tossed it to Ananta, and the naga was so shocked he dropped it and had to scrabble for the stone in his lap for a moment to retrieve it. He held it up and goggled at it for a moment.

"Impossible! Do you mean to mock me?"

"Well, yes," said Michèle, "but the point is this isn't exactly a normal mortal thing to be able to do, is it?"

Actually, I was a little surprised she'd been able to do it, considering the resistance we'd felt to using the creative power here before. Perhaps that had something to do with Ananta's opposing presence. But for whatever reason, I could feel it too, the potential of the creative power. It was almost like an itch that wanted to be scratched.

"No," said Ananta after a pause. "But what does this mean? The power of the gods devolved to mortals … I don't understand."

Rhys laughed. "Damn. If you don't understand, we sure as hell don't either."

Steiner got up and walked over to Ananta, looked down at him.

"Five minutes ago, you were cursing us," he said, "threatening us with destruction, even. You laughed at our ignorance. Despised us for it. Our friend got himself killed, or maybe something even worse than dying happened to him, because of you. And you have the gall to sit there and tell us you don't know what's going on?"

The naga looked down at the stone he held in his hands but said nothing. Steiner made a scornful noise, then he turned on his heel and went back to sit down next to Rhys.

"You know," said Nora, "I'm beginning to wonder about our friend here." Quaid completed their thought. "He may be similar in a way to Sandeep."

Mina looked at them. "How do you mean?"

Nora said, "For most of his time here as a bird, I'm pretty sure Sandeep didn't know who he really was. I think he might only have remembered everything at the very end."

Quaid nodded. "We're thinking that Ananta may have been deceived about who he is, too, though the reasons for his belief may be different."

The naga drew his knees up to his chest and put his arms around them. He was clearly listening, but chose not to respond.

The Professor said, "I had the same notion." She walked over to Ananta, sat down immediately in front of him. The naga looked over his knees at her, an unreadable expression on his face.

"Listen," she said, "before meeting us, who was the last person you talked to, god or mortal?"

"I ... I have been alone for a long time," he said.

"For us it's only been a day since the end of the world. But perhaps that doesn't mean very much. Can you remember anything at all from before we came here?"

"Yes," he said, "of course. The Preserver and his consort. I attended them every day for an age of ages. The two of them slept in my embrace. I served as his bed, his crown, and as his throne. And in the old days there were the other gods, the asuras, my brothers and sisters among the nagas ..."

"Are you sure of those memories?" asked the Professor. "I mean, do they seem quite real to you compared to events of the last day or so?"

"I — What do you mean by these foolish questions?"

"You don't seem to be unintelligent," said the Professor. "What do you think I mean?"

The naga didn't speak for a time. At last, he said, "I will not utter words of blasphemy."

"Very well," said the Professor. "I will. I accept the existence of this world. Of the ocean of milk. Of the sea of stars beyond it. I will even accept that those stars may be preserved human minds, souls if you prefer the word. But based on your performance, on what I've seen and heard so far in this place, I reject the notion that you are actually the naga Ananta Sesha."

Ananta shuddered. "Truly you are a demon. You torture me with your words. Perhaps I should have accepted death at your hands, with rebirth to come in a lower form."

"I am not trying to be perverse or malicious," she said. "I am seeking the truth. Tell me, Ananta, how is it we should be here? How could mere mortals have escaped the ending of the Kali Yuga in their proper bodies? How could mere mortals have overcome one such as you who claims to be one step below the ultimate godhead? Even if we were demons trying to deceive you, surely our force should not be so great as to overcome you in Vaikuntha itself?"

"I do not know," he said miserably, and he turned on his bottom to face away from her. "Torment me no more."

"I will tell you what I think you are," said the Professor. "Consider my words. If you are sure of yourself, then nothing I can say will change your mind. But if you are not sure, then it would be foolish to reject this idea out of hand."

She paused, but he didn't reply. The rest of us were all rapt, though; I wasn't quite sure what she was getting at, though Nora and Quaid must have had the same idea. But I felt like she was talking to me as well as to Ananta, though unlike him I was eager to hear her thoughts. Well; perhaps Ananta wanted to hear them too, because though he remained seated with his back to her and the rest of us he made no further objection.

"What I think is this," said the Professor. "There is indeed someone or something who is orchestrating our presence here. You can call him or her the Preserver if you like, but honestly I would be shocked if it was truly the god Vishnu. Vishnu represents a transcendent power, and the person I'm talking about is much more limited. I'm going to call this person the wizard, because like Oz he's hiding from us. The wizard may be powerful but he's not omniscient because I think he's put you here as an experiment, to see what we'd do with you, or what you'd do to us. I'm guessing you're another human soul plucked from the sea of stars just like we did with Sandeep and Steiner too. I'm sorry, but I think you were given false memories and powers appropriate to the mythological figure of Ananta. The snake form and this human one. The poison or whatever it was you tried to use against us. Perhaps that fear we felt before, that might have been you observing us from afar."

"It can't be," said Ananta. "Yours are a demon's words."

"Perhaps," said the Professor. "But you've heard me out. I have no more torture for you, if that's what it was."

Throughout all this I'd been wondering if the Professor's explanation for Ananta's existence might be true of me as well. If I had false memories for most of my life, that would explain my feeling that I'd only really been alive for the last year or so. But then, the question was why that had been done to me, and maybe to me alone of everyone alive before the end of the old world. I was sure there were no answers to that question, none I could work out here and now anyway.

Ananta said nothing in response, just looked into the golden stone Michèle had duplicated, as if there was an answer of his own he could find there.

"Okay," said Rhys after a pause, "but what do we do now? I mean, with him, and in general, too."

No one had anything to say at first, but after a minute Michèle said, hesitantly, "Mina? What do you think? He — your friend died because of him."

"Fuck," said Mina, "I don't know. I guess he's just a dupe. I wouldn't have minded if we'd killed him at the time, but now, well, I'd feel bad about it if we didn't let him go."

The Professor got up and walked over to Mina, sat down and took her hand. "I'm happy you feel that way," she said. "I don't want to contaminate our lives here."

Rhys asked, "What do you mean?"

"I can't really explain it," she said, "but I want to feel like I'm doing the right thing." She nodded to us. "I'm sixty-three years old, if that means anything here. I've done a lot of things I regretted, things I shouldn't have done. I've told lies, hurt people, and lied to and hurt myself probably even more. I don't want to do anything like that anymore."

"Oh," said Steiner, "I get it. It's like we're starting with a clean slate here, isn't it? I've been feeling kind of bad because this guy Sandeep I never got to meet was killed in a fight that had to do with saving me. I think I wanted to punish Ananta so I'd feel better about it. But now the idea makes me feel sick. What about the rest of you?"

"We agree too," said Nora and Quaid, speaking in chorus. "We talked it over last night," said Nora, and Quaid said, "We decided we'd spent our lives before pretty much just fucking up, so why not try something different this time around."

"Right," said Mina. "No one else wants to punish him, I guess?"

I shook my head. She walked over to Ananta.

"Okay," she said to him, "whatever it is you were doing before you started messing with us, you can go back to it if you like. Just don't get in our way, all right?"

He didn't answer, didn't move either.

"Well?" She stood over him. I don't think I've ever seen anyone look as abject, as pathetic as Ananta did then.

"I ... I don't want to be alone anymore," he said.

"What?"

"I don't know what is real," he said. "I don't — I was wrong. I'm sorry. About everything. Please don't make me go away!"

"Oh, for pity's sake." Mina's voice started out scornful, but it softened along the way. She looked at us. Nora and Quaid smiled at her and nodded. Rhys sighed and shook his head, but there was something histrionic about the way he did it, and we could tell he wasn't really objecting. Steiner chuckled and gave Rhys a mock punch to the arm. Michèle looked at me, and I could see a little quirk in her mouth. And the Professor moved over to Mina's side, put her arm around her waist, and leaned her head against her shoulder.

"Fine," said Mina to Ananta, "fine. I guess you're as lost as we are."

Ananta looked up at the rest of us. He rose and bowed to us, hands together. "Namo vah," he said. "I am yours to command."

Mina reached out to him; the naga flinched but controlled himself. She put her hand over his ruined eye, and a bluish glow played around the back of her palm. When she took her hand away his eye was whole.

"There," she said, "all better."

He goggled at her for a moment, put his hand to his eye. "This is not a demon's power," he said. He paused, and after a moment continued, "I fear I will be useless to you. Your strength and wisdom far exceed my own. And what I thought I knew — perhaps it is all lies."

Mina laughed. "Strength?" she asked. "Whatever strength I have is a gift. And wisdom? Come on, last week I was a clerk in a McDonald's. I didn't know anything. I still don't know anything."

"You're wise enough for me," said Rhys. "But I still don't know what we're going to do next. And I have the feeling we should be doing something. I mean, apart from coupling up and having meals that can't be beat."

"Hey," said Steiner. "Have I been missing out on something?"

"Well yes," said Michèle, "but I think there's likely more to come."

"Kama is essential to purusartha," said Ananta.

"What's that?" asked Michèle.

"Yes," said the Professor. "Please recollect that we don't speak Hindi."

"Pardon me," said Ananta. "I meant to say that the fulfillment of desire in a loved one or in the sensual beauty of the external world is one of the essential pillars of human existence. Or so say the sages."

"Really? What are the other pillars?"

"There are four. Artha is the security of material prosperity. Both artha and kama are subordinate to dharma, righteous behavior according to divine law. But even dharma is no more than a path to moksha, which is liberation from the cosmic cycle of karma."

"Oh," said the Professor. "That's interesting. Do you suggest that the ultimate goal of human existence is freedom from the cycle of the ages?"

"I only repeat what I have heard," said the naga.

"Well anyway, so long as sex and food are okay, I'm happy," said Michèle. "But Rhys, I guess what you meant is: what should we be doing about big things? Like the new world that's supposed to be coming. And like all the people from our old world, if they're out there in the sea of stars."

"Yeah," said Rhys. "Should we just be waiting around for someone else to make this new world for us?"

"Or should we be making it for ourselves?" The Professor completed his thought. She looked at me. "What do you think about all this, Jay? You haven't had much to say recently."

"To be honest, I'm still thinking 'holy shit, giant snakes'," I said. "But yeah, I guess those are the right questions to ask. That's scary, though, trying to take any of that stuff on. Are all those billions of people depending on us? What do you do if you screw up an entire world?"

"Oh shit," said Steiner.

"What?" We all looked at him.

"What you just said. What you do if you screw up the world. Maybe you wrap it up, clean the slate, and let someone else try again with a fresh start the next time around."

I think all of us felt it then, the weight of his words. We just sat there staring at him for a few seconds.

"You think that's what happened," said Quaid, and Nora said, "whoever made our own world decided they screwed it up?"

Steiner nodded. "And maybe they're so sick of it, they've decided it's someone else's turn to screw up now."

"Okay," said Rhys, "I agree with Jay. That's fucking terrifying. I wish I could say it was wrong. Still, though: what next? Any ideas?"

Another brief silence. Then the Professor said, "Well, there's goals and there's next steps. It seems to me that before we can consider doing anything big we have to explore our own capabilities, find out what's possible. First off, we've only been here a day or so, and we still don't know the limits of this power we've been given. Second, we don't even know the extent of this place, Vaikuntha, I mean."

"Yeah," said Mina. "Ananta. Is this pretty much it? A sandy strip surrounding green hills? How big is it? Is there more to it? Does anyone else live here?"

"Vaikuntha is as large as is necessary," said the naga. "During the time of the Preserver's reign, it is a paradise for the gods and for the liberated souls who have attained moksha, and it may be as large as a continent, or even a world in itself. At present, however, it is not so extensive. Perhaps no more than ten or twelve yojana across, all told."

"Yojana?"

"A man may walk three or four yojana in a day, in reasonable comfort."

"Hm. And is there anything else on the island? Apart from what we've already seen?"

Ananta shifted uncomfortably. "Well, of course there is the palace. The Preserver's seat."

"What? A palace? Where is it?"

"At the center," said Ananta. "But it is forbidden to approach it when it is untenanted. Or ... I should say, this is what I once believed.

You people have made me uncertain of things … the last age now seems to me no more than a distant memory of a fading dream."

"Now that's something to do next," said Mina, addressing us all. "Don't you think?"

"Is looking for this palace something we have to do right away?" asked Steiner. "I, uh — I kind of want to try out this kama stuff." He looked up at Rhys, and the bartender blushed but he put his hand on Steiner's shoulder nevertheless.

"Well," said Nora, "one place is as good as another, inland," and Quaid said, "It's not like we've got any luggage to carry."

The Professor nodded. "Yes, we have kama and artha taken care of wherever we go. Is there anything else we should worry about? Ananta?"

The naga frowned. "I don't believe so, not until we actually get to the palace. At that point, the lokapalas might prove … argumentative."

"Lokapalas?"

"The guardians of the four gates," said Ananta. "If you permit it, I will lead us to the west gate. Varuna and I have always been in accord."

"Varuna?"

"Varuna the all-seeing," said Anantha. "Varuna is the lord of the oceans. The stars themselves are his eyes. He has always been a friend to the nagas."

"Hey, wait a minute," said Steiner. "I thought you were supposed to be the only survivor of the last age."

Ananta's face twitched. "I — I can't explain this. I know that I am Sesha, the singular remnant. I know I should be alone, solitary. And yet I also know the palace is guarded by the lokapalas. But even in Vaikuntha, outside of creation, the gods should have retired from their incarnations until the next age. There should be no guardians apart from me."

"Perhaps it's another example of false memory," said the Professor. "It must be troubling, but I suppose we shall find out the truth when we arrive."

12

W E DECIDED TO TAKE A BREAK, partly to bring Steiner up to speed on what we'd done in the last day or so while he was gone, partly to give him a chance to play with the creative power, and partly just to recuperate from the weird events of the night and day so far. It was pleasing to see the joy Steiner took in being able to materialize an ice-cream cone or a butterfly. I realized then I hadn't done much with the power myself. A couple of pizzas, that copy of Proust, maybe some unconscious expression of sexual endurance, and that was it. Surely there was more to it than that? Works of art. Fun and games. Useful stuff, too. I could perhaps have made a drone with a camera to survey the island. Vehicles to ride in. I could have changed my body somehow, or maybe even my mind. I had the sense of unlimited potential, of the power and pleasure that might come with creation, but I decided not to indulge the urge. Something about using it frivolously felt wrong, I guess, though I couldn't say why. And after a few minutes even Steiner had quit messing around with the power. He was sitting and talking quietly with Rhys. Michèle followed my gaze. She smiled and put her hand on mine.

"Okay," I said, "kama may not be the highest priority. But it's nice, though."

So it was afternoon by the time we got ourselves together and set off in a group, following Ananta as he led us on another trek across the fine black sand to the grassy sward that lay inland.

It was a quiet walk. We didn't say much to one another. For my own part I felt like just walking next to Michèle was enough for me to be comfortable, and I let myself relax. It was pleasant not to think about much in particular for a while. Another two hours or so, who knows, and we were back on the lawn, the sullen overcast at the shore replaced by a cheerful yellow sun in a cerulean sky.

"All right," said Rhys, "let's pause a minute. I hate to say we have more to talk over, but let's be sure we know what we're doing, and why. We're going to look for this palace, to see if it's real, and to find out if someone's there. And if it exists, and if they do — what then?"

Nora shrugged, and Quaid said, "Umm, we'll act appropriately to the situation?"

"That's fine for any one of us," said Rhys, "or maybe even any two. But if we're going to actually talk to someone who's, well, who's a god or who is anyway like a god —"

"Yes," said Michèle. "We can't be chatting like this, trying to come up with something. We should know what we want, yes?"

Rhys nodded. "Yeah," he said, "that's what I'm trying to say."

"Okay," I said, "I get it. You've got my vote."

"What?"

"You've got my vote to represent us," I said. "I'd trust any of us with the job, but since you brought it up, why don't you be the one to speak for us?"

Everyone else chimed in with their acclaim. Rhys nodded and said, "Okay, well, thanks then. I guess I'll have to do it. But what do I say?"

"That's the point," said Mina. "That's why we all want you to do it. Apart from just what the fuck, I have no idea what to say to someone like that. Vishnu, the Preserver, some kind of god? The whole idea of talking to him is crazy. But it should be fun."

Steiner laughed. "Exactly. Play it by ear, man, and we'll take what comes."

"Well then," said Rhys, "I'm not sure if we really have to eat any more at all, or even sleep, but I think I feel better when we do. So if you guys don't mind, let's have dinner, and sleep, or —" he blushed, stammered once "— or whatever, and we can head out in the morning."

Dinner was potluck; we each contributed a dish or two. It occurred to me to contribute something I'd eaten as a child and loved, but I couldn't think of anything. And that brought up more questions I'd realized I'd been suppressing. What had happened to my parents? Why hadn't I thought of them even once during the crisis when our world was falling apart? Either I was even more of a useless uncaring jerk than I thought or else, well, maybe they'd never really existed in the first place. Not in my current existence, anyway.

But those depressing thoughts aside, I wound up with a plate of chicken katsu with kare raisu because I'd eaten it at a Japanese fast-food restaurant in my neighborhood and liked it. Other contributions included seaweed salad, shrimp cocktail, consommé célestine, chicken pot pie, chateaubriand, sautéed trout, vegetable bhaji with papadums, potato salad, pistachio ice-cream, cherry pie, a cheese board, and chocolate mousse. I tried to guess who contributed what and wound up only about half right; but yeah, the chateaubriand was the Professor's, and Mina provided the bhaji in Sandeep's honor: it was his favorite snack food. We ate sitting around a nine-sided table with a lazy susan central disk for easier passing. At first, Ananta was hesitant to join us, but when Mina invited him to the table he ate with us, showing a healthy appetite.

That night, however, the naga withdrew from our company at the point we were working out who would sleep with whom. I had been supposing the default couple pairings I'd observed would hold true again when Nora and Quaid approached Michèle and me.

"We'd like to spend some time with you," said Quaid, and Nora said, "we haven't had the chance to talk to Michèle much yet, and there's more we'd like to share with you too, Jay."

Michèle smirked. "Talking and sharing? Is that it?"

"Well, no," said Nora, "sex is part of it too," and Quaid said. "It's an intimate form of sharing."

"In that case," said Michèle, "I am very happy." But she looked at me questioningly. It took only a moment for me to decide. Last week I think I would have been appalled by the suggestion. I would have had thoughts of swingers and wife-swapping and I wouldn't have wanted to sleep with another man in any event. Now though it was just a question of making sure that there was nothing invidious about it, no obligation weighing on Michèle or me. And the idea of sex with Quaid was intriguing, not off-putting.

"I'm game," I said. "I've been curious about you two since that first day you came back to the bar together, but like you said there wasn't a good time to talk. And, well, until recently intimate sharing wasn't really my thing, but I kind of feel like I've got to make up for that now that I have the chance."

13

At first, there wasn't much talking at all, We discovered that four people, all together and at once, was a little awkward just from the physical requirements of sex. Three wasn't bad but it left one person out, so we wound up ringing through all the changes of two couples. I had suspected Nora and Quaid had come up with something like telepathy between them, but I'd never really had the chance to ask what it was. Now I found out.

Quaid and I had just pulled apart from a kiss after lovemaking. I think it was the first time for both of us with another guy, but it was the opposite of awkward. We were sitting next to each other, his arm around my waist, my hand on his thigh. I was going to ask him when the sharing part was going to happen when I realized that I knew where Quaid was coming from, and what his past had been like. I'd always known he had a bad time earlier in life, but I'd never quite dared to ask him, back while our old world was still alive. Now I knew it all.

Quaid had been a pretty regular guy, I thought, lucky in many ways. He'd grown up an only child loved by his parents, and he'd been fortunate enough to avoid most of the abuse and distress that young black men were subject to in our country. He met a lovely young woman named Naomi in college, and they married right after graduation. Even filtered through Quaid's memories, I could feel how happy he'd been. They'd been right together, and they both knew it. The two of them got good jobs, he as a civil engineer and she as a lawyer for a major firm. Over a decade they'd had three children, each in their ways a trial and a burden, but each an endless source of joy as well. Quaid and Naomi had their ups and downs, but their love remained strong and even the bad news that Quaid's father was dying of cancer hadn't been enough to derail his affection and good humor.

But that news was only the first in a parade of horrors. Over the next year it happened like this: Naomi, the most important person in Quaid's life, killed in a car crash by a drunk. His eldest child Hope contracted a rare form of blood cancer and was dead three months later; Quaid was holding her hand as she took her last breath. His second child Orfeo, struck down by a policeman's stray bullet at a playground while he was watching, sitting on a park bench. His mother killed herself a week after his father's death. And then Sasha, his youngest child, died of the flu; one night sniffling with what seemed to be nothing more than a stuffy nose, cold and still the next morning, suffocated by massive pulmonary congestion. Twelve months, and every last person he cared about was gone. Even getting it second hand like that I felt like I'd just been shot in the belly. I couldn't imagine going through it myself. I caught my breath then, realized I was a heartbeat away from crying.

Quaid spoke up. I guess he knew somehow that I'd just internalized all those memories. He moved his hand up to my shoulder, hugged me for a moment, and whispered in my ear.

"It's okay," he said, "it was bad, then. But I'm through it now, mostly. Thanks to Nora. Sorry to do that to you all at once."

"How did you manage?" I asked, turning to face him.

"Of course I considered suicide," he said. "I was a zombie, pretty much, for a few years. Quit my job, just lived off Naomi's benefits, didn't take care of myself at all. But whenever I thought about killing myself, I got angry. It was like the world wanted me to do it, the same stupid evil world that had killed them. It was like an easy way out. 'Screw that,' I thought. I didn't want anything in particular, didn't want to make a new life for myself, didn't have any real goals. But I did think, just to honor all those lost memories, I should at least live on until the world was done with me. So I got a new job, living life just like a machine, and one day I happened to come into Caernarfon on the way home from work. 'Nice place," I thought. Relaxing. The rest you know."

"Not everything," I said. "What about your kids, your wife, your parents? They're out there in the sea of stars, right? Don't you want them back?"

Quaid was silent for a moment. Then he said,

"Oh my God, yes. Nora and I are two mirrors facing one another, two sides of the same coin, but that doesn't mean I've stopped loving my wife and kids. Now that we know it's possible, we want them back, Nora just as much as me. If we eight can get along, as weird and messed up a group as we are, I'm pretty sure that Nora and I could find a way with them. But we need to be sure there's something for them to come back to. It could be some goddamn thing we don't understand is going to end everything for us soon. It's like we're not in a stable place here, you know? So we want to go to this palace or whatever it is. And if there's someone there to talk to, we want to be sure there's a new world for my wife and kids, not to mention for the rest of us."

"Okay," I said, "I get you. I told Rhys this when we were trying to get Steiner back, but the same thing applies to you. If there's anything I can do, I mean anything at all, I just need to be told, you understand?"

"Yeah," he said. "Thanks."

Something occurred to me. "Hey, did you get anything from me like I got from you?"

"I did," he said, "and I know what you're worried about."

"You think I should be worried? You think I'm right about that?"

"I hate to say it," he said, "but yeah, I think you are. I know what my own memories feel like, fucked up as they are. Jay, I guess you never had anyone to compare to before, but, well, you just don't have enough of a past to make sense to me. I'm sorry."

"It's okay," I said, "I think I've known it for a while. I just wish I knew why, you know?"

"Sure. But we all knew you were special. I mean, we're all snowflakes, right? Messed up in our different ways. But beyond that, I mean."

"Oh shit," I said, "you mean that essence stuff?"

"Yeah. Can't be a coincidence, you having a surplus of it, you connecting all eight of us, and you also not having proper memories. Something else to ask this guy at the palace, right?"

"Right."

"And look who's finally finished with their sapphic ardor," he said. Nora and Michèle were standing in front of us.

"Did you boys have fun?" asked Michèle.

"Well, yes," I said. "But this thing they've come up with is something else, isn't it?"

Michèle laughed. "It is like the bible in reverse, no? There it says 'he knew her', and it means they fucked. Here we fuck, and now I know her."

Somewhat later, Nora was in my arms. We were cuddling together, lying down side by side in the soft green grass, in an interlude between bouts of lovemaking. I'd had the idea of trying to track the progress of whatever technique or faculty she was going to use to convey her past to me, but I'd lost track of the intention; she'd distracted me. Now I was lying back on the grass. Nora's cheek nestled up against my chest, and I was wondering if it would happen next time. And then I realized I already knew what I needed to know about her.

Nora: the second youngest of our group after Mina. She'd grown up quick, intelligent, and out of place in an uneducated lower class family that didn't know what to do with her. For most of her childhood she'd felt like a changeling. Her parents never quite managed to show her the affection they were obviously bestowing on her older siblings. School was tough too; she was the smartest in the class, smartest in her whole school in fact, but she didn't have the capacity to hide her sharpness and she didn't have the charm to make friends in spite of it. In high school Nora had gone enthusiastically after boys of her age, eager to get away from the girls she didn't like and who liked her even less. But she had found no satisfaction from the opposite sex, nor from sex of any kind. The spark of desire was there, but it never fanned into the flame she'd sought. Her lovers didn't care for her personally, nor she for them, and in the absence of pleasure she'd gotten nothing much out of the experience except an increasing distaste for contact with other people.

College only confirmed Nora in her isolation. Even with a partial scholarship and grant money she had to work her way through school to supplement her loans as her family was unable or unwilling to provide any support. It took her six years to graduate; and with each passing year she felt more and more cut off from her classmates. After a while Nora found it convenient to keep people at a distance, not that many approached her anyway. She trained herself to deliver cutting remarks as a sort of defense against unwanted intimacy. She'd always suffered from highs and lows, extremes of nervous tension, but now that tendency was becoming a serious problem. Drinking helped a little, as did marijuana, but not nearly enough; and yet she had enough pride in her sharp-edged intellect that she couldn't bear to dull it with harder drugs, or to go too far with alcohol or pot. And she resisted the idea of therapy, though she couldn't have explained why at the time.

So she suffered in silence and graduated with profound relief only to find that she was expected to make her own way in a world even less caring and considerate than the college she'd departed. To the extent anything offered her a distraction, she found refuge in poetry and literature, and perhaps for this reason she wound up with a copy-editing job at a publishing house. But as always Nora found no friends there, and as a result she saw few prospects for promotion or even eventual freedom from debt. She struggled daily to blunt her own sharp edges, always failing, but found a little relief in her own poetry and short fiction, none of which she ever attempted to publish. Every day she grew more disenchanted with life, less able to cope with other people and with the world at large. And then one day, seeking refuge in the form of alcohol from a particularly acute bout of self-loathing, she wandered into Caernarfon. From that day on, her problems didn't exactly go away, but for some reason she found them more bearable, and though she had no interest in intimacy with the regulars at the bar, she began to tolerate them if not appreciate their company.

"Something about that bar," I said. "Really, I guess it was something about Rhys as a bartender. Having Caernarfon to go to made things better for us. For you and me and Quaid and Steiner, and I'm pretty sure for the Professor, too."

She traced the line of my jaw with a fingertip, then kissed me lightly and briefly on the lips, like a gull touching down for an instant in the water.

"Yes," she said, "I thought it had to do with you, you know, that quality the Professor said you had. Now I know you were just as messed up as the rest of us, though. So I guess it was Rhys? But he seems so normal, you know? I mean, don't get me wrong, he's very sweet, a lovely guy, but I wouldn't have pegged him for a walking oxytocin dispenser or whatever it is we were getting out of Caernarfon."

"I suppose there's an easy way to find out. Tomorrow night, maybe."

"Ha." She touched the tip of her nose to mine and made her eyes cross for a moment, giggled and drew back.

"You know," she said, "by the end of high school I was halfway to thinking I must be a lesbian, I got so little out of sex with guys. But then none of the girls were even a tenth as interesting to me as the boys, and I hated most of them anyway, so I never even tried. I pretty much gave up on sex completely. Even a week ago I would have told you I just wasn't interested in it either way, with anyone. Now, though, after Quaid and I hooked up, and what with you and Michèle, I wonder what I was doing to screw everything up. You know us both now. What do you think?"

I smiled. "You're asking the wrong person if you want profound analysis. Michèle's a lot better at that kind of thing than I am. If I really do have false memories, then you're just the second woman I've ever made love with, so what do I know?"

"Yeah, yeah," she said, "that's nice, but I'm pretty sure you're about to say something deep now, so come on and out with it."

"Okay," I said. "On the second day of the emergency, when we didn't yet know what the hell was going on, Michel came to me in my apartment. Michel, not Michèle as she became. At that point my only view of him was of a paranoid macho guy I didn't know hardly anything about. Like the last thing I would have thought was he'd jump into my arms. And the last thing I would have thought about myself is that I'd kiss him."

"Oh," she said, "Quaid and me, we got that from you and from her too. It's like hearing it in stereo. She was surprised as hell at herself, you know. I mean, at himself. Whatever."

"Ha," I said, "Yeah, I know that much. It wasn't a good day for him, and not for me either. Well anyway I turned him away after that. I still feel bad it about it too because after kissing him it was really a pretty lousy thing to do, but the excuse I used was I didn't feel a spark. You know what I mean. I was telling myself I wasn't gay or bisexual or whatever, and I may even have been right about myself then. But now, with you guys ... I feel it. I felt it when I kissed Rhys yesterday, and having sex with Quaid just now, not to mention with you. And when Michèle first approached me, I mean, as Michèle, I felt it then too, even though I knew right from the start she had been Michel the day before."

"Okay," she said, "you're saying you were like me and Quaid too, in a way, right? Oh, I get it. Desire, right? And the power to change the world."

"Yes," I said. "Since the emergency began, we've been able to change in ways we might not have been able to before. Sexual alignment is one thing; I don't know if most people used to be able to change in that way. Some people, maybe. But there's too many people who've lived their entire lives tortured by what they couldn't change about themselves. Gay people who would have changed to fit in if only they could. Transgender people, too, before they were even accepted to the small degree we'd managed in our world, before there was anything they could do about it, and pretty much everyone who's ever had any kinds of private physical or psychological or emotional situation, all of us wishing we could change, but never able to do it. But if you *could* change yourself, maybe one common choice would be to be able to love people better, more easily, wouldn't you? So what I'm saying is with the end of the world, and with this power we've gotten, we've all been able to change ourselves that way. I feel like if we were back in our world, it wouldn't be all that much, that there would be other kinds of contact and support that would be just as good as sex, if not better. But here, amongst us eight in particular, we've made it into something new."

"Yeah," she said. "That's it. I like it a lot. And you know what else?"

"No, what?"

"I like you a lot too. And the others too. Last week, if I'd been forced to admit it honestly, I would have said you and the other regulars at the bar were okay I guess, in that grudging tone of voice, you know? Now everything is different, and better too. Quaid is my other half in a way that's no metaphor at all, and we love how we fit together; but we love you guys, all of you, too. Michèle and Mina as much as anyone, even though we've only known them a couple of days now. And you know what else?"

"Tell me."

"We're wasting time. Some giant snake or Godzilla or whatever might eat us tomorrow, or this world could end too with nowhere else for us to go. We've both got some lost time to make up for. So let's use our mouths for something besides talking for a while, okay?"

"Sure —" and she closed my mouth with a kiss. I knew I'd never mean as much to her as Quaid, and I was okay with that; but just then I did my best, and for a while at least I think we were as close as we could get.

And later still, Michèle and I were sitting and talking by ourselves, having said goodnight to Quaid and Nora.

"So what do you think?" she asked.

"About them? Or about us?"

"Yes," she said, "both, and about penises and vaginas, and love and stuff. And the spark, too. You know."

A good thing Nora had made me think about it before. So I told Michèle my thoughts as I'd just recently formulated them.

"What I think is this," I said after getting through some of the preliminaries. "Back in our old world, we might have been bound partly by culture, partly by biology. Some people were naturally bisexual even then, and others might have been able to make it with a select few of whichever gender they weren't aligned toward, but I think most were stuck with one or the other. Here though … Quaid and I each never slept with a guy before tonight. And it was really good. I mean, we did everything you can imagine two guys could do, and I loved every minute of it. But I spent a whole year of nights sitting next to Quaid at the bar at Caernarfon, and not once did the thought even cross my mind. I would have been shocked if he approached me, and I would have told him no, too, without even thinking about it. And it would have been right for me to tell him no back then too, is what I really mean to say."

"But not now? Now you fuck each other and like it?"

"Oh yeah," I said, "and so I think what we've done is change ourselves to make it possible. I think we started changing on that first day of the emergency or the end or whatever you want to call it, and some of us figured it out faster than the others. Quaid and Nora did, anyway. You should have seen Rhys and the Professor and me staring at them when they came to the pub on the second day, looking like twins. So like you said, now I know Quaid and Nora, better than I've ever known anyone else, and, well, I wish I knew you that well too."

"Why not?"

"What?"

"We know it's possible, now," she said. "And much as I liked doing it with Quaid, and finding out that I still like girls, too, with Nora, well … I just have to look at you, Jay, and I want you all over again, like I haven't had sex in years. So you know …"

Between Quaid and Nora I should have been half-dead. It would have been tough for even a teen-ager to keep up with either of them. But yeah, I just had to look at Michèle, the curve of her hips, the swell of her breasts, and most of all that eager affectionate look on her face, eyes bright, mouth-half-open, and I was ready, and more than ready.

Maybe we were gods after all. Gods of kama. Not the worst kind of god to be, either.

Some time later, she was sitting in my lap, legs locked around my waist, my hands on her hips. We were kissing, enjoying the languorous end of a long slow lovemaking session. *If the world was going to end again,* I thought, *it might as well be now; but it didn't.* I realized I had completely forgotten the vague intention of recreating whatever telepathic or memory-sharing effect Quaid and Nora had come up with. Oh well: and then I realized it had worked after all, that I knew all about Michèle, and Michel before her.

Michel grew up in Marseilles in a middle-class household, his father a cop and his mother a housewife. Old school, and indeed it was a very old-fashioned family, deliberately so. As a child Michel was cheerful, eager, smart and sensitive; similar to the Michèle I knew today. But his adolescence beat those qualities out of him, or rather submerged them for a long time.

Michel's father was in the National Front, the French ultra-right-wing party. In Marseilles with its big immigrant population the party line was even more racist and xenophobic than elsewhere, and there the police bias against Algerians was notorious. He was a stern and unloving authoritarian at home, and he had little to say to his child or his wife that wasn't cutting, chastising, or just offensive. In that kind of atmosphere, it was almost inevitable that at age 15 Michel fell for Meriem, an Arab girl from one of the Algerian suburbs that bordered Michel's carefully segregated enclave. Of course her family were as outraged at the relationship as Michel's father, if not more so. The two young people made plans to run off together; a sympathetic high school friend made his vacationing older brother's flat available to them for a few nights, and it was there that both families found them, united in wrath if in no other way. Meriem's older brother actually pulled her out of Michel's arms, and it was only his father's menacing presence that saved Michel from violence. Later he heard that Meriem had been shipped off to relatives in Oran, but Michel never saw her again. His rescue from Meriem's relatives was no great blessing though; Michel's father was livid and after beating him black and blue he kicked him out of the house. So there he was, a high school freshman with no job, no place to live, and nothing to live on but a pittance his mother managed to set aside from her household budget.

Michel's next few years were pretty tough. He learned self-reliance, but also a wariness verging on paranoia. If anomie had a name, it was

Michel Delacroix. His friends at school cut him off when they discovered his situation. He got his driver's license and a job as a cab driver, and worked days to pay for a night-time technical education at a vocational school. Getting out of school as a qualified mechanical draftsman he discovered that there were no skilled jobs he could get, not just in Marseilles, but anywhere in France. But then he realized he had no ties, he could get a job anywhere in the world, if he wanted. He got an offer from Montreal, used up all his meager savings to get there, and from there he bounced around from job to job until eventually he signed on as a designer in the US. But along the way he'd learned to keep to himself. Cut off from his family, old friends, and his previous life, he'd been unable to make new relationships with people in America. Instead, he lived in my apartment building like a hermit, leaving only to go to work and to shop for himself, spending all his spare time watching television, drinking, and smoking. Every month or so he'd splurge for a prostitute. It was a sign he still had a little life left in him that at least he enjoyed the sex; but he wasn't blind enough to fail to recognize how fruitless it was. But even recognizing his own situation he'd been unable to break out of the rut he'd carved for himself. It wasn't a good life, and it was getting worse, year by year and hour by hour until finally I happened on him unloading his car that day, the first day of the emergency.

I couldn't look down on Michel, though; I thought my own behavior up to that day was worse. At least Michel had fought hard to make a new life for himself, no matter how isolated and alienated he wound up. I hadn't had to do anything at all. I just lived like a slug. I'd been spending down my cash reserves on food and rent, not even bothering to look for a job, doing nothing all day until at last it was time to take refuge in Caernarfon with the other regulars. And now I had to wonder where my bank account had even come from. Was I created a year ago with a bank account and a vague memory of being laid off from — where had I been working? Damn. I couldn't even recall. I must have been set up somehow not to even think about it, lest I get mixed up in an attempt to talk to someone from my past.

Michèle noticed I'd distracted myself to the point I'd stopped cuddling with her. I guess it was obvious what I was thinking about, if she'd gotten my past the same way I'd gotten hers. There was so much less to my life, after all. She uncoiled herself from my embrace, got up and sat down again facing me.

"It must feel horrible," she said, "not having anything to grab onto. My past sucked, but at least I'm pretty sure I actually had one."

"Yeah," I said, "it's strange. But it's not too bad. I think I got off easy compared to the shit you had to put up with. Poor Meriem. And poor Michel too. But for me that last year of sitting around doing nothing is all I know. I guess for me the question is did I even exist before last year, with memories that were wiped out, or was I actually created and, well, installed into the world at that point?"

"It makes you something special either way."

"I guess so," I said, but I didn't feel it.

She heard the doubt in my voice.

"Listen," she said, "this world we're in now may be a set made just to mess with us. It could all be a test like Rhys said, or it could be something like that snake-man says, a place outside the world where we just happened to wind up. But either way, it's designed."

"Yes," I said, "but —"

"Don't you see? We thought our old world was, how do I say it? Natural. And even if it was created, we thought it wasn't something being messed with, you get me? At least not till the end. But if you had your memory erased, or if you were maybe even given a body and false memories like Sandeep or Ananta, but it happened a year ago in the old world, then that means you were being messed with all the way back then. It means this whole thing is a set-up. Maybe all of last year is someone's plan for you, for us. Or maybe all of everything, all of time and space and all of creation, it's all part of the same plan."

I bowed my head.

"Okay," I said. "You're right. I guess I was trying to ignore the idea. But there's nothing special about me. Even if the Professor is right about that essence thing, about me having more of it, it's just a gift from whoever set all this up. Now you've seen it, you've seen me, you know how little there is to me. I'm the opposite of special."

Michèle's face froze and she clenched her fists.

"Fuck, man," she said angrily, "you think I'd turn gay for just anyone? You think when that didn't work, I'd turn myself into a girl for nobody? That I'd fall for you, that I'd love you, that I'd want you more than I've ever wanted anything in my life, because you're a nothing?"

Her voice broke in the middle of that last sentence, and by the end she was almost sobbing. *Oh my god,* I thought. *She's crying. She's crying because I don't think enough of myself.* I felt as bad then as I did when I turned Michel away after that kiss, as bad as when I realized that night that Michel might be in trouble back home when I was at the bar at Caernarfon.

"Oh shit," I said. "Michèle, Michèle, all I meant is that I think you're worth so much more than I am. I love you, Michèle, you know that, right? If I had to, I'd destroy this world for you. And I'd make you a new one if I could."

She looked up at me, eyes gleaming with tears. "You goddamn well better mean that," she said. "Because that's how I think when I think about you, okay?"

And I realized I did mean it. I really did.

"Okay," I said. "Let's do it."

She grinned, and all at once I felt about a million times better.

"You mean let's fuck again, or let's make a new world?"

"Both," I said. "But first things first."

14

B REAKFAST WAS CRÊPES SUZETTES accompanied by fruit: cantaloupes, plums, clementines, grilled grapefruit, and miraculously pitless sweet cherries.

"Grilled grapefruit? What the hell?" Steiner was unbelieving.

"Just try it," said Michèle.

He gingerly took a bite of a slice.

"Oh," he said after a minute, "I see. Apparently the world had to end before I was allowed to discover this. Seems unfair, somehow."

We set out on our journey with no fanfare or speeches, following Ananta's lead through the interior. The landscape was dull, but walking was pleasant enough on the rolling lawn, with gentle breezes wafting around us under a warm sun. Ananta said he thought it would take us two or three days, based on his estimate of the size of the island. After some back and forth we determined that a yojana was around six or seven miles. so a three- or four-yojana leg during the day seemed quite feasible considering we were all in perfect health and had no real need for rest or food. I suppose we probably could have done it faster, either by setting a sharper pace or by creating some sort of vehicles or even mounts to ride, but none of us suggested it. For my own part I felt no great urgency to discover the truth of the Preserver's palace. I think we all suspected it was going to disappoint us, one way or another, but the trip also served to put off any decisions on our part about what we should be doing instead of merely indulging in kama and artha.

We paused briefly at midday. Rhys produced beers for most of us, and a Diet Pepsi for the Professor, but there seemed to be no point in creating an unnecessary small meal, and going all out with fancy food while en route felt like overkill. When we started walking again, Steiner fell in beside me. It was obvious he wanted to chat in private, so we let a little distance open up between us and the rest of the group.

"Thanks," said Steiner. "I wanted to talk to another guy apart from Rhys, but pulling Quaid away from Nora felt weird, so you're it. If you don't mind."

"Not at all."

"So, uh, I guess everyone knows that me and Rhys are together," he said.

"Yeah. I hope that's what you want."

"It is," he said, "I'm pretty sure, anyway. It's just a little embarrassing. I didn't know I was gay until now. Or bi. Or whatever."

"So you're unsure of yourself?"

"Yeah."

"Let me guess," I said, "it's better here with Rhys than it's ever been for you before. Am I right?"

"I wouldn't know," he said. "It's the best thing ever, for sure, but I've never had anything like a relationship before. You know how screwed up I was. Couldn't even think about connecting with anyone with the kind of problems I was having."

"Oh. So —"

"So I don't know," he said, "I just thought I was straight, okay? I could at least fantasize about girls. Now I don't know what I am. It's — it's like I'm not walking on solid ground. You know what I mean?"

"I would have guessed I was straight too," I said, "if you asked me last week or whenever it was all this started, but now I'm pretty sure labels like that don't matter. Not anymore, anyway. You know why?"

He shook his head.

"I don't think we're quite human anymore," I said.

"What?"

"It's not just this power," I said, "it's the ability to change, to be what we want to be. I think we're really only eating and sleeping out of habit, or because we want to."

I told him my theory about how we'd changed ourselves to be able to love each other better. I didn't mention the notion that we'd been grouped by couples, though. I wasn't sure about it, and it seemed a shame to put a damper on his own love just for speculation.

"Well," said Steiner, "I guess that makes sense. Hey, come to think of it, I haven't had to go to the bathroom since you guys pulled me out of the ocean of milk."

"Shit," I said, and laughed as I thought about it. "It didn't even occur to me. But what more proof could you want? I don't know what's happening to the food we're eating, but it's not getting digested."

"But — but I'm still breathing. I've got a heartbeat. I can feel my muscles moving and stuff like that. And when I had sex last night, I came, you know?"

"How many times?"

"What?"

"I mean it," I said. "How many times?"

"Umm. Five. I think. Maybe more, actually. Okay. That's weird, isn't it?"

"Don't ask me for all the answers," I said, "I'm pretty clueless, too. But maybe all that's because it's what we're wanting or expecting? Everyone wants to have all the endurance in the world. And we have no memory at all of any time in which we weren't breathing or feeling our bodies, so we keep that up here, too. But you only used to have to go to the bathroom once in a while, and it's usually not something you're looking forward to anyway, so we've just gotten rid of the necessity, is what I think."

"Huh. So what are you saying, you could chop off my head and carry it around, and I wouldn't have to walk?"

"Maybe," I said. "But I wouldn't try it. Maybe you'd assume that something deadly like that would actually kill you, too, so you'd make it happen. And after what happened to Sandeep, I wouldn't count on coming back from that sea of stars, either."

"Yeah," he said, "you got that right."

"Anyway, just for the sake of your own peace of mind, why don't you and Rhys talk to Quaid and Nora tonight? And by talk, I mean have sex with. If they're up for it, and I think they will be."

"You mean it? Seriously?"

I told him about my experience with them last night.

"So I know what you mean about being gay or bisexual and not knowing it," I said. "I had no idea what it would be like, but sex with Quaid was really sweet. Not to mention with Nora. This thing they've come up with, though, this memory sharing thing or whatever it is. It's really profound. Maybe we should all do it."

"Huh," he said. "Okay. I'll talk to Rhys."

We picked up our pace to rejoin the group. Michèle looked over her shoulder at us as we approached, and I fell into place beside her, while Steiner moved forward to join Rhys.

•   •   •

I stumbled suddenly and lost my balance. Mina whirled and grabbed me before I could fall. She was so strong she only needed one arm to support all my weight as I regained my feet.

"Watch it," she said, and grinned at me.

"Thanks."

I blinked and shook my head. I felt a little strange, almost like I'd just woken up.

"Did something just happen?"

Steiner and Nora paused and looked back at me, and a moment later Ananta came to a halt. He stood calmly waiting.

"I don't think so," said Mina, but she seemed unsure of herself. "Are you okay?"

"Yeah," I said. "I must have been daydreaming or something. It's nothing."

We kept walking for the rest of the day without incident. I figured we must be making at least two miles an hour or maybe a little more, and we walked for maybe ten hours, so, what, three yojana? Of the five or six Ananta had said we'd need to go. So if there was anywhere to get to, maybe we'd arrive there tomorrow.

At last, as the sun was setting, we called a halt. Nora told us she'd take care of the menu. She went with Italian food, starting us off with cold asparagus in a vinaigrette with soft bread and butter (Nora explained she wasn't a fan of oil on bread) with olives and chunks of parmigiano on the side to nibble on. For pasta we had capellini with a delicate garlic-and-oil sauce, and for entrees she let us choose between platters of veal piccata with capers in a buttery lemon sauce and acqua pazza, whitefish in a tomato and garlic broth. On the side, risotto with a mix of pumpkin and nutmeg stirred into the rice. The first course came with prosecco, the second with pinot grigio, and dessert, a rum-soaked cheesecake, was accompanied by tiny cups of espresso and frosted tulips of sgroppino, a sort of alcoholic lemon sorbet.

Everything was exquisite, though I'd never eaten anything like it before and had to have the food explained to me. Ananta chose not to join us. He withdrew around a hillside to meditate or mope; there was no telling which.

The last of the day's light was dying away in the west when the four of us finally rose from the table. We walked around a hill to make it easier for Nora to dispose of the table and the remains of the dinner service, and she joined us as we stood looking up at the sky.

"That was a wonderful meal, Nora," said Mina.

"Thanks," she said. "When I was little, we used to eat that kind of food once or twice a year, but usually we were pretty much a mac-and-cheese household. After I grew up I wasn't really into food at all, but now I guess I'm more of a voluptuary than I used to be."

Steiner put his hand on her hip, gave her a squeeze. "You're voluptuous enough for me, anyway," he said.

Nora smiled, but a moment later she darted her hand out and grabbed Steiner by the balls.

"If you weren't the second to last man on Earth — or wherever we are — you'd be in danger of losing these," she said.

"Pax," he said, a little squeakily, "you win."

"I always win," said Nora, but there was no severity in her voice. And letting him go she trailed a finger up his belly to his chest.

"That was a little harsh," she said more softly. "I'm sorry. You think you can forgive me?"

"I think so." Steiner took a step closer to her, put his hands on her shoulders and looked into her eyes. "In fact, I'm sure of it." And they grinned at one another.

"Well I can see where this is going," said Mina. She nodded at me. "Shall we give these two some privacy?"

Mina and I went to sleep in each other's arms, but we didn't do anything more than that. At some point in the night, I woke up, contemplating her athletic form with a sort of connoisseur's appreciation of beauty, wondering what her past had been like, how she'd become the person I met at that McDonald's window, and a strange thing happened: I realized I already knew everything I wanted to know, like I'd dreamed my way through a summary of her life.

She'd grown up in a working class family, one of her mothers employed as a mail carrier for the post office, the other a daycare teacher. It hadn't been a luxurious childhood, but she'd been well-loved. Elementary school wasn't bad. From time to time some classmate had shied away from the girl with two mothers, but she'd made many friends at an early age before any of that had mattered much, and she had enough of a network through her childhood not to suffer much as a result. Things had changed in middle school and high school, though, as most of the kids there were strangers. The culture there was retrogressive, and any kind of nonstandard connection or preference was cause for ostracizing or worse. So Mina pretty much kept to herself in those years, her only friends coming from outside school, like Sandeep at her McDonalds.

Then came the trauma. Both her parents were killed during their day off in a failed daytime burglary while Mina was at school, aged 15. She'd been shuffled off to live with relatives, an extremely religious and intolerant aunt and uncle who'd taken her in reluctantly, disapproving of her dead parents' lives and only grudgingly giving her any space for herself at all. She'd been stuck in that situation for three more or less miserable years, counting the days to high school graduation and the chance to live on her own, when she'd moved out into a tiny studio that ate up all her pay, which included a very small income inherited from her parents.

As a young teenager she'd discovered Japanese animation. Immersing herself in that world offered a wonderful escape from reality when things got bad. Even recalling her memories as I was in retrospect, titles like *Revolutionary Girl Utena*, *Bubblegum Crisis*, *Ghost in the Shell*, and *Noir* stood out for me, all television series with strong female characters, often featuring girls or women with extraordinary abilities. There was no question where Mina had gotten her new body image from, and she wasn't the least bit embarrassed about it either. And I realized that I was proud of her, for her resilience, for her forthrightness, and for her kindness and humor after all she'd been through.

"Wow," she said, "I — I just — I think I just remembered your past. Is that crazy or what?"

"Yeah, I just got you, too. You were so disappointed in Anthy, weren't you? When she turned out to be just her brother's creature."

I was talking about a character from Revolutionary Girl Utena, Mina's favorite show.

"Yeah," she said, "Yeah. I was hoping — well, she's dark-skinned, you know, and not that many girls are in anime. When I was in middle school, I really identified with her while I was working my way through the series. I was hoping so much she'd really make it work with Utena and they'd just kick everyone's ass. But that thing about your last year is wild. You never told me about that."

"Yes, well." I felt ashamed. I'd meant to tell her. *In fact, hadn't I done so?* I thought I remembered telling her, lying back on the lawn with her in my arms, just like this …

I was going to say something, but I was interrupted by a sharp cry from around the hillside. It sounded like Nora. I was on my feet quickly, but Mina was even faster. I got there only a second or two after her, though.

Nora was huddled on the ground, sobbing. Steiner was on his knees a couple of yards away from her, looking utterly shattered.

"What happened?" Mina asked. "What's wrong here?"

"I don't know," said Steiner. "I swear I don't. She won't let me get near her. Oh God …"

"Okay," said Mina to me, "you take care of Steiner, okay? I'll see if I can help Nora."

And she knelt down beside Nora, who was crying her heart out now, her face turned away from us, buried in the grass.

Fuck, I had no idea what to do. No, scratch that: I did have an idea.

"Come on, Steiner," I said, "let's give them some space. Tell me what happened."

I gave him my hand and pulled him to his feet. We walked a little ways around the hillside.

"Okay," I said.

"I don't know," he said, speaking fast. He reminded me of how he'd been during his bad times the previous year, fighting a battle with himself. "I — I —"

I put my hands on his shoulders.

"Calm down. Take it slow. Just sit with me for a minute."

I used a little pressure, and he sank to the ground. I sat down beside him. He was breathing hard, on the edge of collapse. After a minute or so he regained a little self-control.

"Ready to talk? There's no hurry."

"Okay," he said. "Thanks. So, you know I really care about Nora, right?"

"Yeah."

"I'd never do anything to hurt her." He said it urgently, like I might have disagreed.

"I know," I said. "I trust you. Just tell it, okay?"

"We made love," he said. "It was really nice. We couldn't get enough of each other. It was like we were trying to break down a wall between us, is what it felt like. Oh."

He didn't say anything for a minute, and I let him collect his thoughts.

"Break down a wall," he said. "Like at the end of the world? That may not have been my best-ever metaphor."

"Ha, yeah." But something was nagging me about that now that he mentioned it. It was like my memory of the four of us breaking through that wall was foggy now, even though it just happened a few days ago.

"Anyway," he said, "it was really nice. For all the little digs we get in, I think she likes me as much as I like her. Or I thought that, anyway. I thought everything was fine. I was so happy, you know, to fall asleep in her arms. It made me feel so damn good. And I thought she felt the same way ..."

Steiner trailed off. I could feel him trembling beside me.

"She woke me up," he said. "It was like I was sleeping with an angry leopard for a second. And then she gave this horrible little scream and pulled away from me. I didn't know what was going on."

"Sounds like it was just a nightmare."

"Yeah," he said, "but I went over to her, you know, and asked her what was wrong and I reached out to her and she slapped my hand away. You know how sharp she can be sometimes, if you say something dumb to her? Imagine it a hundred times worse. A million. She said 'You're not him.' And I tried again, and she said, 'Don't touch me,' and oh God, her tone of voice. I felt like a rapist or something. I wanted to kill myself. I still want to, I think."

I wanted to say something comforting, but just then Nora and Mina came around the hillside. Steiner jerked his head up, and then jumped to his feet. He started to say something, but Nora spoke first.

"Steiner," she said, "I'm so sorry. I didn't mean it at all."

"Oh," he said. "Oh. Well then —"

"Well then, 'What the fuck?' is what you should be asking, right?"

"It's all right," he said.

"No it's not," said Nora. "And I'll explain to everyone too, since I got you all up for this. But first I want to say something right now so that there's no question about it, okay?"

Steiner nodded, so she continued.

"I had a great time with you, Steiner. Sex with you was the best I can remember, ever. I'd do it again anytime, and I hope we do it again soon. I love you, okay? And tonight I wanted to be with you. I mean that."

"Okay, yeah," said Steiner, a little jerkily. He wiped his eyes. "Yeah, I feel the same way. That's why —"

"That's why you must have been wondering 'What the fuck?' Well here's how it was."

She sat down on the grass, and we all moved to sit down next to her, making another little circle, like we'd done a few times before. Mina gave me her hand and smiled at me, but there was a troubled look on her face I didn't like.

"All right," said Nora. "It was just a dream, but I think ... I think it's more than that. At least for me it was. I was dreaming I was asleep in someone's arms, and I dreamed I woke up, and I dreamed I was so happy I was in that other person's arms, because it was like they were everything I ever wanted, and it was like they wanted everything I was myself. I felt so complete, so fulfilled, you can't imagine it. I don't think you can, anyway. And then I woke up,"

Steiner flinched, and Nora reached out a hand to him, patted him on the knee.

"I know what it sounds like," she said. "I know how horrible this is for me to say. I want to cut the part of me that feels that way right out of my body, because I know it's hurting you, Steiner, and you don't deserve it, and I do love you. It's just —"

"I'm not that guy," said Steiner. "Is that it?"

"Yeah," she said. "And this is the thing. I've never had a dream like that before. I know I haven't. And you know how dreams are, they fade away when you wake up. You remember having the dream, but the dream itself you mostly forget. The emotions you felt then are smoke in your hands, you can't grasp them anymore. But not this time."

"What was he like?" asked Mina.

"Huh?"

"The guy in your dream."

"I ... That's the thing," said Nora. "I can't remember his face. Just his touch. How it felt to be with him. I know it's crazy though. It sounds crazy when I say it out loud. But I know he exists, okay? I know it. That's what made me freak out, Steiner. If I could remember his face, if it was just someone I used to know, someone who's dead now or in the sea of stars, it would be okay, you see? It would just be a nightmare. I could shake it off. But now, even now, I'm sure he's real. He's just ... not here. And I can't remember. That's what pisses me off!"

She was shouting by the time she finished, angry as hell.

"I believe you," said Steiner.

"What?" Nora looked up, her voice much calmer now.

"You say he's real," said Steiner. "I believe you. He's more important to you than anyone, right? So that makes it more important to you to find him than for us to find some mythical palace that may or may not exist. So let's do it."

"Steiner, I ... I don't know how ... Thank you, Steiner."

"It's okay," he said. "We're friends, right? You'd do the same for me, wouldn't you?"

"Yeah," she said, "I would. For sure. It's just I don't know what to do to find him."

"Hell," said Steiner, "neither do I. But we've got this power now, and maybe we can use it. Let's think it over, sleep on it even, and maybe we'll come up with something tomorrow. Okay?"

We all agreed to that, so for the second time that night we broke up by couples.

"Jay," said Mina, as we walked back to our sleeping spot, "I didn't want to make a fuss back there, but you know, I believe her too."

"Why not?" I shrugged. "So much weird stuff has happened to us lately, who knows? And she's never seemed like the kind of person who could just make something like that up, or be deluded about it ..." I'd started out neutral on the question, but now I was convincing myself.

"Yes," she said, "but that's not why I believe her."

Oh, I thought, *Oh.*

"You mean you feel that way too?" I asked.

"Not exactly," she said. "I mean, I didn't have a weird dream, and I don't feel like there's someone out there who's my perfect other half. But I was thinking about what Nora said, and then I was thinking about Utena and the lesbian girls in that show. And I got to thinking that the feel of a woman in my arms, it was something I knew, something I liked.

Something I was used to, even. But I've never slept with a girl, not that I can remember anyway. But maybe there is a girl out there, somehow? Does that seem strange to you?"

"Well, yes," I said, "but not strange like it's something-wrong-with-you strange. More like it's something-we-need-to-worry-about strange."

"You think someone's been messing with us? Someone's changed our memories?"

"I don't know. But it's possible, isn't it? I mean, after all we've seen here. I just don't know if that's what's happened. And if it did happen, did we lose our memories of these people, or did they give us — you and Nora anyway — false new ones?"

"Man," she said, "that creeps me out. And it pisses me off, too."

"And anyone you get pissed off at had better think seriously about changing their behavior," I said.

She laughed and patted me on the arm.

"So you think maybe Ms. Right is out there somewhere waiting for me?"

"Could be," I said. "Why not? Just to be quite clear, though, just like Nora was with Steiner, if she is out there, it doesn't change the way I feel about you. If you ever find someone you love like that who doesn't happen to be me, I'll be happy for you. But until then, and afterwards too if you want, I'll be here for you."

"That's pretty damn sweet," she said. "And in case that does turn ever out to be true, we'd better spend our time here wisely, don't you think?"

We reached our sleeping spot. Mina put one arm under my bottom and the other behind my back, and her eyes flashed blue for a moment. She lifted me into the air like I weighed nothing at all, like I was a little kid, but then she kissed me, and there was nothing maternal about that. We wound up not using the sleeping spot for sleeping, not for the whole rest of the night.

15

DAWN CAME WHILE WE WERE still doing our best to break down whatever walls might have stood between us. I'm not sure if we quite succeeded completely, but it was fun trying anyway. I'd managed to put any question of my own memory, or lack thereof, out of my mind for the night, but with first light my concerns came rushing back. How could there be people out there we'd lost, or forgotten? And if that had really happened, who could they be? I was trying to wrap my head around the problem of Nora or Mina knowing and loving someone I couldn't remember either.

It wasn't logically hard, of course. Obviously if they really existed, all of us must have had our memories of those people erased or suppressed. Though apparently in Nora's case, and maybe in Mina's too, the process hadn't been perfect. Which raised another question for later. But for me the real problem was more visceral than that. I wanted to be able to trust what memories I did have, because without those, there was no way for me to reason about anything.

"Okay," said Mina, "I guess it couldn't last forever. Too bad."

I was lying back on that familiar lawn while she caressed me. And for the first time I was too distracted to respond.

"Yeah," I said, putting my hand over hers. "I'm sorry. It's like I'm feeling something missing now too. I was thinking before it was that I only had the one year of real memories, but now I think maybe ..."

"Maybe we've all lost something just recently, not just Nora. Or not just Nora and me."

"Yeah. And then I was wondering if it had something to do with breaking through the wall, you know, going into the light. Maybe that messed us up somehow, screwed with our minds. It would explain some things, anyway."

"Huh," she said. "That could be."

She sat up then, and so did I, moved to be right next to her, took her hand in mine, her thigh up against mine, our bodies touching too, side by side.

"I wish we could just be together like this forever," said Mina. "But now I'm trying to remember that myself. Breaking through the wall, I mean. It's like an itch, and I can only scratch it by opening up my skull."

"That whole time is really fuzzy for me. And you know, you'd think it would be clearer, right? I mean, we did it just recently, and it was so important."

"Shit," she said. "You're right. It's like I'm waking up now, and that was all a dream. I think I remember you all supporting me, right? It was me who broke through, wasn't it?"

Her voice was very weak and unsure. Hearing that from Mina, who was usually so strong and sure of herself, made my heart sink.

"We've got to get through this," I said. "This isn't right."

"Yeah."

"At the wall," I said, "we all worked together to get through it, right? We helped you break through. Do you remember that too?"

"Oh," she said. "Yeah, I do. I could feel it. All of you supporting me. But —"

I waited for her.

Mina frowned. She was concentrating. "But there's something wrong there. I feel like something's missing, right there."

"Shit," I said, "I feel it too. Listen, this can't go on. Let's get Steiner and Nora. Maybe we can work it out."

So we both scrambled back up, took another trip around the hillside to where we'd left them. They were sleeping together side by side, Nora's arm draped across Steiner's back.

"Damn," said Mina softly, "it's nice to see them like that again."

"Yeah. Maybe we should let them be."

But it was too late. Steiner opened an eye and looked muzzily up at us.

"'sup?"

Nora awoke then too. She didn't recoil from Steiner, either. He twitched once, though, sharply, and she giggled. I think she must have goosed him — or something like that anyway.

Both of them sat up.

"Good morning," said Nora.

"Feeling better?" asked Mina.

"Well, yes and no." She got to her feet, offered Steiner both hands, and heaved to help him up too.

"I can still feel him," she said. "Or where he isn't I mean. It's like I'm one of those indentured contracts they used to have, that was torn in half. But I'm fine."

"You don't sound fine to me," said Mina.

"Well, okay, yeah. Not 100%. But Steiner helped."

"That's me," said Steiner, "the human consolation prize."

"Hey," said Nora, "better than booby prize. Take what you're offered."

He laughed, but underneath it I heard the bitterness.

"Well anyway," said Mina, "I was thinking, maybe you're not the only one, Nora."

"What?"

Mina explained her own feeling, that she'd lost someone of her own.

"Damn," said Steiner. "You're in the same boat with me then, huh Jay?"

"Maybe," I said.

"Well, it's a fucked-up situation for all of us," said Mina. "Whether we've lost someone or whether someone we care about has. I'm trying to figure it out, though: it doesn't make sense to me. I was thinking that maybe passing into that white light, you know, beyond the wall, it affected us somehow. Made us lose memories of people. But I don't know ..."

"I can remember all kinds of people from the old world who aren't here now," said Nora.

"Yeah," said Mina, "that's what doesn't make sense."

"Name three," said Steiner, abruptly.

"What?" Nora wheeled to face him. "What's that supposed to mean?"

"I mean it," said Steiner. "Name three. People you used to know. Not from way in your past, I mean, but people who you knew right before the world went to hell. I was right there with you when you said you could remember people. I thought I could too. But then I couldn't, you know?"

"I don't know," said Nora sharply. But then she frowned.

"This is stupid," she said after a moment. "All of us except Mina used to hang out at the pub. But ..."

"Just the three of us?" asked Steiner. "Doesn't seem like enough, right? We spent a lot of nights there. There must have been more people there we knew, don't you think? How could you stay in business with just three regulars?"

"Well, of course there were other customers," said Nora.

And Mina said, "What about the bartender? You guys must have known him, right? Or her?"

"Shit," said Nora. "you're right. We must have. But maybe they rotated? Maybe there was a bunch of them? It's like a blur for me now."

"No," said Steiner. There was anger in his voice now. "Yeah, it's like a human-shaped hole for me, too. But I'm feeling ... I'm feeling like it's important."

"Yeah," I said. "I feel that way too."

But Steiner was lost in his own thoughts. He said, "I'm trying to visualize the bar. I 've got a good picture of you, Nora, always working your laptop from one of those high tables in the middle of the room. Jay, you were usually there at the bar with me, listening to whatever goddamn thing I had to tell you that night, nursing a beer. But behind the bar ... I can't even remember what it looked like. Oh shit."

He stopped short. But his tone of voice was such that we all shut up and waited for him.

"Oh shit," he said. "I can't remember the name of the pub. That's fucked up."

"The name? But —" Nora cut herself off, too. Then both of them looked at me.

"I've been trying for the last five minutes," I said. "Since Steiner came up with his name-three thing. But it's not working. I can't remember anyone there but you two. Not the bartender, not anyone else, and not the name of the place, either."

"Okay," said Mina. "I don't know much about your pub. But this doesn't seem even the slightest bit natural to me. It would have been one thing if going through that wall wiped our memories completely. But this is too damn specific."

"So what are you saying?" asked Steiner. "That someone did this to us?"

"Yeah," said Mina. "That's it. Exactly."

"Well, hell," said Steiner. "If there is a someone to be doing this, and if that someone is somewhere in this world, I'm pretty sure our snaky friend is going to be leading us to him. Or her."

"That's an interesting thought," said Nora. "And where is he, anyway?"

Ananta wasn't hard to find. He was seated cross-legged atop the next hill over, watching the sunrise. As we approached, he stood up in a single sinuous motion holding his feet planted, which caused him to turn 180 degrees to face toward us as he rose.

"Are you ready to proceed?" he asked.

"Not quite yet," said Nora. "What happened to the other members of our group?"

"What?"

"When you first noted our presence," said Nora, "how many of us were there?"

Ananta blinked. "Why ..." He trailed off. "Three," he said after a time, but he didn't sound very sure of himself. "And then you summoned this one from the sea of stars, though I tried to stop you." He nodded at Steiner.

"Really," said Mina. She stalked towards him. Even in human form, Ananta had a couple of inches on her, and probably at least fifty pounds, but he flinched as she approached. She planted herself squarely in front of him, put both hands on his shoulders.

"You wouldn't be shitting us now, would you?" she asked. She didn't seem to be exerting much force, but Ananta sank to his knees.

"No," he said, "Please! My memories are ... confused, I think. But that is all I know. First the three of you, then the fourth. I have no wish to deceive —"

She crouched down, put one hand behind his head, and the other over his mouth and nose. I thought to intervene, then changed my mind. I trusted Mina a lot more than I did Ananta. And she wasn't trying to smother him anyway.

"Hush," she said. Her nails began to glow. Her middle finger extended over the naga's nose up to his brow, but the nails of her index and ring fingers were poised just beneath Ananta's eyes.

She spoke in a low voice, but I heard her words easily enough.

"I took one eye away from you, remember. Then I gave it back on the basis of your good behavior. You want to lose both of them? They'll never heal, you know. You can kill yourself if you like, come back from the sea of stars. You'll still be blind. In every incarnation for all eternity. I guarantee it. Now tell me if you believe me."

Shit. She was freaking me out, now. Her tone of voice was chilling. I'd never heard anyone that angry before, not for any reason.

She pulled her hand back, angled her palm so her fingers were pointing directly at his eyes.

"I believe you," said Ananta, and a shudder ran through his entire body.

"Good," said Mina. "Now, one more time. How many of us were there? Think carefully before you speak."

"Eight," he said. And then quickly: "No! Seven! I mean seven! And then you summoned one to make eight, and then later this one, to make nine. But then, eight again."

Mina laughed. A harsh and bitter sound but still lovely withal.

"Why did you lie?"

"When I saw that four of you were gone, I knew it must have been the Preserver's will. I cannot stand against him. And then I saw you accepted the loss of the four. So that must be his will too. And when you asked me just now, I thought — I thought —"

He stopped. Began to cry. Ananta Sesha, the Endless, the Infinite, the Last Remnant, the Throne and Crown and Bed of the Preserver, and the supreme ruler of all nagas, was crying, tears rolling down his purple cheeks.

"Oh for pity's sake," said Mina. But she sat down next to him, put a hand on his shoulder, and it was no longer a menacing gesture.

"Listen," she said, "you're safe from me, okay? I'm not going to hurt you. And I just made that thing up about your eyes."

"I — I know you did," he said, sniffling and rubbing his eyes. "I know it now. You wouldn't — That's why — Oh! I broke my parole. I'm so sorry. You have been kind to me. I have eaten your food. If you had blinded me it would only have been simple justice."

"It's okay," said Mina. "But we're still missing our memories. So please tell us about the people we lost."

"All right," he said, and we were rapt, focused on his words.

He counted on his fingers.

"There was a girl with white hair," he said, and Mina tensed.

"Tell me!" she demanded.

"I thought she was quite young," said Ananta, "but she talked like a sage. And you called her by a title. I forget —"

"Oh shit," said Mina. "Oh shit my God. The Professor. Harriet. How could I forget her?"

It was like standing downstream of a rupturing dam. All those memories of the Professor rushing into my head. And it was as if I'd always known them, of course. But, damn, how stupid I felt now, and how angry! Mina was taking it harder than me.

"Motherfucker!"

Mina jumped up, and Ananta scooted away from her, panic written on his face. Mina's nails and eyes were blazing blue now. She looked like an iconic representation of a goddess of wrath. She screamed in rage, and it was a piercing sound that went through me like a sword. A hawk's cry maybe, or yeah, maybe Garuda's. Mina raised her hand, which was glowing so brightly it looked like a star brought down to earth, and she smashed it down into the ground. There was a blinding actinic flare and a thunderclap, and the earth around me shook. When my vision cleared, she was kneeling there before a big mound of ripped-up earth and grass, her arm buried in the soil up to her shoulder, with a half-dozen lines of torn lawn and shattered earth running radially away from the point of impact for a dozen yards. One had passed right by Steiner, bowling him over.

"Jesus, Mina," he said, getting back on his feet. "What the fuck?"

"Uh, yeah, sorry," she said, pulling her arm out of the ground. Her nails and eyes had lost their brilliance. "I need to figure out how to control myself better. But man this pisses me off! I care about you guys, right? And you Jay, a lot, I care about you a lot. But her, the Professor ... well shit. What I just did? That was fucking *nothing* compared to what I'm going to do if I don't get her back soon."

"Yeah," said Steiner, "me too, and I'm beginning to think I'm maybe missing someone also. Ananta, hey, tell us about the others. I promise we won't explode or anything. Right Mina?"

"Right," she said. "I won't do that again. But we have to know."

Ananta returned. He managed to avoid staring at Mina, which I thought was pretty ballsy of him.

"Very well," he said. He turned to Nora. "There was a man who looked very much like you. I thought at first you must be brother and sister, but after a time I realized you were lovers. You were always together as we journeyed. Never once did he leave your side. Always you were touching, talking. His name —"

"Quaid," said Nora. "Quaid. My God." She had been sitting up, alert to what Ananta was saying, and now she sagged back, as if she'd been sapped. And I remembered Quaid too now; or rather I remembered them. They'd seemed like two halves, yeah, but together they were more than just two pieces, they were something bigger, more whole, more profound than any couple I'd ever seen before. And someone had torn them apart, and worse than that they'd made her forget him.

Mina said, "We'll get him back, Nora. I swear it."

Nora was still processing her revelation, but after a minute she nodded. "Yes," she said. "That's what we're going to do. And someone's going to pay."

Steiner nodded. "Damn," he said. "Yeah, Nora, I can see why you freaked out last night. Shit, I'd have done the same thing if I had someone like Quaid as my other half, and then I woke up and this jerk Steiner was all over me instead."

Nora smiled. "Hey. Don't think you're sleeping alone tonight. And when we get Quaid back, it's going to be a threesome. Or, wait, do you have someone lost too?"

"Yeah," said Steiner to Ananta. "Me next. Was there someone ... someone I was with? Who I don't remember?"

"I did not have as much time to observe you," said Ananta. "But in the last day I believe you spent much time with the bearded man."

"Bearded man?"

"Jesus," said Nora, "Rhys. There was no rotating bartender. It was Rhys, every night. He owned the place. It was all down to him. He was the only one of us who wasn't messed up. The one who was there for all of us. We all owe him, big-time. And we forgot him just like that. Now I feel sick all over again."

And again, it all came rushing back. Rhys's reassuring presence behind the bar, making Caernarfon the one place I could stand to be around other people, night after night.

Steiner started to laugh. There was a little hysteria there, but he got it under control.

"I was so sure it was going to be a girl," he said. "But Rhys? Ha. Oh man. Oh shit. Rhys. Goddamn it."

"How do you feel about him now?" asked Nora.

"Oh hell," said Steiner, "you want me to cover it up? I love him. Of course I do. I think I have since I met him, but I didn't know it until you guys rescued me. When he hugged me that first time, coming out of the sea of milk. Goddamn it, I want him back. But like Mina said, all of you. I care about all of you. And especially about Nora's sweet ass."

She snorted.

"Hey," he said, "it's the sweetest part of you. Listen, taking any one of you away is horrible, But the people we actually lost? It's like it was selective. The Professor and Mina. Nora and Quaid. And me and Rhys. Wait, shit, that's still just seven."

They were all staring at me now, and I felt it. The gap. The hole in my life. A shadow cast by someone I couldn't see.

"Ananta —" said Mina, but I interrupted her.

"Stop, please. I want to try to work it out myself. Give me a minute, okay?"

Maybe it was just obstinacy. But if it wasn't for Nora and her dream last night, I could have gone on forever thinking there was just the four of us. But Nora had woken to the realization of missing Quaid, even if she didn't know his name. And then the others had worked out their own losses, even if they'd only gotten their memories back with help. Mina had her intuition regarding a girl, the Professor, and after a while Steiner felt something was missing too. But even now, even after all these revelations, I still had no clue who or what I was missing. Maybe it was because there wasn't much to me in the first place. Maybe because I was used to being meddled with, took it for granted. But I wanted to try to fix myself now, with no prompting.

Rummaging through my memories did nothing. I could tell now there were some fuzzy spots, where I must have had my memories adjusted, like when we broke through the wall. The eighth person must have been there. And probably at many other points as well. Like my memories of hooking up with Mina the first time. Maybe that was wrong too. Maybe we'd just made love for the first time last night. But wrestling with these recollections wasn't helping me find what I wanted. So I decided to do something different.

"Okay," I said. "I'm going to try something."

I closed my eyes, imagined my mind as pink cartoonish-looking brain floating in space. Corny, okay, but that's how I saw it. And there: a black railway spike rammed through the top of my head, down deep into the hippocampus. That spike represented the false memories someone had shoved in there. I was going to pull it out, mentally, when I realized it would just leave a gaping bloody hole if I did that. So yeah, sort of floating nearby, a narrow wedge-shaped chunk of brain, Those were my lost memories, the real ones.

And now I had a real sense of trepidation. Consciously using this power, well it was fine to make a meal or a book or whatever. Screw it up and maybe you'd get something inedible or illegible, no harm done. But this was mental surgery, and I wouldn't have dared to even try anything like this if I wasn't so angry at what had been done to us all.

But still I hesitated. And then I realized after a moment that it was now or never. So I did it. The brain gave a sort of pulsing squeeze and the black spike slithered out like it had been excreted. I visualized the cut-out wedge of brain aligning itself with the hole and sliding back in —

"— Jay! Jay!"

I was lying down, which was unexpected, and so I sat bolt upright even before I opened my eyes. Bad idea. I bounced my forehead smartly off Mina's chin, which sent me right back down to the lawn again.

"Shit! Shit. Jay, are you all right?"

"Uhh, yeah," I said. "I think."

I opened my eyes first this time. Mina was leaning over me, and Nora and Steiner were at my side, looking anxious. Ananta was there too, a few yards away, the expression on his face unreadable now.

Mina sat back on the ground, right next to me. Her eyes were closed and she was breathing hard. And yeah, those were tear tracks on her face.

"We thought you were dead," said Nora.

"What?"

"You collapsed all of a sudden," said Steiner. "You weren't breathing. We tried to use the power on you, but nothing happened. Mina gave you mouth to mouth."

"How long?"

"It felt like a goddamn year," he said, "but I don't know. Might have been five minutes."

I scooched over on the ground next to Mina, put my arms around her. She was sobbing. Goddamn it. "Thank you," I said. "I'm okay,"

"Oh," she said after a minute. "Oh, I'm so happy." And then after a beat. "What did you do?"

"Something stupid," I said, and told them.

"Holy shit," said Steiner. "Did it work?"

And like that it hit me. What really happened breaking through the wall. Michel and Michèle. And what we meant to each other. Everything we'd said to each other. All the love we'd shared in under a week. I'd forgotten her like she'd never existed and I never would have remembered her either if I'd just gone on in my usual way, going with the flow. I couldn't stand it. I just couldn't. I screamed.

I don't think I'd ever done it before. Screamed, I mean. It was a loud and angry sound and I liked doing it, but after five seconds or so, I saw the others were gaping at me, astonished. And Ananta a few yards away was cringing, hiding his head in his arms. I couldn't do it anymore, so I stopped.

"Michèle," I said. My throat was already raw. It felt good. "They took Michèle away, too."

I could see from everyone's expressions they were remembering her now. It only took the slightest prompting and the suppressed memories were released. Like breaking a spell.

"Oh Jay," said Mina, "I'm so sorry."

"Yeah," I said, "so am I. But you know what? I'm not sorry about us. And I'm pretty sure Steiner's not sorry about Nora."

"You'd better not be," said Nora.

Steiner grinned. "Not in a million years. Wanting Rhys back doesn't change that."

"That's it, exactly," I said. "Before we go, anyone have any clever ideas what do next. Apart from the obvious, I mean?"

Mina bared her teeth. "The obvious is good enough for me."

I got up from the lawn.

"Okay," I said. "Ananta, get a move on. We're going to the palace."

As a group we were quiet for a while, following Ananta through the gentle rolling hills. I guess we all spent some time dwelling on the people we'd lost. For sure I was thinking about Michèle for most of that time, anyway. Where she was, what she was doing. If she was okay at all. I didn't want to think about the worst possibility, but I couldn't help it. Maybe she'd been deleted, removed from the world completely. The idea was a burning coal in the pit of my stomach.

Then it occurred to me that maybe if we made enough of a fuss, we all might be deleted. But there was something a little strange about that thought.

"Hey," I said, "I've been thinking."

"Nice," said Nora. "How's that working for you?"

"Not so hot," I said. "Trying not to think about some of the possibilities, you know. But I was wondering why someone with the power to do all this stuff would bother to use it on us this way. You know, splitting us up like this. Setting Ananta on us. It seems kind of, well, petty. I mean, if we're a bother, we can probably all just be killed directly one way or another, but how can we even be a minor annoyance for a god?"

"Yeah," said Steiner. "That's a question, but we still don't know enough to have an answer."

"Sure," I said, "but it doesn't hurt to speculate. So I was thinking, one answer is this is all a test, like Rhys was saying a while back. A test of what, I don't know, though."

"Okay," said Mina, "maybe, but I don't buy it. A real god would know from the start if we were going to pass or fail, don't you think? And a fake god, someone like us, say, who just has this power but isn't omniscient … I think anyone who was anything like a normal person would know how pissed off they were making us with this shit. You said 'one answer', though. You got another?"

"Could be the power is limited some way we don't understand. Could be we really are a big threat, or someone thinks we are anyway, but for some reason they were only able to split us up, not get rid of us completely."

"Sorry," she said. "Don't buy that one either. But don't let me stop you from doing some more thinking. Could be the truth isn't that far off one or the other."

"The problem," said Nora, "is that until we learn the truth, we're just going to have to blunder forward without a clue. And I don't know if anyone is going to be so kind as to tell us."

"Hey," said Mina, "that suits me. If someone gets in my way, heading for the Professor and everyone else, I'll talk to them first. Only fair to see what they have to say. But if they don't make me very happy very fast after that, well, fuck it. They had their chance. I know it sounds kind of brutal. But what else have we got to do?"

Steiner laughed. "I have to admit, I'm feeling kind of what-the-fuck myself just now. I don't know how much help I'll be, but I'll be right behind you, Mina, if it comes to that."

Nora said, "Sure. If nothing else we can pump you up, Mina, the way we did at the wall."

I was going to say pretty much the same thing, but Ananta surprised me by speaking up first.

"I — If you let me, I will support you in any way I can," he said. "I know I have not earned your trust. And I … I think I cannot go up against the Preserver. Even if it turns out I am not who I think I am. But should any lesser power oppose you, I wish to fight by your side. I owe you at least that much. And I too wish to learn the truth, if indeed I have been deceived."

Mina glanced at us. Nora nodded at her, but I think Mina already understood we were giving her the lead in this situation. She turned to face Ananta.

"Sure," she said. "It's got to suck to be you right now. I wouldn't want to think my whole existence was a lie, either. And it could be, you know, for any of us. All we've got to go on is who we are, right? So let's go. We'll take it as it comes."

"Thank you," said Ananta, and we returned to the journey.

16

THE SUN WAS LOW OVER THE HORIZON when Ananta called a pause. We'd been traveling a little west of north by my estimation. "We approach the palace," he said.

"How can you tell?" asked Steiner.

"Follow."

We went with him as he climbed to the top of the nearest hill, pointed. In the distance, perhaps three miles away, a ridge line of slightly higher hills could be seen.

"The palace lies in the valley beyond those hills," said Ananta. He paused. "I am relieved to find them where I expected."

"Good job," said Mina.

Ananta bowed. "If you will heed my advice, I will lead us around to the west."

"To meet your friend," she said. "I forget his name."

"Varuna," said Ananta. "I would not say he is truly my friend. But — I am more in accord with him than with any of the other guardians."

"How many are there?"

"There should be four," said Ananta. "Yama guards the south way. He is narrow-minded and wrathful, a lover of slaughter and inflicting torments. Indra is to the east. A pompous arrogant buffoon, always recalling past glories. Impossible to speak to him. To the north, Kubera. A greedy coward, never willing to grant a favor."

"Quite an assortment," said Nora. "These are gods? Divine servants? They don't sound very appealing. How do you reconcile such unpleasant characters with the divinity of your Preserver?"

"I ... cannot," said Ananta. "And though I remember each of those three as I have said, also I recall them in other circumstances. Just and unswerving Yama, the pure-souled judge and chastiser of the sinful. Great Indra, master of the skies, matchless in his nobility, eyes flashing with lightning. And Kubera the munificent, the wise, the bountiful friend of humanity. All of them servants of dharma and of the Preserver."

"Huh," said Mina. "Well anyhow, we may as well go around to the west."

It took us another hour or so, going at a trot. At last, we stood on the approach to the ridge line, this time with the dying remains of the sunset at our backs.

"Okay," said Mina. "Here we go, right? No turning back now. But if — if something goes wrong ..."

"If something goes wrong," I said, "it went wrong because we were trying to discover the truth of this world, and to rescue the people we love. No regrets from me."

"For sure," said Nora. "There's no question in my mind. I love you guys, I do! But without Quaid — oh God, there wouldn't be any point."

Steiner reached out and put a hand on her shoulder. Nora said nothing, but she put her hand on his.

"There's no question for me either," he said after a moment. "Don't get me wrong. I want more than what we've been given so far. But I've had a couple of really sweet nights, Nora, one with you and one with Rhys. That's more than I ever thought I'd have in my life, back in our old world. I'm happy with what we've done so far, and with what we want to do. What we need to do. But if it had to end here, I couldn't complain. So I'm ready, is what I'm saying."

It was just a hundred yards up to the top of the ridge, which only deserved the name because it was a more or less uniform contour a little higher than the surrounding hills. We had to scramble to get up over the top of it.

All of us stopped to look. We saw below us a large circular valley several miles across, and most of the valley was taken up by a lake. A real lake too, full of water, not milk. Four narrow causeways in the cardinal directions crossed the lake, meeting at the center where indeed a palace could be seen. It was an enormous structure made of some sort of pink-gold stone, heavy and turreted and baroquely intricate in design. There were eight secondary wings, each a stepped angular form emerging from the central space of the palace, which was roofed by a large golden dome. On the exterior an elaborate portico enclosing a golden gate faced the western causeway, and from the symmetry of the layout it looked like there would be similar gates to north, east, and south. From two miles or so away we couldn't see any details clearly, but the setting and architecture was impressive, for sure. No sign of life could be seen down there, but that hardly meant anything from this distance.

"Behold," said Ananta. I think he took some proprietary pride in what we saw, and for that matter he was probably relieved that it was actually there. I'd had my doubts, myself, and after all this rather bland landscape it was something of a shock to see something so obviously the result of artifice.

"Where is Varuna?" asked Steiner.

"If he is present, he will doubtless emerge to challenge us when we reach the west gate."

We worked our way down the hillside towards the lake. As we approached the red stone causeway the lake took on the appearance of a reflecting pool; the water was absolutely still and the surface was a perfect mirror. Here and there enormous lotus pads and blossoms floated motionless on the water, the only plants apart from grass we'd seen thus far in all of Vaikuntha. Ananta took a tentative step out onto the causeway, paused, turned his face up to the heavens.

"Impressive," said Nora.

"It is lovely at night," said Ananta. "Stars above and below."

Steiner said, "It's quiet, though, don't you think?"

"Quiet?" My voice sounded small and flat in this wide-open space.

"If this was a real place, I mean, in the real world, there'd be life," he said.

"Yes," said Nora. "You're right. There would be frogs. Bugs. Birds. It might still be a serene and beautiful place. But it wouldn't be so still."

"Is it dead?" Mina asked. "Or only sleeping?"

"In the span between ages," said Ananta, turning to face us, "this is meant to be a place of repose."

"Sleeping, then," she said. "Well we're bringing a wake-up call." And she strode forward, past Ananta onto the causeway.

Watching Mina take that first step filled me with admiration. Whether it was the scale of this place, or its serenity, or something else, I'd almost forgotten our purpose in coming here. I'd been feeling humble and small, and maybe that's how I should have been feeling, too, but realizing that shamed me, deep down.

"Right," I said. "Let's go."

Our five minute walk down the causeway to the palace felt strange to me, like an interval cut out of time. The expanse of water to either side was weird, to be sure. The perfect undisturbed mirror surface of the pool seemed more like a video special effect than a real thing. Nearby, to either side, the pool reflected the sky, a cream-orange glow behind us in the west, shading to deep blue overhead, and a darker purple over the ridge line to the east. Ahead of us the palace itself reflected off the water, appearing like an inverted edifice beneath the surface. I was feeling pumped up too, my heart racing with excitement, and yet with nothing to do but walk onward. But beyond this I had the feeling we were taking an irrevocable step forward here, and whatever happened, I was sure there would be no turning back.

That feeling lasted as long as it took us to get to the palace. From close up the complexity of the architecture became more apparent. The portico we approached was around a hundred feet tall, with dozens of broad shallow steps rising to the enormous coke-bottle-shaped columns that supported the roof over the approach to the west gate. Every exposed wall and column was intricately carved with a fantastic complexity of intertwined figures: humans, animals, and all shades of in-between.

We stood facing the gate for a few moments. No one challenged us. The gate itself was gilt metal, possibly solid gold. Either way it must have weighed many tonnes, because it stood a good ten meters tall, with each side of the double-doors five meters across. An elaborate lotus was carved in relief to the door.

"What do we do, knock?" asked Steiner.

We all looked at Ananta, and he shrugged, which seemed a strangely normal and out of character gesture.

"I have never seen the gate closed before," he said.

Steiner stepped forward and put his hand on the door.

"Yeah," he said, "this isn't going to work." But he knocked hard anyway. There was no audible sound at all.

"Well, this is kind of insulting," said Nora.

"Maybe no one's home," I said.

Steiner snickered. "I've got an idea," he said. "Here, watch this."

He walked back down the stairs to where the causeway started across the lake, and we all followed him. He turned his back on us for a moment. When he turned back, he had something in his hand.

"This place is so pretty," he said. "So perfect. It's pissing me off, you know?"

He held the thing in his hand up for us to see. It was a hand grenade; or it looked like one anyway, the old pineapple type, with a ring pull and a handle safety.

"Jesus, Steiner," said Nora, "do you have any idea what you're doing?"

"Not really," said Steiner, and he pulled the pin.

I was wondering what he intended to do with it for a second. There was no way he was going to get through those doors with a grenade. But he surprised me by throwing it into the lake. It made a plopping sound and a beautiful series of concentric rings spread from the point of impact, disrupting the perfect mirror plane. I wondered how long the water had gone without a touch.

After a couple of seconds, I was convinced it wasn't even going to explode. But then came the detonation. A rather moderate boom and a spray of water that drenched all of us. For a few seconds the surface of the pool was pure chaos, and then it resolved into a spreading region of ripples. In a minute all the lake around us had lost its eerie mirror beauty; it just looked like water now.

"Well, that made me feel better anyway," said Steiner. Mina laughed. Nora glared at him for a moment, but then she too started to chuckle. It was infectious, so I joined in. All of us were surprised when Ananta approached Steiner and bowed very low to him.

"You — you chastise the very water in your anger? And then you mock it with your laughter? Truly you are bold."

"Sure," said Steiner. "Very brave. It's not like it fights back, though."

"Sir," said Ananta, "are you not aware that Varuna is the lord of water? And of all the water to which you might give an affront, you chose the sacred pools surrounding the Preserver's own palace, of which Varuna is the protector? I honor your audacity, and your courage."

"Ha," said Steiner. "As if any of that had even crossed my mind. But the fact is I'm too ignorant to know what you're talking about. And too angry to care. If only I'd had to use a toilet the whole time I was here, I'd be happy to piss in it too if that would help any."

Ananta shook his head. But there was a strange expression on his face. I didn't know how to interpret it at all.

"I guess we'd better get through that door," said Steiner. "Can't be any harder than the wall around the world, can it?"

He turned to walk up the stairs.

At this point the twilight had progressed to the point of that half-darkness in which everything looks clearer and sharper than ever it does during the day. The sky to the west was still a dusty rose while overhead it was deep dark blue, and to the east bands of darkness stretched upwards like shadowy fingers. It would still be the better part of an hour to full darkness. Or rather, that's how long it should have taken. But it grew much darker in just a few seconds. I looked up, and the sky had turned a deep, velvety black, with the stars shining piercingly bright, glimmering with coruscating rainbow auras, like tiny diamonds illuminated by an arc lamp.

"What the fuck?" Mina said it, but I'm pretty sure we all thought it.

"He comes," said Ananta, and pointed upward. "The eyes of Varuna."

The stars of the southern hemisphere weren't familiar to me at all; but it took no great astronomical lore to realize something strange was going on. One of the stars was moving. Slowly at first, but then faster and faster, bending a graceful path around the zenith. And then others followed. As we watched, the entire celestial sphere began to move, stars spiralling inwards like glittering lights circling a drain. After a minute all the stars in the sky had formed a long curving streak. And then I realized something else was happening. Some of the stars brightened, others dimmed, and though the whole was still in a spiraling motion, a structure was emerging. The stars were forming a shape, individual stars moving to outline a three-dimensional structure. A snake it was; no, a vast serpentine dragon, with the two brightest stars for its eyes, wings unfurling now to stretch across the dome of the heavens. The paranoid fear I'd felt walking under the stars the previous night, and Ananta's fear that we'd fought through in rescuing Steiner; both were pale shadows of the feeling I had now. This vast creature was heralded by fear and terror and dread and there was no escaping it. And yet at the same time it was beautiful, so lovely indeed that the star-dragon's celestial glory was greater even than the fear that surrounded it.

The gigantic thing flowed through the heavens. Its head turned, stars shifting places like gems adorning the dragon's skin. For a moment the huge creature paused, regarding us from an unimaginable distance. And then it dove towards us, mouth gaping open, starry fangs stretching across the sky as if to swallow us all.

"Holy shit," said Steiner, and the fear in his voice matched my own.

And Mina laughed. She wasn't afraid; she was delighted. The contrast with my own emotion was shocking. Though she didn't say the words, I knew she was thinking, *I was born for this!* And her joy lifted my spirits like a rocket, banishing the dragon's fear. Mina's eyes began to glow, and her nails; she extended her right arm, pointing at the descending dragon, and I could feel the power rising in her, and a sort of pull too, like a magnet calling on something in me as well ...

"Support her!" cried Nora, and she put a hand on Mina's left shoulder, and then she stepped forward, and put her other hand on Mina's hip.

Steiner hesitated a moment. He reached out, placing his palm against Mina's belly. She shifted her stance a little, and I could see her pushing back a little against the contact. Steiner had to brace himself to support her, and he wound up kneeling in front of her, both hands on her abdomen.

I stepped forward as well, and I rested my hand at the small of her back. I remembered what had happened to Sandeep. *He'd gone all out, used himself up,* I thought, *in striking down Ananta.* And more than anything else I was resolved that wouldn't happen to Mina, or if it did, it would happen to me too. I could feel the connection between us, feel the energy pulsing up from me and entering her body through the point of contact, rising up through her spine, a pillar of light within her body like the contained power of a sapphire laser rod, building, growing stronger ...

"Now!" she cried, and I could feel Mina releasing the energy, a great fountain bursting forth. A coruscating blue flare surrounded her outstretched hand, and a perfectly straight line of light, at once the deepest ultramarine imaginable and the brightest cyan, streaked straight up toward the descending dragon.

For a frozen moment all of us stood there, locked in a tableau, heads turned upward, watching the clash of energies. The dragon's celestial radiance contending against Mina's will, against her essence, against all of ours, taken together. And then: a blinding bright flash overhead, an immense soundless sound, like the world's largest flash bulb going off in the distance, and everything went dark.

I came back to myself caught up in a four-person twister-game of tangled limbs. Ananta was sitting nearby by himself, looking upward, his mouth open and his eyes wide. The four of us had all fallen together, and it took a few moments to get ourselves sorted out. I had the feeling it couldn't have been more than a couple of seconds, though, no more than that.

"Hey," said Steiner in a pained voice, "watch where you put your weight!"

"Sorry," said Nora. "But that was pretty orgasmic, I have to say."

I finally extricated myself from the others, looked up.

"Oh," I said.

"Oh," said Mina, who'd likewise pulled herself back from the others. She took a deep breath. "It's so pretty!"

All around us, stars were falling like incandescent dandelion seeds, drifting slowly downward in a cascade of glowing sparks, blue and green and purple and gold, the aftermath of the explosion of a cosmic firework. There was no sign of the dragon except inasmuch as these drifting motes might be the broken and scattered remains of its celestial body.

We sat there, watching in awed silence as the stars fell. After a while it became clear they were tiny things, each no bigger than a firefly, emitting glowing auras just a foot or so in diameter. Thousands of them fell all around us into the lake and, when they touched the water, they floated there suspended on the surface until the whole lake was transformed into a field of sparkling lights, all of them slowly fading, guttering out one by one.

Mina held out her hand, and a last trembling blue spark drifted downward to rest delicately on her open palm. And then she closed her fist and grinned, showing her teeth. She stood up.

"All right," said Mina. She called out, projecting her voice. "All right. Varuna. Show yourself. I know you're there."

Almost at once a light appeared in the water to the side of the causeway. A dim golden glow from deep down below, rising higher, expanding and growing brighter as it approached. As it neared the surface the light expanded into a sphere ten yards across, raising a bulging lens of water for a few seconds before the source of the light erupted through the surface in a wild spray of shining fluid.

The sphere vanished like a ruptured soap-bubble and there he was, larger-than-life, a huge silver-skinned man, bald with a large mustache, wearing golden armor. In one arm he held a noose, and in the other a trident. He was standing on a large lotus pad by the side of the causeway.

"Ananta Sesha. I thought better of you."

I think Mina was about to say something, but Ananta turned and gestured to her, that slight movement of the hand that means "back off", and she fell silent. He stepped forward to the edge of the causeway. Ananta might once have assumed the form of seven gigantic cobras each hundreds of meters long, but as a slight young man unarmed and dwarfed by Varuna he seemed entirely overshadowed.

"Lord Varuna," he said. But he didn't bow.

"Have you betrayed your master?"

Ananta blanched, but he answered strongly.

"My master? Not yet."

"What sort of answer is that? You have thrown in with these interlopers, have you not? They have struck down my star-steed."

"Lord Varuna, you are the protector and the ultimate ruler of the naga race," said Ananta, and after a brief pause: "Or so it is said."

Varuna said nothing, but at that last remark he frowned.

"But you are not *my* master," said Ananta. "You know I serve a higher power."

"Do you? I wonder."

"I admit," said Ananta, "I have some questions regarding my terms of service."

"Blasphemy? Or treason?"

"That is yet to be seen," said Ananta. "I hope neither. But however it may fall out, we require entrance. It is your function to open the gate."

"Say, rather, to guard and protect it."

Ananta sighed. "Varuna, I know you have no regard for the prowess of mortals. But if you rouse their anger my companions will surely destroy you. Have you forgotten what Prince Rama did to you in days gone by when you failed to heed his request for passage?"

Varuna growled, and he gestured angrily with his trident. "Rama was an avatar of the One we serve. And he wielded the Brahmastra, the ultimate weapon. Else I never should have been overcome, even by him."

"Yes, Lord Varuna," said the naga. "And yet you knew neither of those things at the time."

"What are you saying?"

"Merely that having expended all your power in a futile attack from the stars, it behooves you to let us pass."

"Hmm. Hm-Hmm." Varuna paced back and forth, glowering down at Ananta. He thrust his lower lip forward and puffed out his mustache. At last he shook his head.

"I am a lord of dharma," he said. "The natural order is my mantle and my shield. I will not give over my charge to play host to a group of usurping mortals, nor even to the Preserver's own body-servant, if he turns traitor."

Ananta said, "I regret your decision, Lord Varuna. Out of respect for our past friendship, I offer you a final chance to recede from your position."

"Never!" cried Varuna. "Even if I am slain, I shall hew to my honor and my duty. In the next world I shall be reborn and restored to my position as a reward for my service! But you, false friend and betrayer ... I shall have your heart here and now, and if you are reborn, it shall be as a worm!"

Varuna pulled his arm back, and the barbed points on his trident began to glow with a bloody red light. Ananta simply stood there, however, and made no move except to bow his head.

"No," said Mina quietly. Her eyes flashed blue, once, and Varuna's glowing trident guttered out. Varuna himself remained frozen in position for a thrust. His eyes bulged, and he trembled in place, but it seemed he was unable to move.

Mina stepped forward, moving up to Ananta's side. The naga was looking up at Varuna, apparently not quite comprehending what was happening. "Thank you," she said to Ananta. "You spoke well to him. That was pretty cool."

Ananta goggled at her for a moment, stammered, seemed to be unable to speak.

She kissed him lightly on the lips. "I'll take it from here, kay?" And then she whispered something in his ear.

The naga blushed, purple rising in his cheeks. The tracework pattern of scales stood out on his chest and arms, and he stammered again. He turned back to the rest of us and saw us all smiling at him, and I think that staggered him too. He took a couple of steps toward us and stumbled, might have fallen except Steiner and I both moved to prop him up. And holding him up like that, my arm around his shoulders, I had the strangest feeling, like he was my younger brother, a kid who had just done something to make me proud of him.

"Nice work," said Nora, "that was great, what you just did."

"I can't believe I said all that," said Ananta. "I'm amazed. I should have been struck down."

"No way," said Steiner. "You're our friend. Mina wouldn't let it happen."

"But I was your enemy."

Steiner slapped him on the back. "Not anymore."

Mina strode up to Varuna, who was still helplessly paralyzed.

"Right," she said, "enough is enough, okay?"

Varuna said nothing.

"You can talk," said Mina. "Do you really want to die?"

Nothing.

She shook her head. "Our friends have been taken away from us. All we're trying to do is get them back. We're not here to fight with you or with anyone else. You're the one who thought that was a good idea, and you're still alive only because it was so damn easy to beat you."

Varuna tried to turn his head away, but Mina grabbed his chin.

"I won't leave an enemy alive behind me," she said. "I hear you are a protector of this place. Well if that's what it takes I promise you I will annihilate it utterly. I swear to you on my honor if I get no satisfaction here, I will destroy this world and everyone, god or mortal, who stands in my way. And if you don't yield to me right now, I'm going to kill you, and believe me it will be your fault, dharma will not save you, your master will not save you, and you will *not* be reborn again. This will be the true death, the final death. I will annihilate you utterly."

"I — I —"

Mina drew her own arm back, and once again her nails began to glow.

"I yield!"

Behind us we heard a grinding noise, and we looked to see the great golden doors opening.

We left Varuna there, his head bowed, kneeling on the causeway, fingering the noose he'd carried in one hand. He'd dropped the trident into the lake when Mina freed him from his paralysis.

As we filed through the open doors, Steiner whispered to Mina, loud enough for us all to hear, "Holy shit, that was powerful, what you said to him. Did you mean it?"

She paused, and we waited for her to answer.

"I felt it that way," she said, "and the first part, about destroying this place, I know I meant it. I still mean it. And I almost wanted Varuna to say one more stupid pompous thing, so I could kill him. It would be like, I don't know, like I was proving myself somehow. But even when I was saying it, I was remembering what the Professor said a while back. About doing the right thing. And I couldn't help wondering if Varuna was just maybe another poor fool planted in this place with false memories or something. So yeah, I don't think I would have unless he forced me to somehow."

"Ah," said Steiner. "I get you. But I wanted to say how cool that was. What Ananta said to him, and then what you did. I don't know if I could ever come up with something like that on my own, but it made me feel really good, hearing you say it. And when he backed down, man, I just wanted to cheer."

"Thanks," said Mina, "that means a lot to me. But you know it's all down to you guys, right? That's how I could do all that stuff, blast the dragon, paralyze Varuna like it was nothing. It was all down to you."

"Huh?"

"You all charged me up. I still feel it, like there's a reactor in my belly, where you had your hands, Steiner."

"Oh, ah," he blushed, stammered, "I hope that was all right. Not like it was creepy at all, or anything."

"Come on, Steiner," she said, "if we survive another day or two, I'm going to take you to bed. You can count on it. And when we do, those fireworks from blowing up Varuna's dragon aren't even going to be in the running."

"Oh jeez," he said weakly. But then he recovered, smiled at her. "Yeah, Mina, I'm looking forward to it."

"You'd better," she said. "Anyway, let's finish this up, okay? I like cartoons and computer games, so I know how the dialog is supposed to go, but these boss fights are getting kind of old."

17

W E PASSED ON INTO THE PALACE. The first chamber we entered was enormously impressive but at the same time desolate and barren. The walls were paneled with plates of stuff that looked like gemstone. Maybe that rich deep blue was the lapis lazuli I'd read about and never seen in real life; but other panels were lustrous pink, a delicate pale green, brilliant yellow, and a shiny iridescent black that looked oily but was smooth and dry to the touch, like polished glass. Each panel featured incised script inlaid in complementary colors of precious metal: gold, silver, and some kind of bluish metal. I supposed the elegant curving characters connected through horizontal bars at the top must be Sanskrit. Enormous marble columns every twenty feet or so were minutely and elaborately carved with figures in relief, like those on the outer walls but even more detailed and delicate. The ceilings were vaulted, painted over with frescoes showing mythological or devotional scenes featuring Hindu gods I couldn't identify. Fantastic gold and silver chandeliers bearing brilliant oil lamps illuminated every room. A luxurious carpet of midnight purple lay in a stripe down the center of the polished pink marble floor, with complex paisley patterns woven into the warp in golden thread.

And yet, gorgeous as it all was, there was no sign of life in the halls, no furniture, and I had the feeling the five of us were the first people ever to walk on the soft fabric of the carpet.

"You know what this is?" asked Nora. "It's like one of those fake Disneyland buildings, that you think from the outside might be a real place, but it's just a sort of false front and false interior too, someplace for tourists to take pictures of. Sure it's pretty, but no one will ever be reigning in this palace. There won't be courtiers gathered in these halls, and if there's a dining room anywhere in this place, which I doubt, no one is ever going to eat there. No prince and princess will be dancing in the ballroom and no pages or maids will ever make love in the garden. It's not even a proper temple, not without any priests. It's just a sort of phony Hollywood idea of one."

We walked through hall after hall, each one grander and more ornate than the last, and all of them just as barren and deserted. We ignored cross-passages, abutting wings, vestibules and side doors. Heading straight for the center. And after a time — a long time, it felt like hours — we got there.

It was a vast octagonal room with a central dome held up by a dozen twisted columns of gold, with an open skylight at the top like that of the Roman Pantheon. Eight halls radiated from the center, including the one we'd entered from. A shallow reflecting pool took up most of the space in the room, forming a layout like the lake and palace in miniature. Four walkways crossed the pool to the center. Around the edges of the pool, eight large objects were placed in a symmetric ring. Each looked like a folded-up lotus bulb, grading from buttery yellow at the top through pristine alabaster white to a luscious pink at the base. And at the center, where the four walkways met ... an enormous circular bed, crafted in the form of a gigantic lotus blossom. No; as we approached it became clear: it really was a lotus blossom, flowering open, growing from an equally enormous pad in the center of the pool. From the ceiling above the lotus drapes of sheer gold netting fell to the floor on all sides.

We filed down the walkway, and Mina pulled the netting aside.

"Ah ..." her voice trailed off.

Revealed were two figures, a man and a woman, both nude, reposing supine on the bed of the lotus flower. The man was blue-skinned and the woman's skin was a pink-gold hue. Both had four arms. Although their other hands were by their sides, one of their hands was clasped lightly in the other's grip as they slept side by side.

The beauty of the two was awe-inspiring. They had a supernal, exquisite impact I could never have imagined the human form — or something reasonably close to it — could possibly have. I wanted only to stand there, drinking them in with my eyes.

Behind me Ananta took a breath. "I cannot believe it," he said. "They are here. And in their higher forms. Oh!" He sank to his knees,

"Om Namo Narayana," he chanted slowly, eyes closed. And after a pause, he repeated it, then repeated it again; it seemed he had no intention of ever ceasing. The sound of it was strangely soothing. I felt a sublime calmness coming over me as I listened to him, as I gazed at the two beautiful sleepers. And I felt myself relaxing, letting something go ... it was the need to act, the petty goals and desires I had brought with me to this place. There was no need for them anymore, now that we had won through to the immanent presence of divinity.

And so I felt no surprise, no alarm when my body began to move of its own accord. I walked back down the path away from the lotus bed and the two sleepers, to one of the four giant lotus buds that had opened silently while we were standing there admiring the two sleepers. I saw that my companions likewise were walking away from the lotus bed, each towards their own opened bud, except for Ananta, who was still on his knees, still chanting. My feet took me to the northwest bud, and Steiner, Nora, and Mina each walked to their own position around the circle. Neither was I surprised when I found myself ducking my head to crawl into the opened blossom. I sat down on the soft fragrant tissue of the opened bud and the leaves closed around me, and the warmth and the darkness were reassuring. I sat there inside the lotus bud, cross-legged.

After some time in this state, it wouldn't be right to say that I was bored, or anxious or truly interested in anything outside; not really. But I couldn't hear Ananta chanting anymore, and so it occurred to me to wonder what had happened to him. It was the faintest velleity, the merest wisp of will that sparked my curiosity, but nevertheless I found that I could see through the opaque flesh of the lotus bud as if it wasn't there at all. The scene in the central palace chamber was much as we had left it, the eight lotus buds like huge pods surrounding the central flower in which, presumably, the Preserver and his Consort still lay sleeping. Ananta was nowhere to be seen, however.

Having established this seemingly magical point of view, it was an even more trivial exercise of will to move it around, like the invisible camera in a video game that you can fly through the air with the press of a button. The effort required to do this was so negligible that it was a form of idle play to rush through the palace corridors. I could zoom in to examine the finest detail on one of the figures carved into a pillar, or zip through the halls so rapidly that everything turned into a blur. After some time, I moved my camera-eye outside the palace. I came out on the south side, and no one was there at all, so I moved around to the west, skimming the water until I moved my viewpoint up onto the western causeway. And there I saw Varuna, or rather his body. He had fitted his noose around his throat and tightened it to the point of asphyxiation. Varuna died sitting in the yoga lotus position, which seemed fitting.

The north side of the palace was as barren of interest as the south, and already I was so bored with this toy that I almost returned to meditation in my lotus bud; but for completeness I zipped around to the eastern approach as well. And there I must admit I did feel some mild surprise at what I saw.

Golden-skinned Lord Indra was there, an ornate rod or mace that I supposed must be a weapon on the ground at his side and a golden goblet clutched in his hand. He was sitting slumped against a pillar next to the eastern causeway. At first, I thought he must be dead, but when I zoomed my point of view towards him, I saw Indra was only sleeping, his mouth hanging open, his big pock-marked nose bobbing gently with his breaths.

And then I saw my four missing companions passing the gate and entering the palace. They were accompanied by Ananta. Michèle was there, joking with Rhys about something, while the Professor paused to study one of the engraved gemstone panels. Quaid looked over his shoulder, right at my viewpoint I thought, but then I realized he was looking at Indra. Perhaps he was concerned that Indra might awaken while they were still present. It didn't occur to me how strange this was, to see them all here, free and at large, nor did Ananta's presence signify anything to me either. But the group did hold my attention, so I followed them into the palace, and as I moved my viewpoint closer, I heard them talking.

"That was easy," said Michèle.

"Yeah," said Rhys. "Good thing we had Ananta with us. That was a good idea, that soma drink you came up with."

Ananta nodded gravely. "Thank you," he said. "It wouldn't have worked on the other lokapalas, but Indra in his lower form really is something of an imbecile."

"Let's get a move on, okay?" Quaid was anxious, more on edge than I'd ever seen him before. "Every minute we waste …" he trailed off.

The Professor looked up from the panel she was studying. "Oh," she said. "Yes. We must hurry. If they're there, if they're waiting for us —"

"They're hurting," said Rhys. "Yeah, I know. And I have the feeling someone there is going to be able to answer our questions, too. Hopefully not another pompous dipshit like this Indra guy."

The five of them hurried inward, deeper into the palace. For a minute I wondered idly who "they" was, but the question wasn't important to me, so I merely continued to watch them. It was only a few minutes before they emerged into the central lotus bedchamber.

At first, they just stood there a moment goggling at the view, and then they filed along the east-side walkway to get to the lotus-bed. Rhys thrust aside the netting.

Ananta reacted just as before. "I cannot believe it," he said. "They are here. And in their higher forms. Oh!" He sank to his knees.

"Om Namo Narayana," he chanted, "Om Namo Narayana."

The other four staggered. Each of them took a step back from the bed. And around me I saw the four giant lotus buds at the cardinal points begin to open, slowly and gracefully.

For some reason I felt a little sad then, seeing the four of them start to file toward their respective buds. But then Michèle paused, staggered.

"Hey," she said, "wait."

The other three ignored her.

"This isn't right," she said, a little uncertainly. "Rhys? Quaid? Ha-Harriet?"

The other three began to enter their respective buds.

"Wait!" she cried. "What are you doing?"

Michèle tried to grab Rhys, to hold him back, but he was too strong for her, though he wasn't really fighting against her so much as just striding forward. Breaking free of her grip, his elbow caught her in the side of the head, and she rocked back a step, and then fell to the ground.

She looked up then, saw the other three buds slowly closing and gave a sort of choked off sob. Then she got to her feet.

"C'est des conneries," she muttered. She took a deep breath, looked around the room. "Fuck," she said, "Eight of them. Well, then."

She strode back down the walkway to the end, at the lotus-bed, where Ananta was still chanting.

"First," she said, "would you just shut up already?"

Ananta ignored her, so she bent over, put her hands under his arms and hauled him to his feet.

"Tais-toi!" she shouted in his face.

"What?"

"Shut up! What do you think you're doing, idiot?"

Ananta was taken aback. "I — I am —"

"Our friends are in these — these pods! While you sit there like a fool chanting!"

"I — This is the Lord Narayama. The Preserver's higher form. And his consort, Lakshmi. The great goddess. They are supreme —"

"Supreme? Supreme? Supreme shit! Haven't you figured it out yet? Pauvre con! You've been even more screwed around with than the rest of us!"

She pushed him, and Ananta staggered back, surprised.

"Don't worship the one who fucks you over," she said. Ananta just stood there blinking, his mouth an O of shock and dismay.

"Ah, ah, to hell with you too," she said. She looked around the room. "Ha, yes," she said. "Right there."

Michèle reached behind the still-open petals of the lotus bud on the north side of the room, the one that was meant for her, and she pulled out a machete. She ran to the northwest bud and hacked at it, but the fibrous material of the bud was tougher than she expected, and the machete rebounded in her grip.

Michèle screamed then, a cry of rage and frustration, and chopped again at the pod. The blade barely bit, but she swung again and again, without making much progress. After a time, she fell back, panting heavily.

"Shit," she said, "I'm an idiot too."

She paused, closed her eyes briefly, and the machete began to glow, a bright blue sheen coming off it.

"Ha," said Michèle. "I may not be Mina, but —"

She swung the machete again with all her strength, and it sliced through the giant lotus bud with no resistance at all. I saw the glowing blade pass within inches of my face, using my eyes, my real eyes, not this faked up mobile viewpoint. Her next few swings were more controlled, and she quickly made enough cuts to make it easy to tear the whole top of the thing away, which left me there sitting within it, my head poking out of the torn section of bud. There was a jarring moment of double vision, and the ghostly remote perception went away.

"Jay," she said. "Jay! Mon dieu! It's you!"

She made a few vertical cuts through the remaining husk of the bud, but I didn't respond, didn't say anything, didn't help to free myself. I didn't feel any need to. And then she looked at me and I could see her joy turn to horror, but it didn't register at all for me as anything significant. And then she reached out her hand and touched my cheek. And it all came rushing back. What I was and who. Will and desire. And regret.

"Michèle," I said, "Michèle." I couldn't think of anything more I could say.

"You stupid!" she said, "Putain de merde! How could you let this happen?"

I pushed open the flap of bud she'd cut free and clambered out. I was in a hurry because I needed to hug her. I was crying now, rage and dismay and the horror of having everything I was taken away from me like that mixed with the knowledge I had hurt her. I felt like I couldn't stand it. But then she wrapped her arms around me in a fierce embrace, and I knew what had happened didn't matter. It didn't matter at all. Neither of us spoke for a minute, but I think we communicated everything we really needed to make things right without words.

As last I said, "I thought I was supposed to be rescuing you. Michèle. But somehow everything got turned around."

"Okay," she said, "okay. Someone or something has been fucking with us. Maybe that bastard in the bed over there, I don't know. We lost our memories before. When they took you guys away from us. And then — Shit. Let's cut open the others. We can talk later."

I produced a machete of my own, imbued it with the idea it would cut through anything, and tacked on a blue glow just for the hell of it. We spent another ten minutes cutting open the other lotus buds. The others were all in the same state I had been in, so passive they might as well not even have been alive, but it only took a touch to restore them, just like me. Three more pairs of lovers' reunions followed; three more confused exchanges. I got the idea that a strange symmetry had been applied to us somehow; each group of four of us supposed it was the others who'd been vanished. And both of us had been accompanied by Ananta the whole way. Each of our groups had been afflicted with removed and false memories, and each of us had eventually realized the deception.

During this time, Ananta sat by himself on the floor, his head in his hands.

At last Michèle crouched in front of him. She put her hand on his shoulder, and he flinched away, but then he looked up at her.

"Listen," she said, "you didn't mean to screw us, did you?"

"I swear it," he said, "I swear on my name, on whatever I am, whoever I really am, I don't know — I did not know. I didn't mean to lead you into a trap. But I remember it now. I remember being two. I took you four from the north side of the island. That was where I thought we had come from, where I had first found you. I took you south from the north side of the island, and then when I told you about the lokapalas, we agreed I should try taking you to the east gate, to Indra, because he might be the easiest to deceive. And at the same time —"

"You're saying you were with us too at the same time?" Steiner asked.

"Yes. I know it makes no sense. But I led you, from the south, and to the west gate, to Varuna, because I thought I remembered we had been friends. Though now I don't —"

He shook his head, hit the ground with his fist. "I know I betrayed you," he said. "A second time. You must hate me."

"Come on," said Michèle. "We've all been fucked with here. You as much as anyone. We know you didn't mean to hurt us."

"But I brought you here. To His presence. And I — I couldn't — I was just overwhelmed. In their lower forms I would entertain them, you know. The two of them, Lord Vishnu and Lakshmi, they would make love on my back. I would carry them through the ocean of milk like I was a boat, and I would shield them from the sun with my hoods! That's what I remembered. Maybe it even happened! I don't know — I don't know!"

Mina joined Michèle and Ananta.

"I remember how you stood up to Varuna," she said. "And the Professor told me you came up with a way to get them past Indra, too."

"Yes," he said miserably. "But you wound up here. Perhaps it was all part of a plan."

"Did you bring us here thinking you'd be betraying us?"

"N-no."

"That's all I care about," said Mina. "You're not responsible for having your brains scrambled any more than we are. So cheer up, okay? Now we've gotta decide what we're going to do about those two." And she gestured at the lotus bed in the center of the chamber.

"We must confront them," said the Professor.

We all looked at her standing there among us, a slender naked teenager with white hair and a girlish voice. But there was something in her tone, her calmness perhaps, that commanded attention.

"They may just be sleeping dolls," she continued. "And even if they're real people, they might be more poor creatures who've had their minds altered, who really believe they are gods. But they are here, at the center of this place, and just looking at them was enough to turn us into mindless idiots. So I don't think there's any question of us having to find out for sure."

"Yeah," said Rhys, "there's no point in leaving without facing them first. But what if it happens again?"

"We'll be prepared," said Nora, and Quaid said, "We know it's possible now. Maybe we can fight it."

Of all our little reunions, I think I was happiest to see Nora and Quaid's. Their embrace had a sort of symmetry to it that was beautiful in itself, and I could see them both relaxing from moment to moment, the wound that the other's loss had left healing visibly on their faces, in the lines of their backs, the motion of their bodies.

"Hey," said Steiner, "how did you not get sucked in too, Michèle?"

"I'm not sure," she said, "but maybe it was something I did. The night after we got split up, the Professor figured out something was wrong with our memories. And I was the last to remember, you know? When Jay came back into my mind, I was so pissed off. I remember thinking, this is so wrong, this can't happen again. I can't let it happen. And so I think, maybe, I used the power, you know? Maybe I changed myself, or gave myself a defense or something? Because I was so pissed off."

"Good enough for me," he said. "I don't want anyone else screwing around with my head either, but I was too stupid to come up with that idea. I'll try it."

We all tried it, for what it was worth. For my own part I imagined a sort of invisible net surrounding my head that I decided would be able to intercept any external influence or change. I concentrated on it, tried to pump energy into it. No idea whether it worked, or whether anyone else had any success either, though. At least no one's head exploded.

"Okay," said Rhys. "Are we ready? To wake them up?"

"One minute," said Mina. "I want to ask Ananta about something. Just in case."

"Just in case?"

"Yeah. I like the way you came up with a way to get past — Whats-his-name? Indra? — Better than the way we got past Varuna. We had to fight him. But just in case."

She whispered a question in Ananta's ear and they moved apart and began talking quietly. I was curious of course, but I figured she had her reasons for keeping whatever it was private.

"All right," she said, after a minute. "I'm ready."

We returned to the lotus-bed again, stood outside the canopy of gold netting.

"I'll do it," said Rhys. "Maybe you guys should stand back or something?"

"Not me," said Michèle. "I want to be right there."

None of us retreated so Rhys shrugged. "Here we go," he said, and he drew back the netting once more.

There was no immediate response from within, so once more we approached the bed. Looking at the two sleepers, once more I was impressed by their beauty, but this time it was less of a hammer-blow between the eyes. And whatever effect it was that had taken away my will last time, it didn't seem to be operating now. Whether that was due to imaginary psychic shielding or something else there was no way to tell.

Mina was on the woman's side of the lotus bed, and Rhys was on the man's, and the rest of us stood in an arc around the bed. It was a weird situation. If they were ordinary people, it would have to be a bit of a shock to wake up to a crowd of strangers expecting something from you.

Rhys reached out, put his hand lightly on one of the sleeping man's two left-side shoulders. There was no response.

"Huh," he said. "Now what?"

"Let me try," said Mina.

She put her hand on one of the sleeping woman's right shoulders. She didn't even stir. But then Mina's eyes flashed blue, and the woman's eyes opened. She started, seeing all of us standing around her, and she gave a little shriek. Then she jerked her knees up to her chest and wrapped her arms around herself, pulling one of her hands out of the man's grasp to do so.

"Oh! What is this?" The woman's voice was shocked, horrified even. She didn't sound like a goddess, anyway.

"We mean you no harm," said Mina.

"What? But — my arms!"

The woman flailed for a moment, and one of her elbows caught the sleeping man in the side, but he didn't even flinch. After a moment, she brought all four of her hands forward in front of her, holding them up.

"I have four arms!"

Rhys said, "Maybe we'd better talk to her without all looming over her like this. Let's get out of here. Mina, can you talk to the lady? When she's ready, lead her over to us, okay?"

And once more, we filed out from the lotus bed along the walkway to the outer area of the central chamber. A minute later, the woman and Mina joined us, Mina leading the woman by the hand — by one of her hands.

"This is Joy," said Mina. "She's from our world, and she's a little confused."

"Joy Nielsen," said the woman. "And it's a lot more than a little."

We introduced ourselves in turn, and Joy shook each of our hands. When she got to me Joy said, "Wait. Don't I know you, young man? Haven't we met?"

And the way she said "young man" made me think. It sounded familiar. And it wasn't the sort of thing someone who looked like her would likely say. Then it hit me.

"Oh! You're the — the lady I met on the street. Coming back from the supermarket!" I had to stammer not to say "old" before "lady".

"I remember!" She laughed, a full-voiced note, full of pleasure. "I remember now! Yes! Did you ever get your groceries?"

"No," I said, "I went to McDonald's instead."

"Well," she said. "I suppose it doesn't matter now. But would you please tell me what's going on? Did we die? Is this some kind of crazy afterlife? Who was that in the bed? What happened to my body? And —"

She cut herself off. "I guess I should shut up and listen, huh?"

We started with an eager babble that only abated when Rhys told us all to shut up, and then we went through our explanations a little more calmly. I think what it was at first, we knew so little about what was really going on we wanted to try to explain it to ourselves, too. Anyway, after a half an hour or so we ran down.

"So anyway," said Rhys, "here we are."

"So why didn't I have a false memory, too?" asked Joy. "If I'm supposed to be this goddess, Lakshmi? Shouldn't I think I'm her?"

"Uh well," said Mina, "I think that's down to me. See, we haven't done so well talking to people who think they're gods or whatever." She nodded at Ananta. "Though Ananta here is our friend, now. But anyway, I was thinking, maybe she's going to be all crazy like Varuna was. And then I thought, 'Well, when we had our own memories messed with, it was easy enough to fix them.' So when I woke you up, I tried to use the power that we've been given to give you your memory back. And maybe it worked."

"Ah," said Joy. "Well, thank you, dear. And thank you all for being so kind and telling me all this. I must say it sounds horrible and sad, but … well, kind of wonderful too. All those people, gone, everyone I used to know, all my children, all my grandchildren … but maybe they're not gone after all. I don't feel like they're gone, anyway. And well, the four arms *are* a bit odd, but it's nice to be, oh, sixty-five years younger all of a sudden."

The Professor laughed. "Only forty-five years for me, but I know how you feel. Still, this must be an enormous shock, coming all at once. It was hard enough for us, and we had a few days to work it all out."

"Well, what can you do," said Joy. "I've never been one for carrying on when there's no alternative. And I'm too young and healthy now to keel over. But what about that man in the — the flower with me? Shouldn't we wake him up too?"

"Yes," said Rhys. "We'll do that next. But listen, Joy. We don't have anywhere for you to go. What we've been doing is not exactly safe. Going up against gods, or against people who think they're gods, anyway. There's no telling what will happen to us if we keep pushing up against things like this."

Joy smiled. "You're very kind, but don't worry about me. I went to bed one night and woke up just sort of floating someplace, and then I went back to sleep and woke up here with four arms, in a flower with a strange man. I was eighty-eight years old, you know, and all alone and I wasn't expecting there to be an afterlife at all, to be honest. So whatever I get here is like a bonus, isn't it? I guess I'm still kind of shaky on what's going on, but one thing I do know is you're all doing your best. I'm with you, my dears."

18

So yet again we filed back to the Preserver's bedstead, the ten of us standing in a circle around the open lotus flower.

"What you did for Joy worked out pretty well," said Rhys. "So Mina, if you would do the honors …"

"Sure," said Mina, and she reached out her hand to the sleeping man. She reached out her hand —

— and my eyes were drawn to the man's navel …

— there was a lotus flower there in his beautiful belly, growing, unfolding its petals …

— and I felt myself falling …

— Michèle screamed and I reached out to her …

— and we all were somewhere else entirely.

The whole world was an open lotus blossom, shading pink to cream to white, seemingly miles across, countless petals overlapping, extending to the horizon. Above us a golden sky swirled with light, streamers of radiance spiraling overhead. The floral aroma was delicate and overwhelming at the same time. All ten of us were arrayed in a scattered circle of bodies around the center of the enormous lotus, and there we saw him, a hundred yards tall, the glistening blue-skinned form of the god. When he'd been reclining before us on the bed in the palace I'd thought of him as a man, but now there was no question in my mind he was a god. In one hand the Preserver held a lotus blossom on a scale appropriate to his size, ten meters across, and in the others he held a giant conch, an ornate mace or scepter, and a sort of bladed disk with a hole in the center that he twirled idly around one upraised finger like a weapon-grade hula-hoop.

The god smiled. It was a blissful serene smile, and all around us, in a ring at the edges of the vast blossom on which we lay, thousands of ethereal human forms appeared. Thousands of adoring worshippers, alternating blue and gold skin, male and female, kneeling, genuflecting, raising their arms in perfect unison and singing in chorus.

Om Namo Narayanaya, the chant arose. Om Namo Narayanaya …

The impact was awesome, overwhelming. I couldn't take it all in at once. I felt my insignificance here, like I was something entirely negligible, a grain of sand caught up in a tornado, or a mouse balanced precariously on the precipice of a volcano. In the distance, as it were (really it was probably only a dozen yards), I heard Michèle cry out again, and that brought me back to earth a little.

I struggled to my feet. The spongy petalled surface of the world-flower made running hard, but I scrambled over to Michèle, who was likewise trying to rise and having difficulties in this crazy place.

"Are you all right?" I helped her get to her feet.

"Yes! But this — this is so cool, isn't it? Psychedelic!"

I was taken aback for a moment, because she seemed so delighted and amused. But then it hit me, the combined impact of the cosmic beauty and outrageous absurdity of the situation. I laughed. I couldn't help it. It was just so ridiculous and terrifying at the same time; there was nothing else I could do. And after a minute I was still laughing. A little hysterically, maybe, but now Michèle was laughing with me, laughing cheerfully, too.

The others had recovered too by now, and maybe it really was a funny situation, or maybe it was just Michèle and my own inappropriate hilarity that triggered it, but Mina pointed up and started laughing too. I followed her gaze. The god was wearing a sort of golden kilt now, but from our vantage far below, there was no mistaking his enormous blue penis dangling up there, reminding me a little of Ananta as a giant cobra. And the thing was it was a beautiful penis too, like everything else about the god was beautiful, awesome, and divinely inspiring; but it was funny too, and there was no way to avoid that.

So we were all standing now, laughing at the supreme deity and his supreme genitals bobbing gently high above our heads. Ten of us, Ananta too, and Joy as well, gathered together in a group now, laughing; and laughing with a sort of purpose. There was a power there in our laughter, a sort of buoyancy that brought confidence, and it banished the awe we felt, until after a minute or so we were just ten people, standing around an eleventh. The god was much larger, to be sure, and the setting was visually impressive, but I didn't feel like I was an ant perched on the edge of a volcano anymore; somehow the psychic, emotional, and even the moral tables had been turned. All around us the chanting still rose up, Om Namo Narayanaya, but now it was a mere distraction, no longer words of power but simply repetitive and meaningless sounds.

The Preserver frowned and he slowly and gracefully gestured with the hand holding the lotus flower. Holding the stem between giant thumb and forefinger, he lowered the blossom until it was facing us all. The lotus flower had been at a sort of half-bloomed stage like a partially unfolded bulb; but now its petals opened completely. And there above our heads, upside-down in the opened blossom, we saw a tall blue form standing, and around him we saw ten tiny figures gathered in a group. And the god above our head was at the same time the god in the flower. And we were at the same time standing together in a group at the god's feet on the world-flower, and we were also up there in the smaller blossom opening above our own heads, and there we looked up at a smaller version of the god, holding a smaller version of the flower, and in the flower another god, and around the god, there we were again, looking up at another flower ...

So yeah, it's hard to laugh when you've suddenly grown a million pairs of eyes and you're stuck in a hall of mirrors, and all you can see is more eyes. I guess that's not really how it was, but that's how it felt. I was dizzy, floating, lost, adrift somewhere and I had trouble focusing on anything. Except, I guess, the figure of the god himself. From wherever I was, from whatever viewpoint I had, I could see him pretty clearly. The chant was still rising up around us: Om Namo Narayanaya ... Om Namo Narayanaya ... and now it seemed to me it was easier not to fight it. All I had to do was look at that glorious blue-skinned form and listen to the chanting to avoid that terrible vertigo.

"Well fuck this shit," said Mina's voice from nearby. "Ananta. Deal with this stupid flower. would you?"

"Yes, my lady," came the naga's voice. "But how?"

"Your poison," said Mina. "That hala-whatever-it-was stuff."

"As you command," he said.

A few moments later I heard a whuff from nearby, and I had the impression of something large looming overhead. Then a whooshing noise came. All this time I was still focused on the image of the Preserver floating before my eyes. But after a minute the chanting suddenly stopped, and it seemed a spell was broken, and once more I felt free to look around. We were still there, gathered at the Preserver's feet. Ananta had resumed his gigantic serpentine form, seven enormous cobra heads and necks connected to a vast elongated body that seemed to go on forever. He breathed a roiling cloud of blue-purple mist, and where it touched the lotus, the petals withered. As I watched, the necrosis of the flower tissue spread beyond the extent of his poison at a rapid pace, racing outward towards the perimeter of the lotus. After a few seconds, huge acre-sized petals began to fall away around the perimeter, taking hundreds of the ethereal chanters with them.

"Ha," said Rhys, "look at that." He pointed upward.

The Preserver's lotus, the one he was holding in one of his four hands, was decaying along with ours, and petals were falling from it, creating a rotten shower of drifting withered flakes a yard across, but so light they were being wafted about by the gentle breeze. A sour smell of decay rose up all around us, replacing the heady floral scent. Then I noticed that the inner area of healthy flower tissue was beginning to erode as well.

"Ananta," I said, "can you stop your poison? We're running out of space here."

"What? Oh! No, it's happening on its own," he said, in a seven-fold chorus from all his heads at once. "I can't stop it."

The rot must have penetrated below the surface to the stem, because all at once I saw the entire remainder of the lotus in the Preserver's hands fall to pieces, the heart of the lotus withering and tumbling from the stem. And at the same time, the fleshy flower surface on which we'd been standing tipped over and fell away beneath our feet. And beneath the Preserver's feet as well.

The fall seemed to last forever, a dizzying descent through a psychedelically colored void. I hit the ground hard, but the impact just knocked the wind out of me. The ground? Yes, the grassy lawn of Vaikuntha, the sward near the lake surrounding the Preserver's palace. I looked around, saw the rest of us (Ananta had resumed his human form at some point) sprawled out nearby. The beautiful blue-skinned god stood on a hill, shrunk now to a mere eight feet in height. He had replaced his lost lotus with a sword with a long golden blade, and instead of a conch he now bore a long-hafted battle-axe. Together with his scepter-mace and the jagged-edged disk still twirling on an upraised finger these accoutrements gave him a rather martial appearance.

It took us a minute to sort ourselves out again, during which the Preserver watched us placidly. At last we were arrayed in a half circle and Rhys took a step forward.

"Is it okay if we talk now?" he asked. "It's been kind of a pain getting to this point."

The god ignored him. He held out his scepter and pointed at Ananta, who quailed for a moment before his gaze. But then Mina slapped him on the back, and he regained his composure.

"Ananta Sesha, my servant. You disappoint me." The god's voice was sonorant and lovely. I decided that I wouldn't want to be the one to disappoint him and I was glad that I wasn't being picked out for chastisement.

"I —" Ananta stammered, hesitated. He looked like he was choking on his own words

"You can do it," said Mina softly.

"I am not Ananta," he said.

"Of course you are," said the god. "Have I not said so?"

"I ... I am Carlos Jiménez. I am a police officer! Not your servant. I am a free man!"

And then I looked at him, and I saw what I should have seen long ago. His face had changed very little since the first time I saw him. Take away that golden gem in his forehead. Change his complexion. Give him a pair of mirror shades. Yeah, he was the cop, the one I'd given the hamburgers to on the first day of the emergency.

The god glanced at Mina and nodded before turning back to Ananta-Carlos.

"Yes," he said. "You were once called Carlos Jiménez. In a past life. But then I raised you up. In this cycle of the world, you became my Ananta Sesha. You served me loyally. Until your faith was corrupted. A pity, but so be it."

Joy spoke up. "What," she said, "Are you going to tell me I was your Lakshmi, now? What kind of monster would make me sleep like that? Like a four-armed doll?"

The god sighed.

"It was necessary that you fill the role of my consort," he said, "for form's sake. Once there was another Lakshmi ... but she is gone now. I kept you asleep beside me to protect your sensibilities. It would not be fitting to coerce you, and had you awakened it would have been impossible to avoid distressing you. I regret that these ones" — he nodded at us — "saw fit to disturb you. But you must know that I have done you no harm."

"Hmph," said Joy. "If this was the world I came from, I'd have Officer Jiménez arrest you for kidnapping. No harm, indeed!"

"Anyway," said Rhys, "what about the rest of us? You've been playing us like pawns. It hasn't been fun. Do you have any explanation for that?"

"You guessed correctly quite early on," said the Preserver. "You were being tested. For strength. For creativity. For stability. For resourcefulness. For resolve."

"For fuck's sake," said Steiner. "You can't be serious. You're supposed to be a god. Don't you know enough about us already? And anyway, testing for what?"

"You must have realized the purpose of the testing as well. A new Creator must be appointed for the new cycle of the ages."

"And you want us for the job? Or just one of us?"

"One is sufficient."

And all my friends looked at me. Me!

"No," I said. "You can't be serious."

Nora and Quaid nodded solemnly at me. "You would be our choice," they said.

Michèle punched me on the arm. "Yeah," she said. "Mine too. But you knew that already, right? You'd better have known it."

"But it doesn't make sense," I said. "I've just been following you guys around, more than anything. It's always been someone else taking the lead, and doing a great job, too. You really want me to have that kind of power?"

The Professor spoke up then. She'd been silent for quite some time, frowning at the god. But now she turned to me.

"I'm afraid it's going to be unanimous," she said. "You're our keystone, Jay. You must realize that. You've connected with all of us, one way or another. You're the real reason we're all here, and not disintegrated or lost in the sea of souls."

I was going to say how worthless I was, and how undeserving of the role, but I'd already gone through this with Michèle not too long ago.

"But do you really all want me to do this?" I asked. "I have to hear it."

"She's right," said Rhys. "You're it, if anyone is."

Steiner said, "Sure, why not? Seriously, Jay, just think about what's happened to us all. You might not have been the lead on everything, but you've been in the middle of it all. I don't think it's an accident."

And Mina laughed. "Of course," she said. "Ever since you stopped at my window that day for hamburgers, I knew it. There's something about you, man."

I was really taken aback. All those votes of confidence. Honestly I don't know what I would have said. But before I could organize my thoughts the Professor spoke up again.

"There's just one problem." she said.

Nora nodded. "We said you would be our choice." And Quaid said, "Yeah. Why don't you explain it, Professor?"

She nodded, and turned back to the Preserver, who'd been watching all this byplay with no change in his serene expression.

"We were told the Creator is meant to be subordinate to the Preserver. Is this true?"

"That is the natural order of things," he said.

"The power of the Preserver is superior to that of the Creator, then?"

The god frowned. "Yes. How could it be otherwise?"

The Professor sighed.

"I suppose in the circumstances there's no avoiding this," she said. "I was hoping for a simple conversation with no roleplaying, but I suppose there was never much chance of that."

She turned back to me. "May I?"

"Sure," I said, though in fact I wasn't sure what she was intending to say.

She addressed the Preserver. "In the Hindu faith there is a transcendent godhead, a truly supreme infinite and omnipotent power. The storied actions of the lesser gods reflect and symbolize subordinate aspects of this higher power. If Vishnu the Preserver is the highest expression of the godhead, then he must have those transcendent attributes. And yet it's evident that you do not possess these qualities. To put it plainly, you are a fraud."

"You think it impossible that I have restrained myself, or that I have lowered myself to your level as a courtesy? I remind you that your very existence in this world is due to my action."

The Professor shook her head. "As for our presence here, well perhaps you may have had something to do with that; but if indeed you did, it is hardly proof of divinity."

The god pointed his sword at the Professor.

"You may wish to explain yourself to your companions," he said. "But beware. I am judging your words."

The Professor laughed. "It's a bit late for intimidation, don't you think? But let me lay it out for you. First of all your speech and behavior is that of a poseur. You've attempted a whole series of deceptions, of lies, of attempts to control our minds. A case in point is that lotus-world illusion or whatever it was. You began with an attempt to dazzle us; it was lovely, I must say, very impressive, but it didn't last long before Carlos here was able to destroy it using only the power you yourself appear to have given him. When that failed, you followed up just now with bribery, the offer of godhood. And now at last we hear threats. This is not how a person I respect behaves, much less a god; much less the true transcendent God herself. Then too your servants have all been less than impressive in their performances. Carlos here in his own person has far more dignity than Ananta Sesha, who presented himself to us at first as a pompous and arrogant buffoon. It was only as he overcame his programming, if I may use that word, that we became aware of Carlos' real qualities, his true nobility. I understand that Varuna was nearly as bad, and Indra was nothing more than a clown. With servants like those, what are we to think of the master?"

The Preserver gestured angrily, but the Professor, no more than half his size, unarmed and entirely meek in appearance, rode over whatever he was going to say. And she shut him up too; he subsided to hear her speak.

"Perhaps you will cite the power of the phenomena we have experienced. The destruction of our world. The creative powers we've been granted here. The power you've exerted over our memories, and recently over our wills. I am willing to grant the reality of these things. But just as I was able to create a living tiger despite having no understanding of what I was doing, I suspect you have been using that same resource, an Instrumentality that is not truly yours. While I must concede a great power exists in this world, that power is not your power.

And since we've gained access to that same power you've been unable to confront us directly. To the extent you have indeed used or abused us over these last few days, it's been through deception, or by the exercise of power against naive and defenseless people who weren't expecting an attack. You took away our memories when we had no notion this was a possible danger; and yet it was less than a day before we realized the deception. You dazzled us with illusions but again this has come to nothing. And where your servants have employed force against us directly, they have failed. Failed completely."

The Professor paused, as if to allow the god his chance to speak, but the Preserver said nothing.

"So," she continued. "Tell us again it was all a test. Tell us you have the power to kill us, or to eradicate us completely from the world. Try to give even one of us false memories, or to overcome our wills. I challenge you to make the attempt. It should be a trivial thing for a god to overcome a mortal's will, should it not? But I warn you now, fellow, whoever and whatever you really are, you are the one in danger if you attack us. So why not come clean? We are not your enemies. Admit your weakness. Explain the reality of this place, whatever it is that lies behind the illusion. How can it harm you to do this?"

The Preserver didn't answer immediately, though it was clear the Professor's words had affected him.

Thinking about what she'd said, I was filled with admiration for the Professor's stance. If it had been up to me, I might never have come to the conclusions she had. I might have accepted things at face value. Even now I wasn't sure that all she was saying was entirely right. But enough of it was right that I couldn't think of the Preserver as a god anymore. And if he wasn't a god, well then what justification was there for the things he'd done to us? He'd abused all of us, but Carlos-Ananta worst of all. And maybe Sandeep had destroyed himself, but he'd done it for us, and it never would have happened if the Preserver hadn't set Ananta against us. So yeah, I was feeling something now. Before all this, I'd supported everyone, and followed Rhys or Mina when they'd stood up for us against the destruction of our world, against Ananta, against the loss of our memories, and against Varuna. But I hadn't felt the fire on my own behalf; I'd felt it at one remove, for Michèle's sake, and for the others. Maybe I should have been more aggrieved before. Maybe I should have been more active. I could point to the unreality of my past life as an excuse, but now I was thinking I was just weak, weak and lazy.

"The degeneracy of the Kali Yuga must have sown its malignant seeds in your soul," said the Preserver, at last. His voice was heavy and solemn. "I had hoped for better of you, Harriet Thorne. Tell me, Dr. Thorne, have you shared your life with your friends? Do they know of your crimes? Of your shame? I would have thought one with your guilty past would be eager to seize any chance for redemption. And yet it seems you wish for nothing less than to drag them down with you."

The Professor flinched a little when the Preserver used her full name. But she answered strongly.

"Unlike you, I have nothing to hide," she said. "It's true that I have much to regret. But now I have much to embrace. And it's my friends who have given me that, not you. I believe in them. And I hope they believe in me."

Mina stepped forward and put her hand on the Professor's shoulder. "To the end," she said.

"Yeah," said Rhys. "The Professor is worth a hundred of you, Mr. Blue. There's nothing you can say to change that."

"You have our faith, Professor," said Quaid and Nora said, "and our love."

Steiner said, "Shit, do I have to actually say it too? Professor, you fucking amaze me. I am in awe of what you've been able to say and do. This jerk" — he nodded at the Preserver — "not so much."

Michèle raised her hand. "Is it my turn? Well, if I didn't know you at all, what you just said would make me love you, Professor. But I do know you, and this — this cafard can't say anything to change that."

I pointed at the Professor. "What everyone else just said goes for me too. I want to hear about your past sometime, Professor, but only because I want to know you better. But I know enough now to trust you with everything. I want to say something else too. I feel like I've been confused for a while. But listening to you has made things clear for me. This guy is no god, at least no more than we are. I won't submit to him."

The Professor bowed to us. "Thank you all," she said. "You honor me more than I can say. If we are all resolved, I would like to ask Rhys to address this Preserver one last time. To make our position entirely clear."

"Okay," said Rhys, and he stepped forward.

"Speak, mortal," said the Preserver, and Rhys laughed.

"Mortal?" asked Rhys. "You think you're different from us, when you say that? Listen, buddy, you've given us a lot to be angry about, but we're not threatening you here. We're calling you to account. You can still get out from under this if you want to. Just tell us the truth. We've had enough divine bullshit in the last couple of days to last a lifetime. No more illusions, okay? No more deception, no more fucking mind control. Cards on the table or fold your hand. That's all there is to it."

"Very well," said the Preserver. "As you wish." He flicked the finger around which the bladed disk had been twirling and sent the thing flying, as casually as you might toss a frisbee. It was only around six inches across, not very menacing really, and now it began to hover in the air mid-way between us and the god.

"I agree with you, Rhys Gwalchmai. There is nothing more to be said. The corruption of the Kali Yuga has seated itself too deeply in your souls. Indeed, I see now the new Creator must have a pure soul. But soul purification is within my power. The Narayanastra will eradicate your physical forms entirely if you do not submit to my will."

The disk began to shine with a golden light. It was spinning faster and faster and I heard a hum coming from it now. And as I stared at it, my vision blurred for a moment, and I saw six new disks appear, spinning in a hexagon surrounding the original. The hum was replaced by a sort of chord, rising slowly, like a bank of charging capacitors.

"My turn," said Mina. "Everyone get behind me."

She strode forward. Her eyes and fingernails flashed blue.

"Right," said Rhys. "You guys know what to do. Support her."

Michèle stood beside me. "Yeah," she said, and she put her arm around my waist. "Let's do it."

Maybe because we'd done the same thing a couple of times before, it felt easy now. Even fun, in a way. I didn't close my eyes this time, didn't even move to touch her, but I could feel Michèle and my connection to Mina, and hers to the rest of my friends.

The whining sound in front of us went up an octave, and multiplied its intensity. I blinked and saw now there were 36 more spinning disks; each of the orbiting six had spawned its own cluster of satellites. The whole stretch of lawn between us and the Preserver was glowing with golden light now, and still the disks continued to power up.

"Okay," said Mina. "The Narayanastra? Sandeep told me about that thing. He was really kind of a nerd for this stuff. I never learned anything from him about, you know, Hinduism, but the Great Weapons? That I know about. So check this out."

She raised her hands, and a blue glowing aura manifested above her head. Within it, the shadow of something like a spear, or maybe a giant arrow appeared. And I could feel it, too, all of our wills focused on Mina, and hers on that thing.

"I guess the Narayanastra is the Preserver's weapon," she said. "If Brahma is the creator, and we're it, then this is our weapon. The first level: Brahmastra!"

A blue radiance shone from the tip of the bolt. Where it played on the golden glow of the Narayanastra, the power of the Preserver's weapon diminished visibly.

"Blasphemy!" The Preserver muttered the words, but I heard them nevertheless through the commotion in between us. "Very well. I invoke the Destroyer. Shivastra!"

The ghostly appearance of a vast warrior appeared above and around us. Miles high, the spectral form raised a golden trident high above his head and brought it plunging downward. The weapon was so enormous that I thought a single prong would be enough to eradicate the whole valley, but it shrank as it descended, growing brighter and more tangible, until at last the weapon was ordinary size when it pierced the central disk of the Narayanastra's formation and disappeared in a flare of bright light.

The warrior vanished, but the Preserver's weapon immediately regained its strength, resisting the light of Mina's manifestation. As I watched, each of the 36 satellite disks expanded and developed 6 disks apiece of their own; and then the process repeated. And repeated again. A vast galaxy of bladed disks was floating there now, spinning about one another in intricate patterns, wheels within wheels within wheels, the whole vast formation slowly rotating around its central point.

"Ha!" Mina shouted it, and she really sounded happy, joyous even. I felt a vicarious thrill of pleasure on her behalf. "We can go up a level, too!" she cried. "Watch out, Preserver! This is Brahmashirsha Astra! The godslayer!"

I could feel the demand increasing from the connection we had with her. It was like turning up the power on a vacuum cleaner; but the power or the essence or whatever it was, it was there within us, and it was there for her. I could feel all eight of us networked together now; no nine, and ten, too, as Carlos and Joy joined in.

From the head of the glowing blue weapon, a brilliant light began to shine, brighter and brighter with every heartbeat; and then the whole thing multiplied itself four-fold in size and in structure; now four separate bolts of brilliant blue energy, each with a four-pointed star blazing at the tip. The whole thing was chiming now, resonating like four tuning forks, drowning out the humming horde of disks across the way.

"Ah!" The Preserver's cry pierced through the din the weapons were making. "There will be no purification for your souls! To preserve the world, I must destroy you utterly! I invoke the ultimate power Vaishnavastra!"

The night wasn't exactly dark just then, the illumination from all these fantastic weapons and effects lighting up the whole valley; but for a few seconds night turned to brilliant day as a vast golden arc like a monochrome cosmic rainbow appeared in the sky, stretching from horizon to horizon. And then the whole brilliant arc rose toward the zenith of the heavens, and I saw it really was a bow, a strung bow with an enormous golden arrow pointed at our confrontation. The bow shuddered once and the arrow launched itself towards us like a blinding firework rocket. Again it looked at first as if the impact would be enough to eradicate all of Vaikuntha, but once more the weapon shrank as it approached, penetrating the central disk of the Preserver's array, and once more increasing its power and proportion. Another series of six-fold increases of the disks occurred, and another after that, until at last it seemed the sky was full of the things, a myriad myriads of disks whirling around us.

"Nice one," said Mina, "but if you really wanted the ultimate weapon, you shouldn't have granted us the Creator's power. Let us show it to you. Brahmanda Astra! The Unmaker!"

At first all that happened was that a fifth blue bolt inserted itself in the center of the bundle of four, making a quincunx of brilliant stars. But then the whole thing rose up into the sky, expanding and growing brighter as it rose. I could feel the demands on us increasing as Mina sent more and more of whatever it was we were providing her upward, into the ultimate weapon. And now the thing was a fivefold sun, far too bright to look at directly.

The Preserver's voice drowned out everything for a moment. "I will destroy you," he shouted, and across the field I saw him slashing downward with his sword like a commander ordering the attack. And that whole vast galaxy of bladed disks spinning around our group collapsed inward on us, each individual disk rocketing toward us in a straight line, a billion blades screaming through the air all at once.

"No," said Mina, "you won't." And everything froze in place. The screaming whirling disks hung there in the air, motionless like sequins frozen in resin and we were left in utter silence.

"Okay," she said, "we win."

The million disks vanished as if they'd never been, and the blue sun faded from the sky. For another moment all was silent, and then I distinctly heard the thump as the Preserver collapsed to the ground, and the clatter as his remaining weapons fell along with him, the scepter-mace rolling all the way down the hill on which he'd stood.

"Holy shit," said Steiner. "What just happened? I thought you guys were about to destroy the world or something."

"Could have done," said Mina. "But that was the idea, to convince him something like that was about to happen."

"I don't get it."

"After the Professor told him off, he showed us he was just as batshit-crazy as the other gods. So we were going to wind up facing off, right? And that was good, because we'd have none of this stupid mind-control stuff, it would just be power against power."

"That's good?"

"Yeah," said Mina. "Because there were eight of us. I mean ten. And because we had our secret weapon on top of that." And she nodded at me. "What I wanted to get him to do was to throw everything he had at us. And I had all this mythical weapon knowledge from listening to Sandeep talking about it all the time at McDonald's, so I figured maybe it would work to provoke him. Instead of running away or doing some other clever fucking thing with the power we haven't thought of yet. This way if we had more total power like I thought we did, we could just sort of cancel his out, right? So we wouldn't have to blow everything up. The asshole isn't even dead. He's just lost as close to everything as you can lose without winding up like Sandeep."

"Speaking of which," said Rhys.

"Yeah," said Mina, "here's where I'm going to pass the buck back to you guys. But I guess we can do three things, right? We can kill him, which maybe sends him to the sea of stars and maybe it doesn't. We can try to eradicate him completely, which maybe we can do, and he'll wind up like Sandeep, maybe gone forever. Or we can try to fix him."

"Fix him?" Rhys asked. "What do you mean?"

"Like if he's not really Vishnu, either he was faking it all along or he really thought he was the god."

"Oh. False memories for him, too? I feel stupid now."

Mina nodded. "Yeah, well, that's as far as I've gotten. I don't know if he was faking it or not. And I have, uh, mixed feelings about those choices."

"Excellent analysis," said the Professor, and she and Mina shared a moment just grinning at one another. "But I think it's most like he truly believed himself to be the Preserver."

"Yes," said Michèle, "I think so too. But I want you to say why so I'll know why I'm thinking it."

"Ha," said the Professor. "But it's not that hard. None of us are Hindu. Why should he come up with this complicated deception based on a system of belief and a cultural background none of us share? Except for Sandeep, who probably wasn't even supposed to be there, none of us really know much about Vishnu. He could just as well have made himself seem to be Jesus or God the Father, or Metatron maybe. But he chose Vishnu. So either there's yet another power behind him, messing with him like he messed with us, or he managed to do it to himself somehow."

"Oh," said Quaid. "How obvious, once you set it out." And Nora asked, "so that means we try to fix him?"

"Well, no," said the Professor. "That's the problem."

19

S HE PUT HER HANDS TO HER FACE, rubbed her eyes. We waited for her, and, in a moment, she continued, speaking softly.

"I'm more ashamed of what I'm going to say now than about anything I've ever said or done in my life, or about any other mistake I've made. And like that bastard said, I've made plenty of mistakes.

"By all logic, by all of morality and ethics and compassion we should definitely try to make him well, help him to recover whatever memories he's lost or suppressed. But I don't want to do it. I'm afraid of him. I hate the feeling, but what if we wake him up and he has enough resources to do something else to us, just as Mina said, something we haven't thought of, something we can't defend against? I know now what I put Rhys through, back when I got lost in our own world, when you all forgot me for a while. So yesterday, when I realized something was wrong with our memories, when I made myself remember Mina, oh my God, I wanted to kill myself. I hated myself so much for forgetting her. And here he is, the person who did that to me. To all of us. I know we should be merciful. I said it myself a while back, and so did Steiner, we're starting here with a clean slate. But oh God, I can't make myself believe it."

The Professor's face twisted, and she started to cry. Really cry. She was sobbing and tears were running down her cheeks, and in just a second or two she looked totally desolate. Mina wrapped her up almost at once in an embrace.

"Listen," she said, "it's all right. I'm here. We lost each other, but now we're found again. It's all right."

"But what I just said —"

"You want to kill him," said Mina. "For me, right? Because you don't want anything to happen to us. I got it. And that's why I want to keep him alive."

"What?"

"For you, Harriet. Don't bullshit me, now. It's only been like three days, but I know you. I know you all the way. If you were alone, just facing him by yourself, you'd never kill him in a million years. It wouldn't even occur to you. For you it would be like a dagger in your heart forever knowing you'd killed him. But you'd do it, right? You'd take that dagger in, for me. To protect me. Well think about this, okay? I care just as much about you. And I'm not going to let you do it."

"Oh. Oh, Mina —"

The Professor was still crying, but it wasn't desolation now. It was happiness. It was catharsis. And it was relief.

"Wow," said Joy, speaking in an aside to Carlos. "Are they like this all the time?"

"Yes," he said. "It amazed me when I thought I was Ananta. It still amazes me."

"Kinda nice, though."

"Well, yes."

A minute passed, and the Professor recovered her composure.

"That was embarrassing," she said.

"Oh no," said Michèle. "That was beautiful."

"All right," said Rhys. "Enough screwing around. Let's do it. I've got to say though, if he makes a wrong move, I'm not in favor of any more last chances."

We walked up the hill to where the fallen god still lay on the grass.

Mina knelt by his head.

"How is he?" asked the Professor.

"Yeah," she said, "he's still alive. I mean, if that means anything here. He's breathing, anyhow."

"So what are you going to do this time?" asked Rhys.

"Same thing I did for Joy, and also for Ananta to help Carlos get himself back. I'm just going to try and purge whatever false memories he's got, try to restore him to what he once was."

"And if he doesn't have false memories?"

Mina shrugged. "We'll see, I guess. He might be just the way he's been so far. He might or might not have the ability to mess with us, still. But I think it's worth a shot, anyway."

"Okay," said Rhys. "Anyone have any problem with this?"

No one said anything.

"Right," said Rhys. "Go for it."

Mina put her hand on the Preserver's forehead. She looked like a child beside his larger-than-life form, still beautiful even in repose. Her eyes flashed blue for a split-second.

"That's it," she said.

Nothing happened for what seemed like a long time; probably five seconds or so. And then it happened: a series of black marks appeared at the top of the Preserver's bare chest, tracking downward toward his groin and disappearing under the waist of his kilt.

"What the fuck?" Rhys pointed at the marks, which looked like tiny railroad tracks, except that instead of rails on either side of the ties, a single line ran down through the middle of them.

"Is that … a zipper?" Quaid and Nora asked.

And it really was one too; it's just that the idea of a zipper appearing on the Preserver's body was so impossible I couldn't see it until they pointed it out.

"Shit," said Steiner. "It's opening."

With a faint whir the Preserver's chest opened up and a much smaller man climbed out of his body, leaving a deflated blue human-shaped bag on the ground behind him.

"Shit," said Mina, and she dropped into a stance, her nails and eyes flashing blue once again.

"Peace," said the man, and he sank to his knees in front of us, raising his hands above his head.

I had a chance to look at him now. He was short and slight with black hair and medium brown skin. He was dressed in pale gray slacks and a charcoal nehru jacket that flared out over his hips like a skirt.

"Who are you?" I guess it had to be asked, so I asked it.

The man looked at me and his lips turned up in a half-smile.

"I'm the wizard," he said.

"What?"

"A few days ago, the Professor guessed there was someone behind everything that happened to you all. She refused to believe it was an actual divinity, so she called the person the wizard. She was right. And it's me."

It was a few seconds before anyone answered him.

"All right," said Rhys. "You don't seem to be insane at first glance. You want to explain yourself?"

"Yes, actually," said the man. He lowered his hands and sat down cross-legged. "It's going to be a longish story if you don't mind listening to it. But I promise you I am entirely at your service as regards answering questions."

"Okay." said Rhys. "We'll hear you out."

"Thank you," said the man. "I was once a man like any other. My world was much like yours. In fact, it was a predecessor to your world. Earth for all intents and purposes. Anyway, I had a life in that world, and I died in it along with everyone else. We didn't wait for the world to run down like yours did."

He raised a hand when it was obvious the Professor wanted to interrupt him. "I'll explain that. I promise, okay?

"Anyway," he said, "we did ourselves in. It was a nuclear war. We'd built our arsenals up to the point that there were no survivors. I was an atheist back then, so it was quite a surprise to wake up in a place rather similar to this. No sea of milk, though. I did have a sort of a welcome, a recorded message from the previous wizard, the one responsible for creating that world. She told me she herself was once human, someone who'd lived at the end of the world before mine, and she'd been selected by her predecessor to manage a new world, just like she was choosing me. She'd screwed it up, though. She told me that everyone in my world was dead and stored, awaiting rebirth, and it was up to me to create a new world for them. She'd been so devastated by her failure she'd eradicated herself completely, so apart from that message there was no one for me to talk to about what was going on."

He paused, looked around at all of us. "Is all that reasonably clear so far?"

"Jesus," said Steiner. "It's a lot to take in all at once. You say you created our world?"

"More or less," said the man. "Not from scratch, though. More about that later. Anyway, I felt the weight of the obligation, you know.

There were four billion people alive in my world when we destroyed ourselves. All of them now stored as souls, awaiting rebirth. And it was my job to make a new world for them."

"So you made our world?" asked Steiner.

"Eventually I did," said the man. "But it wasn't my first try. I should stop here to explain something else, though. A couple of days ago Dr. Thorne here deduced the existence of something she called the Instrumentality. An excellent name for it."

He nodded at the Professor who inclined her head in return but said nothing.

"The Instrumentality is a vast intelligence," said the man. "But it's not a god. It's totally passive. It has no will, no agency of its own. All it does is obey. Where did it come from? Your guess is as good as mine. There could be some higher order beings — true gods maybe — who set it up, but they haven't seen fit to make themselves known to me. But anyway, the thing is it has a sort of a resource. Something like fuel, something like stored energy, but not either of those things. Dr. Thorne guessed its existence even before your world came to an end. She called it essence."

Michèle asked, "Are you saying our world ran out of it?

"Yes," said the man. "I'm convinced that the Instrumentality and its soul-storage capability was meant to enable a self-sustaining system. But we — I screwed it up. Just as my predecessor did before me."

"Self-sustaining?" asked the Professor. "Does this essence regenerate, somehow?"

The man nodded. "In fact, it does. Existence itself consumes essence. But life regenerates it. And humans have the potential to generate a great deal. Moreover, uncreating the world reclaims the essence invested in it."

Mina raised her hand. "So what was the problem with our world?"

"Humans generate essence only in the proper conditions. When they are healthy, happy, fulfilled. When the components of purusartha that I had Carlos convey to you as Ananta are present. Material security and comfort. Emotional connection, community, love and worldly pleasure. Mutuality and compassion, not just for individuals, but for all persons. For all living things. For the entire world."

"Shit," said Mina. "Then why —"

"Why would I make a world in which people find those things so hard to achieve, so hard to offer one another? Yes, I know. I have failed you, and every last person who has lived and died and lived again for the thousands of years my world-system has been operating. But as I said, your world wasn't my first try.

"I started with the idea of a golden age, an elysium, a paradise. I didn't want anything like my old world: I was going to make a world without scarcity, a world where no one would need to or want to hurt anyone else. I chose a million people who in the previous world had been net positive generators of essence. I brought them back to life with their memories intact, as adults in their prime. I shared everything I knew with them, and I provided a world in which food, energy and land was abundant. The idea was this core group would develop a system of living into which they would add souls over time, starting with others who would be allowed to continue their mortal lives from the previous world, and regenerating, purifying the souls of the depraved, the despairing, and the heartbroken. These souls would be born as children to my cadre, growing up healthy and happy, and eventually the enlightened society would come to number the full roster of all the lives that had been lost in our last terrible war. It was a nice dream, don't you think?"

"So what went wrong?" asked Joy.

"Nothing and everything," said the man. For a hundred years there were no problems at all, really. Nothing that couldn't be gotten past easily enough. But after a time I realized a certain spark was missing, if I may reuse a metaphor that Jay here has employed lately."

Michèle laughed. "What? You mean people didn't want to fuck?"

"You joke," said the man, "but in a way that was the problem. I had expected rapid population growth. After all, there was no reason for restraint. This new world had every comfort. And yet the population remained quite flat. And while the initial rate of essence generation amongst the people was positive, it declined over time. The arts languished, and no one bothered to work in the sciences at all. There was no engineering, no application, no direction forward for progress. People didn't have bad lives, not like in the old world. But my goal of restoring the lives of the billions had been lost to provide comfort for a mere million, and moreover I could see that eventually society would fall into a complete stasis. And in such a state, they would consume essence instead of producing a surplus. At last, after millions of years, even this small population would exhaust the essence supply, having accomplished nothing whatsoever."

"Do you suppose your presence might have influenced them, might have diminished the urge to grow, or to discover?"

"Yes," said the man. "I tried to live as humbly as possible. I had no servants, and I made no overt use of the creative power. After the first few years, there was no need for me to exert myself at all. But still I thought that perhaps the knowledge that a god was living amongst the people was somehow retarding their growth. So I subtracted myself. I removed myself completely from the world, retreating to a place much like this one. Of course everyone in the world knew of my existence, knew that I'd created the world specifically for them, for their happiness and their contentment. So I had to change that."

"Ah," said Rhys. "I can see where this is going."

"Yes," said the man. "I rolled up the old world. destroyed it completely, reclaimed the essence that had been bound up in all those lives. And then I recreated it, and re-installed the same population with false memories of a world-cataclysm of which they were the sole survivors. I made sure the world provided them the same comforts, the same bountiful existence. But this time there would be no god living among them, however humble and human. And again, I gave everyone long vigorous lives free from care and pain, long lives in which they could raise many children."

"I suppose it didn't work either," said Rhys.

"Indeed. Or your world should never have arisen. In fact it did work out somewhat better than the first attempt. But the population stabilized at a mere ten million. And they showed decreasing interest in their lives, just as in my first world. Evidently there was some social defect in humanity that I hadn't anticipated."

"What was your next attempt?"

"Oh, there was more than one," said the man. "So many attempts. Experiments, trials. The potential of the Instrumentality is vast, but it doesn't provide an oracular view of the future. For a long time everything I tried failed and failed abjectly too, disintegrating or decaying in mere hundreds of years at most."

"And then at last you tried to recreate your own world? And wound up with ours?" The Professor made the suggestion.

"You're skipping ahead," said the man. "In all those failed attempts, I hadn't installed fictional histories. The idea of creating false religions and so on was repugnant to me. Instead, each time I installed the vague memory of a natural catastrophe that had reduced population to the million or so I wanted my perfect world to start with. But after so many failures I decided that perhaps the abruptness of the societal transition was to blame. So I invented an ancient past, invested a great deal of the Instrumentality's resources in faking up records, artifacts, ruins, and so on. I created societies, mythologies, language systems, and all manner of historical and prehistorical records, many scavenged from the history of my own world, which the Instrumentality had stored in full.

"I don't feel so happy about that choice," said the Professor.

"Neither did I," said the man. "But it did have some effect. The idea that they had once enjoyed a higher civilization appeared to spur some more activity among the people. But in the end the population never expanded as expected, and society once more became stagnant. Another failure."

"Did you ever think that humanity just wasn't capable of what you wanted for them?"

The man nodded. "Yes. But I knew my own civilization, miserable as it had been in many ways, had done better than any of the ones I'd created. And so at last I found myself restoring scarcity. Disease. Competition. Short miserable lives, in the absence of technology, with no such knowledge provided by me. My first generation were memory-less children cared for by memory-altered parents. People would have to work to produce food and shelter for themselves. They'd have to defend themselves against wild animals, and they'd have to secure themselves against the forces of nature. The sad thing is that approach worked better than my early attempts."

"So step by step you found yourself tending towards the same sort of world you yourself had been born into," said Nora. And Quaid said, "It must have been a bitter pill to swallow, after the idealism of your first trials."

"You really have no idea," said the man. "Every failed life, every criminal, every war, every torment, and every suicide. It's all my fault. The weight of all those terrible things is on my back, and it's made worse, doubled and redoubled, by being all for nothing. All that pain, all that striving, for nothing. I understand now, you see, why my predecessor eradicated herself completely."

"And you feel the same way now," said Michèle. "Don't you?"

"Yes," said the man. "And here is where I have to explain what you yourselves experienced over the last few days. What was done to you is unforgivable, but at least you are owed an explanation for it."

"Yeah," said Rhys. "We're listening."

"The Preserver was insane, of course. The power of the Instrumentality is hard for a human to stand. Over time, over thousands of years, he grew more and more deranged, until at last he came to believe himself a god."

"I don't understand," said Rhys. "How could that happen?"

"Imagine yourself in his position. You're alone, cut off from the rest of humanity. You are constantly using the Instrumentality to monitor human development around the world; and the stress of integrating your mind with the vast power of the Instrumentality is terribly wearing. Naturally you find ways to occupy yourself as time goes by. You try to enjoy yourself. You play games. You resurrect people from the soul bank to be your friends, your lovers, and at last, your pawns. By this time you've gotten a little full of yourself. The ultimate power is yours, but you're not bearing up very well under it. Not with all those failures, all those lives wasted, all those tormented souls you're responsible for. Nothing pleases you anymore. You begin to wonder whether you should find someone else to give power to yourself. But you're only half-way through the current world, and even though it's not doing very well, you feel like you should at least stick it out to the end. And that could be five, maybe even ten thousand years away."

"Ugh," said Michèle. "That sounds horrible. But how could you go from that — that kind of pain to thinking you're Vishnu, the Hindu god? You didn't believe in Hinduism in your old, world, did you?"

"No," said the man. "Hinduism didn't exist. But that's the thing. I was monitoring your world's development. And I saw that an interesting belief system had developed out of the purely pagan and animistic beliefs that had earlier dominated humanity. That belief system was Vedic Hinduism."

"Ah!" said the Professor. "A light begins to dawn."

The man nodded. "The Vedic mythology is wrong, of course. Or rather I should say so far as I know it's wrong. Who knows, perhaps there is a true Lord Indra out there somewhere, a higher and nobler soul than the poor old man I resurrected to play the role here, and maybe he's observing us with sadness even now."

The man shook his head. "But somehow the early Hindus got the broad strokes of their cosmology mostly right. With no evidence whatsoever, they still managed to come up with fairly accurate notions of the eternal recurrence, the sequence of creations, and the cycle of metempsychosis, too. The idea that these people had gained insight into the true workings of the world fascinated me. So I watched them carefully, for many hundreds of years. I was eager, anxious even, to see how their society and beliefs would evolve.

"And then the Vedic system developed into the more advanced Puranic form, with the emergence of notions of transcendence and universality. The Trimurti, the system of the Creator, the Preserver and the Destroyer, especially intrigued me. You can guess why of course; I embodied all three of these divinities in my own person. And yet I myself was far from divine; I was only leveraging the vast power of the Instrumentality, and doing so incompetently, at vast cost in lives and suffering."

"So you took refuge in the mythology," said the Professor.

"Yes," said the man. "It was a slow descent at first. But there came a point not long before the end, around 1000 BC I believe it was, when I saw that the decline of essence production was inexorable even though the population was increasing. Apart from wiping the slate clean yet again, the only hope was a profound alteration of the underlying system. And yet in my own person my mind was far too weak to envision a path forward. So I came at last to believe that total integration with the Instrumentality was the only way to achieve a successful outcome. And I convinced myself that doing so would in fact elevate me to a truly transcendent godlike stature. I would literally become the Preserver."

"Oh no," said Nora, and Quaid said, "I'm so sorry."

"Yes, well," the man said, "it was pretty bad. A human mind doesn't accept that degree of vastness very well. I never even came close to the degree of integration I intended, and when I recoiled from it what was left of me was the Preserver, not the person you are speaking to here and now. Still it's possible that the Preserver was actually able to prolong the end for a while. You did after all pass through the threat of nuclear war. Your own Brahmastra, as Edward Teller called it, was withheld after its first two terrible uses. However unpleasant your world became, at least you didn't wipe yourselves out completely. My own people never managed to land on the Moon. Even the Preserver smiled when he saw Yuri Gagarin lift off that first time. It was only the global collapse of essence production that triggered the end."

"But why all that messing about with us here?" asked Carlos. "Why did you have to use me as your — your puppet?"

"I can say nothing even slightly redeeming," said the man. "If indeed you had annihilated the Preserver after defeating him, it would have only been just. But even at his most demented and delusional, there was a part of him — of me — who held you in high regard. I had long planned to pass my mantle on to a group, albeit a group with a clear leader. I thought the mutual support of a circle of friends would soften the blow of isolation from the rest of the human race, and might also allow for expanded exploitation of the Instrumentality without such danger of self-dissolution."

"Ah," said the Professor. "And you chose Jay as the prime candidate."

"Yes," said the man, turning to me. "Of everyone in the world, you had the highest capacity for essence. The perfect repository for the Preserver's own capacity, at a time when he could no longer trust himself to make use of it wisely himself."

"What?" I asked. "You gave it to me? Why?"

"It was a moment of relative sanity," said the man. "I think I secretly recognized I was lost, that my mind was out of control. But at the same time I told myself I was the Preserver, immortal and perfect. If I could overcome you, despite giving you all that power, it would prove I was the god; no that I was God himself. It was my plan to create yet another world of my own, a world of eternal adoration in which everyone would join in worshipping the Preserver ..." He trailed off.

"Om Namo Narayana," said Carlos.

"Yes," said the man. "It would have been the most grotesque and horrible failure imaginable, a failure to crown a personal history of total failure, which itself has been the end result of who knows how many previous failures. At least my predecessor had the courage and the strength of will to destroy herself before she fell so low. But I — I deserve no such praise."

He came to a pause, and together we regarded him in silence for a time.

"Oh yeah," said Rhys. "If you were insane and all that, how is it you are back to normal now? You seem like a regular guy to me."

The man smiled. "Thanks," he said. "But really that's down to your actions more than mine. On his own — on my own, the Preserver would have only grown more and more insane. But you triggered a safety mechanism I had installed."

"A safety mechanism?"

"Yes," said the man. "I imagine you'll want to come up with something along the same lines. Very early on I realized that in making use of the Instrumentality I might inadvertently damage myself beyond repair. So I created a contingency mechanism whereby if any radical change was made to my mind in a single stroke the Instrumentality could revert my consciousness to a prior state of sanity. You triggered my restoration by trying to clear the Preserver's mind of false memories."

We sat in silence for a moment, and then Michèle spoke up.

"Monsieur Nameless, I have one more question."

"Yes?"

"I understand why you gave your power to Jay. He is special, even in a crowd of weirdos like us. But why did you have to take away his memories back in the old world? Did you give him his memories a year in advance of the end of the world, or did you make him a body and a past to go with it at the same time?"

"Oh," said the man. "He was dead, you see. I mean, his soul was awaiting rebirth. But there was no time for him to grow up as a child. The Preserver let affairs go until it was almost too late. The world was running down too rapidly. So I had to install him in life as a grownup."

He turned to me.

"Jay, I took your mature mind as it was in your previous life, installed false memories along with an aversion to thinking about your past, and gave you a body to match your memories. What was done to you was hasty and ill-considered. You have my apologies, but I know that's not enough."

"I knew all that," I said. "I've known it for a while now. Even before the end of the world I think I had an idea there was something wrong with me compared to other people. But it's okay, really. You understand how cool all this has been? How wonderful?"

"What?" The man was taken aback.

"Joy said it first," I said. "And I agree. This has been great! I mean, okay, we were kind of desperate at times, and that false memory trick was pretty low. And what happened to Sandeep is … well, it's really bad. But look at us. We're all alive after the end of the world. I doubt any of us really expected that. We had a hell of an adventure. We fought the gods themselves and won. Or Mina did, anyway; and we helped. And all of us, all of us unhappy, broken people, we've managed to repair ourselves, somehow. We've found love. If you set us up for that, or if the Preserver did, we've got to thank you for it, don't we?"

"But —"

"Ha, yeah," said Michèle. "If it wasn't for the end of the world and for you, I'd be Michel living my miserable little life alone. I'd never have met Jay. And the rest of us, we're all lovers now. Did you plan all that?"

"No," said the man. "I assumed you'd work out arrangements of some sort. But the Preserver didn't even pay close attention to the rest of you. You were just Jay's closest links, the ones it was easiest for him to connect to. But what you've actually done? Even before learning the truth of the world? To be honest, I remember the Preserver being shocked. You just all meshed somehow. In couples and as a group. That's why he — why I split you up. I was afraid of what you'd done, and resentful too. It was a cruel and unnecessary test, but you passed it more successfully than I could have imagined. I could never have done what you did."

"I think it was breaking through the wall that was the thing," said Mina.

"What?"

"Remember?" she asked. "We had to sort of link up to do it. I think we broke down more than one wall then because it was such a desperate moment. We'd all started changing before that. But that was when we changed together, you see what I mean?"

"Ha," said Steiner, "typical. I missed out on it."

"Yeah," she said. "But we were there for you afterwards. You must have felt it. Probably you fit in with us when we rescued you. And we linked up afterwards. I bet Joy and Carlos are with us now, too."

"Hm," said the Professor. She was gazing off into the middle distance. I wondered what she was thinking.

"One more thing," said Mina to the man, who had been watching all this with a look of astonishment on his face. "Sandeep. Is he really gone?"

The man bowed his head.

"I'm sorry," he said. "Sandeep was desperate during that fight with Ananta. He committed all his essence, including that which was bound in his soul. And when I say 'soul' I mean the repository of his personhood that the Instrumentality is designed to conserve between lives. Essence is beyond the grasp of terrestrial physics, but it's still not transcendent. The metaphysics of the Instrumentality are really just a higher order of natural laws. The souls managed by the Instrumentality are neither absolutely immortal nor transcendent. They can be destroyed, just as my predecessor destroyed herself in despair at the failure of her own creation. And so the Instrumentality obeyed Sandeep's will. He invoked Jnana Agni, the fire of knowledge; but he gave himself to the fire in order to defeat Ananta. In the end, there was nothing left to sustain him."

"So he's gone, then? Forever?"

"Beyond my power to recover, even if I had full control of the Instrumentality. But listen: the Instrumentality is not infinite. When you try to use the Instrumentality to its full extent you will eventually come to an end of your ability to grasp at time and space. It's a place that is not a place; I think of it as an abyss, like the Ginungagap of the Norse religion, which you may know is closely related to Hinduism. I have always felt there must be something on the other side, though I could not reach it myself or even perceive it. If there is a higher order of creation, perhaps it lies beyond ... And if there is a true transcendent soul — a divine memory of Sandeep's existence — then perhaps the potential to resurrect him is there as well."

The man bowed his head. "His death was my fault. The first true and final death of any of the souls in my care. Another terrible, unforgivable failure. So now I think I have come to an end. An end of this shameful accounting to you, and an end of my own existence as well."

"Is that it then?" I asked. "Hail and farewell? You won't stay to help us? You won't accept another go-round as a reborn soul, even?"

The man shook his head. "No," he said. "I have done too much harm. I cannot be redeemed here. Oblivion would be a kindness, and far more mercy than I deserve. But if there is a higher creation, if there is a reckoning with those who put the Instrumentality in place, then I welcome it. I yearn for it. I have questions of my own, you see."

Michèle said forlornly, "We don't even know your name."

The man nodded. "I don't deserve one. Let no trace of me and my world continue. My world was the true Kali Yuga, the ultimate degeneration of humankind. It was fitting that we destroyed ourselves. You will find the Instrumentality recalls every shade and nuance of your past world in perfect detail. But nothing before that. Let the dead worlds perish from memory."

"Surely there was some good there," said Michèle. "Works of art. Lovers and families. Your world didn't fall apart immediately. It must have lasted many thousands of years. There must have been worthy remnants."

"Perhaps," said the man. "But all I can remember is vileness and despair."

"But you know, we remember our own world with much fondness," said Michèle. "Yes, there were terrible things done there. All manner of horrors. But also there was love, and pleasure, and kindness and creation. We won't — I won't let it all go."

"Good for you," said the man. "That is why I have high hopes for you."

"Idiot," said Michèle. "You miss the point."

"What?"

"We like our world more than you did yours. Who made your world? Who made ours?"

"What? I —" The man was taken aback.

"You failed," said Michèle. "So you said. But you succeeded better than your predecessor did. We were all messed up, lonely people in our world. None of us were making your precious essence at all I bet. But we liked that world pretty well even so. Bad smells and all. So maybe we can use your help. Maybe we can work together. Maybe giving up now is being weak and is failing worse than ever. What do you think about that?"

"Listen," he said, and the man's voice was filled with passion. "I made the world where the Nazis put millions on trains to be gassed and processed for the gold in their false teeth. In my world Temujin piled up a mountain of Persian skulls. I created a place where the Khmer Rouge slaughtered their own innocent people for no reason but the sheer murderous joy of it. Over a thousand cruel generations countless victims of my incompetence died of starvation and neglect when they could have been fed and cared for. All those lives wasted, and all those souls condemned to rebirth again and again with no growth or progress, and none of it their own fault. And none of it was due to karma, either. Just the bad design of an incompetent demiurge.

"So what does a concerto or a moon shot or a kiss between lovers count against that? When the concerto score will be burned along with the orchestra, along with the city? When the same rockets used to reach out into space also carry nuclear weapons to destroy an entire world in a single ugly paroxysm of self-hate? When the lovers are about to be pulled apart and executed for daring to kiss someone of the wrong race or the wrong gender?"

"Perhaps the lovers could answer you," said Michèle. "Perhaps they would thank you for the chance to kiss at all. As I thank you. As do we all."

The man stared at Michèle. Actually, we all did. He got back up to his knees and bowed to her, resting his head on the grass at her feet.

"You are far more worthy than I to have this power," he whispered. "How — How is it I have never heard such words before?"

"I think you did not listen," said Michèle. "You must have been alone within your own head for a very long time. Perhaps you could read similar words in the Hindu holy books if you looked for them."

She put her hand on his head, ruffled his hair.

"Now get up," she said. "We all have a great deal of work to do. Indra must be waking up by now. He must be very confused. And we should take care of poor Varuna. Then Quaid has his wife and children to resurrect. And the rest of us too. We all have friends and lovers to embrace once more, parents and children to reunite, and enemies to forgive. Perhaps that is how we will build our new world. One soul at a time."

ABOUT THE AUTHOR

Laurence Raphael Brothers is a writer and a technologist with five patents and a background in AI and Internet R&D. He has published over 40 short stories in such magazines as *Nature*, *PodCastle*, and *Galaxy's Edge*. His noir urban fantasy novellas *The Demons of Wall Street*, *The Demons of the Square Mile*, and *The Demons of Chiyoda* are available from Mirror World Publishing.

To learn more about the works and world of Laurence Raphael Brothers, you can follow him on Twitter at *@lbrothers* or visit his website, *laurencebrothers.com*.

YOU MIGHT ALSO ENJOY

GODDESS CHOSEN
BOOK ONE OF THE "GODDESS RISING" TRILOGY
by Jay Hartlove

The man who would beat the devil isn't a hero, but a ruthless madman.

THE INSANE GOD
by Jay Hartlove

A meteorite fragment cures a teenaged trans girl's schizophrenia, but leaves her with visions of ancient warring gods annihilating each other in space.

RULES OF THE CAMPFIRE
BOOK ONE FROM "STORIES IN GLASS"
by Paul S. Moore

If you woke up one day and realized you had memories from more than seventy lives, fluent in every language you'd ever spoken, and recalled all the texts you'd ever read, would you wonder why?

Available from Water Dragon Publishing in
hardcover, trade paperback, digital, and audio editions
waterdragonpublishing.com